i

ISBN-13: 978-0-578-51623-3
Library of Congress Control Number:2019910793

Novels by J. E. O'Rourke

Leaving Major Tela

The Young Molly Maguires

WHAT'S YOUR STORY?

J. E. O'ROURKE

Published by GAELWRITER PUBLISHERS
An Imprint of J. E. O'Rourke

ACKNOWLEDGEMENTS

Credits are given for quotes from author articles, interviews, and book publications where they are referenced, including The Writer's Chronicle, New York Times, NY Review of Books, London Review of Books, National Public Radio, and others, as well as from published fiction.

INTRODUCTION

This book is comprised of a series of essays, presented in four major sections. Part 1, the largest section, discusses State Of The Art practice in fiction writing, including author recommendations. Each essay focuses on various story elements used in writing a literary book of fiction. One or more published works are generally discussed in each essay to illustrate good practices. In Part 2 the essays discuss innovative or experimental works, or challenging themes, for fiction writing. Part 3 contains essays discussing controversial or problem areas in contemporary fiction writing. Part 4 discusses various avenues for publication, including the traditional agent or publishing house, and some of the newer internet platforms.

.

TABLE OF CONTENTS

PART ONE - STATE OF THE ART

THEMES

Difficult Themes Cloaked in Metaphor

Occasionally one pauses early on when reading a new novel to reflect on whether there seems to be a compelling story arc, or some difficult thematic material that might enrich one's imagination or life experience. Such questions can arise when reading *The Vegetarian*, by Han Kang. The considerations can be very subjective for different readers, as we shall discuss.

The Vegetarian was translated from the Korean by Deborah Smith, and won the prestigious English Man Booker International Prize. It's a short, compact novel at 188 pages, and one of the qualities that captures the reader is the good writing. In broad brush outline, the story concerns a Korean housewife, Yeong-hye, her sudden plunge into a haunted, vegetarian eating obsession, and the tumult it causes in her own life and the lives of her husband, sister, brother-in-law, and parents.

Perhaps the vegetarian obsession was brought on by an onset of mental instability--Yeong-hye has begun to suffer dark, violent, carnivorous related thoughts--and her new eating practice is, in various degrees, distasteful or repugnant to her extended family. Some book critics suggest it may reflect a broader, Korean attitude toward vegetarianism. At a family dinner the father tries to force a piece of meat into his protesting daughter's mouth, and ends up slapping her, whereupon she slashes her own wrists.

Yeong-hye's husband divorces her, and the husband of her sister, In-hye, becomes attracted to Yeong-hye. He's an artist and filmmaker (oddly unnamed as a character throughout), and clandestinely arranges for Yeong-hye to help him make a film. He paints her body overall with botanical art, and films her making love with a similarly painted young man. In a subsequent filming, he paints his own body as well as hers with the botanical theme, and films them making love together. Sometime later, they repeat the same performance in Yeong-hye's apartment, and are discovered there by the sister, In-hye. In-hye is so shocked she telephones a municipal Emergency Services number, and the authorities bundle the assumed deranged couple off for an examination. Yeong-hye is committed to a mental hospital, where she is visited by her morose sister.

At this point, Yeong-hye's mental condition has deteriorated to where she imagines she is becoming a tree, and no longer needs to eat any food. We shall stop short of giving a complete, 'spoiler' description, in hopes that readers will try Kang's worthy book.

One critic, Diane Johnson, in the NY Review of Books (Crazy in Korea, 8/18/2016), presenting a review of *The Vegetarian* writes:

> a short, absorbing novel that readers and reviewers have declared to be about--besides meat-eating--marriage, obedience, caregiving, adultery, art, human violence, post-human fantasy, taboos, the resolution of the desperate, "the crushing pressure of Korean etiquette," and much more. One of the glories of novels is that their complexity allows for different interpretations, and

perhaps this partly explains the Vegetarian's appeal for judges specialized in literature and translation from various language traditions and with, no doubt, different perspectives.

There are metaphorical constructs so flexible and capacious as to allow for all of these meanings: generally, the more terse and minimalist a narrative, the more adaptable its metaphorical repertory to a wide range.

Johnson's suggestion that there are many metaphors folded into this novel, seems quite compelling. It is a recommended study for ambitious writers.

Writing the Generational Saga

As a guide for discussion we shall use a relevant novel that has an intriguing place setting, thematic material of interest, and all in one tidy package. The novel, *No Country*, by Kalyan Ray, stands out as a good choice. The novel is a family generational saga spanning about 150 years, beginning with the mid-nineteenth century famine years in colonial Ireland, and moving to India in the years of the British Raj before India's independence from England, and finally to North America-- Canada and the United States.

Over that span of time, there are more than a few generations to deal with. Throw in a complicated roster of intermarriages, with some difficulty to clearly track family lines, so that it seems likely the author started this novel with a good initial outline. The average reader will be challenged by the sweeping themes of the family's struggles, reversals, and successes. The book is only moderately long; nonetheless, Ray moves his characters through a number of epochal historic events: the famine that destroyed perhaps a quarter of the Irish population, and the resulting pestilent voyages of *coffin ships* loaded with immigrants fleeing the famine for North America and elsewhere. A principal character fled to India, where his Irish-Indian descendants coped with years of terror and revolution before India gained her independence from Britain, and the family's later immigration to the New World and tough decades following. Their harrowing experiences gained them an inner tempering and annealing of spirit, preparing them for life in the new, industrial age unfolding there.

Some readers may be disheartened reading of the callousness and politics that exacerbated *The Great Hunger*, and may be no less shocked by measures used to smother a storm of Indian rebellion against the colonial rule by Britain. Ray uses a deliberate massacre of an unarmed civilian population in an Indian village to stunning effect. However, one has to remember we also had our own My Lai during the Vietnam war, lest we think modern humanity has consigned all such events to the past.

One can be disturbed reading of the oppressive use of police and intelligence services, paid or coerced informers, and repressive laws, in the dying period of the Raj, and in pre-independence Ireland, all designed to contain threats of public dissent to political and economic interests. One recognizes this is perhaps not much different than what is practiced in many places today.

Perhaps one difficulty with the structure of *No Country* is the blurring sweep of characters as the story moves through the generations. There is not much space to become acquainted with each character. The main progenitor of the family saga, Padraig, in a cascading line of descendants, is aptly characterized in the beginning as a young man living in Ireland, as well as descriptions of his best friend, Brendan. When Padraig is compelled to flee to India, the situation of Brendan and Padraig's daughter, Maeve, becomes desperate owing to the famine, and when there is no news of Padraig for over a year, they board one of the coffin ships for North America. We get to know young Maeve fairly well on the voyage, and it's an endearing characterization. After a harrowing ordeal they reach Canada, and that's about the last of rich characterization for any one of the successive generations.

Another concern from a writer's viewpoint might be the introduction of startling coincidental material into an already ambitious plot. One of the later woman protagonists travels to New York City to seek a young man she had known in Canada, and becomes employed in the Triangle Shirtwaist factory in the garment district when the historic fire tragedy occurred. It was a dramatic episode in the telling, certainly, but it seems not entirely organic to the story thread. Another coincidental element was a chance crossing of paths with a psychopathic character when
descendants of Padraig purchase their home, and which led to diabolical consequences.

All in all, *No Country* is an engrossing read and a useful example for writing the generational saga.

Writing Historical Fiction without too much History

One of the writer's novels is set in a period of American history--an era in the mid-1870s--when an organized labor movement began its contest with the laissez-faire business interests of the period. The story moves through the violent birth and tragic demise of the Molly Maguires, a secret society of Irish immigrant mine workers who struck back at the railroad owners of the mines, who also effectively owned the lives of their mineworkers. The railroad owners, sometimes called 'robber-barons' in American History, controlled the justice system of Pennsylvania, a state where the deep underground anthracite coalmines were fueling American industry. After the robber barons crushed an early attempt by the miners to form a labor union, they embarked on a campaign to exterminate the new, often violent resistance of the Mollies to the desperate wages and deplorable working conditions in the mines.

The Young Molly Maguires was conceived as a YA novel, and looks at the lives of several teen-aged boys and a girl, the sons and a daughter of Molly families in a local *mine patch* of Pennsylvania mountains. Some of the details of life in the mining patch-small clusters of housing generally built and rented out by the mine owners-can be found in newspaper articles and other writings of the time, searchable on the internet. There is a Sherlock Holmes story that revolved around the existence of the Mollies, though only peripherally. Much of the early writing portrayed the Mollies as a totally villainous band of outlaws, and the newspapers of the time described them as worse than the secret society of Thugs in India, robbers and assassins devoted to the goddess, Kali.

Sensationalist views, but that sort of press coverage effectively distracted readers from any sympathetic concerns for the desperate attempts of the workers to win a living wage from the mine owners.

More objective and factual information about the working conditions and lives of the mineworkers became available from newspaper articles and essays written by labor union leaders following the failed efforts of the earlier union organizers. By then, the Mollies had been crushed, and the new immigrant waves shifted to arrivals from Eastern Europe. Labor conditions were still very harsh, but they were beginning to improve as union organizing sprang up nationwide. The most thorough and engaging documentary book on the time of the Mollies was written by Kevin Kenny, a professor of history, titled, *Making Sense of the Molly Maguires*, and published in 1998.

It is an important point to keep in mind, relative to all such intriguing old and new data sources, to use only as much historical data as might enhance the 'fictional dream' (described in *The Art of Fiction*, by John Gardner). There was a *Writer's Chronicle* essay (Sep. 2014) by Debra Spark, Raiding the Larder--Research in Fact-Based Fiction, which addresses this point. Among the ideas Spark discusses:

> *when it comes to fiction, information is only interesting because it is part of the story, because it has an emotional or narrative reason for being,* and, *Indeed all the research for authenticity can get in your way...and not just because it's a time suck. Colum McCann*

distinguishes between what is true--or perhaps what is actual--and what is honest in fiction.

Similarly, Sparks quotes the author Jim Shepard: "you're after a "passable illusion," not the truth. This is fiction, after all. It's a lie. You're just trying to make it convincing." And, discussing author Lily King's use of research for her anthropology-based novel (*Euphoria*): "The important thing isn't the information but (quoting King) how you get your imagination to play with all that information."

These seem good guidelines for writing an engaging story that doesn't get mired in too much historical detail. You would not want to suggest fiction that flies in the face of actual history; however, there is often a tendency to want to include too much of the historical research one does, but which may serve only to interrupt the 'fictional dream' of the story.

Intricate Themes or Universal Themes

Within any theme, a casual reflection on what has made some classic fiction linger in memory suggests character and place were important, compelling reasons. Character often includes a memorable physical appearance, personal traits, and voice. Place in memorable fiction might be a character's interior state of mind: think of Kafka's stories; or, the external, physical world: think of Faulkner's Yoknapatawpha County, or Llewellyn's coal mining region of Wales (*How Green was My Valley*). More generally, memorable fiction tends toward universal themes: love found or requited; bravery or cowardice; faith or lack of it; and so on. The trappings or settings of any time period may add to the interest of the story: for example, the clothing worn; the profession or trade of the character; the tools or machines of the time.

The framework of elements found in memorable fiction came to mind while reading Roberto Bolano's "Third Reich." The novel is worth reading, and time will tell how memorable it becomes. Two German couples, including the first-person narrator, Udo, are on holiday in Spain, do a lot of drinking in local bars, become acquainted with two local characters, nicknamed the Wolf and the Lamb, and another withdrawn character, called El Quemado. He tends a fleet of rickety paddle boats on the beach, and sleeps among his boats each night. Grotesque burn scars cover much of his body, and he is a very withdrawn man. Almost all the elements we have discussed are at work in this novel.

Consideration of story framework brought to mind some of the structure of Hemingway's "The Sun Also Rises," another story set in Spain, with endless bar hopping and drinking, and portraying relationships of the men and women on holiday. Where Hemingway uses sport fishing as a balancing literary diversion, Bolano uses Udo's passion for playing a war game, called "Third Reich," a board game based on WWII. The game includes all the fighting units of the combatant armies, with details right down to the names, strengths, and weaknesses of the individual generals who commanded the actual fighting units. Depending on the competing players' abilities, the outcome of a game may be different than the actual, historic outcome.

Udo is a renowned expert on the game in his homeland, and he keeps a game board set up in his hotel room while on vacation to help in research needed to write a current article on the game for publication. Udo eventually teaches Quemado the rudiments of the game, and they begin to play an ongoing game for a few hours every day. Unsettled by the presumed drowning of a compatriot, Charly, and the subsequent departure of their two girlfriends back to Germany, Udo's game begins to suffer and the German Army positions wither. Quemado's skill with the Allied Armies fortunes meanwhile improves rapidly, partly aided by the hotel's German expatriate owner. He spies on the games progress in Udo's room while he is away each day, and advises Quemado on strategies each night in his hut on the beach. The story ends on a very somber, life-is-almost-over note for Udo.

A point of interest for a writer reading this story might be whether the inclusion of a somewhat specialized contemporary interest, i.e., the Third Reich board game, could need whole pages of narrative exposition. Such a diversion could diminish the universal appeal desired for the story. Bolano, however, does a pretty good job of telling the reader just enough to imagine the rules and mechanics of the game, and the strategies and goals, as well as allowing the reader to contrast the game's action with the parallels or reverses to well-known, actual, historic campaigns. He injects some passion into the fate of the set pieces on the board by expositing on the real flesh and blood attributes of the professional soldiers waging the battles. Bolano is obviously thinking his story through to enliven it and keep the reader engaged.

Still Life and Bread Crumbs—Universal Themes

Still life and bread crumbs, by Anna Quindlen, is a recent novel
that moves at a comfortable pace, fully engaging the reader
with characters whose lives seem to follow a script of
diminished expectations, which we recognize from our own
experience of the world, but the characters seem unique
enough to maybe prove us wrong. At the same time, we might
feel it would not be very literary if the writer allowed things to
finish up too nicely, with our admired protagonist still on her
feet unbowed by all the challenges, but if she doesn't exactly
win, surely she must show some true grit. The so-called
Hollywood ending—think *Rocky* and on through *Rocky-4.*
However, we also harbor dark premonitions from reading the
classics—think *Anna Karenina* or *Madame Bovary*—and that
everything is just going to turn out horribly. And yet, when
done well, with a feeling of genuineness in plot turns and
attention to intelligent language, it could turn out to be fine, and
the reader might feel a little bit ennobled by the time spent with
these characters. What actually does happen?

In *Still Life*... Rebecca had been a renown photographer in the
art world and her work had been featured in galleries and
covered by art critics nationwide. The title of the book is taken
from one of her most famous photographs. However, her
career has lately been in decline, she is now 60 yrs. old, and
her agent hasn't been selling many of her photographs. With
her income falling off, and the financial burdens of paying
expenses for her mother in a care facility, while also attempting
to help her son, Peter, a recent college graduate, she's

beginning to become worried about solvency. Divorced from her philandering, Oxford-educated, professor husband since Peter was a boy, she needs to cut her living expenses—by renting out the expensive New York City apartment she owns and moving to a less expensive setting, perhaps renting a rustic cabin in rural upstate New York. Turns out, the new place has been badly misrepresented to her and is quite primitive, but Rebecca is determined to see it through, at least for a while.

Like many such locales, it has its share of characters and they are mildly interesting. The gruff roofer, Jim, who helps her keep her house intact, becomes a fairly well-developed character and an interesting counterpoint to Rebecca's character. In addition to his trade, he's a volunteer environmental worker and a subsistence hunter--a unique combo. Jim has a bipolar younger sister whom he is trying to help as she copes in survival mode at her trailer home nearby in the woods. A key turnaround experience for Rebecca occurs on her daily walks in the forest, where she begins to find strange little sites, each exhibiting crude wood crosses accompanied by some small object, like a doll, or an athletic trophy, and she artfully records each of these sites on film. The mystery is eventually revealed and the photo collection becomes a key to her reentry into her profession. Her relationship to Jim goes through several wrenching turns--he is sixteen years younger—but always the relationship is so well done by the writer, it holds true.

The author taps into a number of universal themes in constructing this story:

- A decline in professional recognition of a story character, whether in arts, business, or academia (usually in that order of severity) as she ages.
- The challenges to physical and mental well-being of a story character displaced into a very altered environment.
- An Autumn-Spring romantic relationship of two story characters.
- A social class hurdle existing between attracted story characters.

That comprises a formidable list, and so Quindlen is able to tap into the psyches of a great many readers with it, and she does it very well.

Themes of Mortality

There seems to have been a steady flow of profound books touching on a theme of mortality in recent years: *Gilead* by Marilynne Robinson, *Being Mortal* by Atul Gawande, and *When Breath Becomes Air* by Paul Kalanithi. The first is fiction, about an old preacher nearing death and writing a long letter to his young son. He wants to explain to the boy before he dies his views on life, and God, and how he came to marry the boy's much younger mother. The second book is really that hybrid, a creative non-fiction book, and includes the selected experiences of a practicing physician. The theme illustrates the attitudes of patients, and their families, who face serious health issues: perhaps resigned, or unrealistically hopeful, sometimes angry, and often frightened when little time may be left, regardless of attitude. The third book, another creative non-fiction book, is by a doctor, written over the course of his internship as a neurosurgeon, and covering similar ground to that in *Being Mortal*. The book takes a dramatic twist when the 38 year-old neurosurgeon is discovered to have a serious illness himself: major lung cancer. Now it is he chronicling his own stunned responses to increasingly dim prospects, as he tries to carry on with his marriage and his work. He did not quite finish the book in his last year of life; his wife had to write the last chapter for him. A good read, and a lesson on writing mortality.

When one reflects on past reading, much of literature deals in some degree with mortality, either as a major theme or as a hidden or secondary theme. The failing marriage, for example, may be the major theme, but it may be an expression of the midlife crisis, or lack of success in a career "growing long in the tooth," with both tensions being heightened by fears of impending mortality.

As the demographics of the country trend toward an aging population, the interest in reading about how others face issues of mortality, whether in fiction or creative non-fiction, seems likely to grow.

Metaphysics in Literary Fiction

Perhaps one of the most profound mysteries we are confronted with might be simply stated as "why is there something instead of nothing?" Countless philosophers, theologians, and scientists have addressed this question, some from the seemingly unprovable first cause principle—there must be a prime mover, or God. Others, most often the scientists, are apt to suggest there has to be a more scientific rationale for life. We will eventually uncover this, we just are not quite there yet. Nonetheless, look how far we've already come in understanding our universe. We can even demonstrate all that exists today, starting from a distant Big Bang event, which happened some 14 billion years ago, and the complete, scientific answer to why is there something instead of nothing is just around the corner.

Well, many of us are disinclined, or at least hesitant, to delve too deeply into the philosophical or rhetorical arguments that support either camp. Nonetheless, writers and readers may sometimes ponder about what view of God's existence might be held by certain characters in the story? If the author sees an opportunity to seamlessly integrate a spiritual viewpoint into the fiction, might it add greater depth, some flesh and bones to the character, and the choices he makes in the story?

Some of this thought process springs from the reading of *The March*, by E. L. Doctorow. The historical fiction covers the devastating Civil War march through the southern heartland, by General William Tecumseh Sherman. Sherman's army of about 60,000 Union soldiers carried out a scorched earth campaign through Georgia, South Carolina, and North Carolina, as the war neared a close and a collapse of the Confederacy. Like many, if not most soldiers in either army, it seems safe to assume from writings of that era that the existential view of the combatants was Christian, fundamental Protestantism. However, most of the officers of that conflict were trained at West Point Academy, which would have had a tradition from the Founding Fathers of the U.S. for a belief in God, but not necessarily in a dogma of any established religion. Accordingly, the concepts of sin, resurrection, and eternal life in heaven, may not have been the uniform view of officers from the Academy. It was dramatic to read the following by Doctorow, given as the internal dialogue of Gen. Sherman before the battle of Savannah:

> But these troops, too, who have battled and eaten and drunk and fallen asleep with some justifiable self-satisfaction: what is their imagination of death who can lie down with it? They are no more appreciative of its meaning than I...In this war among the states, why should the reason for the fighting count for anything? For if death doesn't matter, why should life matter?

> But of course I can't believe this or I will lose my mind. Willie, my son Willie, oh my son, my son, shall I say his life didn't matter to me? And the thought of his body lying in its grave terrifies me no less to think he is not imprisoned in his dreams as he is in his coffin. It is insupportable, in any event.

> It is in fear of my own death, whatever it is, that I would

wrest immortality from the killing war I wage. I would live forever down the generations. And so the world in its beliefs snaps back into place. Yes. There is now Savannah to see to. I will invest it and call for its surrender. I have a cause. I have a command. And what I do I do well. And, God help me, but I am thrilled to be praised by my peers and revered by my countrymen. There are men and nations, there is right and wrong. There is this Union. And it must not fall.

Sherman drank off his wine and flung the cup over the entrenchment. He lurched to his feet and peered every which way in the moonlight. But where is my drummer boy? he said.

And where else might a writer go to study a moving portrayal of the metaphysical views of a major literary character? Perhaps from Ahab in *Moby Dick*, by Herman Melville?

What is it, what nameless, inscrutable, unearthly thing is it; what cozening, hidden lord and master, and cruel, remorseless emperor commands me; that against all natural lovings and longings, I so keep pushing, and crowding, and jamming myself on all the time; recklessly making me ready to do what in my own proper, natural heart, I durst not so much as dare? Is Ahab, Ahab? Is it I, God, or who, that lifts this arm? But if the great sun move not of himself; but is as an errand-boy in heaven; nor one single star can revolve, but by some invisible power; how then can this one small heart beat; this one small brain think thoughts; unless God does that beating, does that thinking, does that living, and not I. By heaven, man, we are turned round and round in this world, like yonder windlass, and Fate is the handspike. And all the time, lo! that smiling sky, and this unsounded sea! Look! see yon Albacore! who put it into him to chase and fang that flying-fish? Where do murderers go, man! Who's to doom, when the judge himself is dragged to the bar? But it is a mild, mild wind, and a mild looking sky; and the air smells now, as if it blew from a far-away meadow; they have been making hay somewhere under the slopes of the Andes, Starbuck, and the mowers are sleeping among the new-mown hay. Sleeping? Aye, toil we how we may, we all sleep at last on the field. Sleep? Aye, and rust amid greenness; as last year's scythes flung down, and left in the half-cut swaths—Starbuck!

But blanched to a corpse's hue with despair, the Mate had stolen away.

Ahab, too, is of an earlier era when fundamental Protestantism was the rule of the land, though his First Mate, Starbuck, finds Ahab to be of a frighteningly blasphemous nature. Note the ornate dialect, almost as if reading from the King James bible, and which makes the passage doubly dramatic.

So far, the discussion relates only to how a central character struggles to express some understanding of a God-based meaning of life, usually falling somewhere within the tenets of written Scriptures of three major monotheistic religions, and on reflections of the character's own life experiences. A big hurdle is that, however inspired the Scriptures may have been, they were written about two thousand years ago and by men of uncertain erudition. Since then vast amounts of human learning and experience has occurred, but religious dogma, once established, changes only at glacial speed. It might be refreshing to have a few characters express new visions of what a God-based vision of life is for them, where some rational account is taken of the exponential growth of experience and knowledge gained in that two millenniums.

The strange perplexities of quantum mechanics comes to mind as a potential backdrop for new, innovative fiction. A recent NY Times article discusses ongoing confirmations for a proof of entanglement theory in subatomic physics. In essence, subatomic particles, like electrons and photons, have an infinite but measurable range of possibilities in properties of velocity, location, and spin. However, as soon as a measurement is made for one property in one particle of any entangled pair, the complete range of possibilities collapses into finite, related values in each of the particles. For example, the spin direction of one particle will be found to be exactly opposite the other particle. Experiments demonstrate that this happens no matter the distance scientists might establish between the particles, and theoretically would occur for a distance even to the far side of our universe. This implies that the particles must be able to transmit data to each other at speeds exceeding the speed of light. This is impossible according to Einstein's theories, and he did not like the idea. He and other major scientists disputed it; there was 'the finger of God' aspect in it for them. Nevertheless, the theoretical underpinnings and the experimental data of quantum mechanics have continued to hold up.

What new kind of characterization of God might this prompt in literary fiction writing? Perhaps it might lead to concepts far more complex and sophisticated than the anthropomorphic characterization of God we have generally assumed in our stories.

Elemental Tales of Penance

One can enter a mesmerizing and penitential world of biblical dimensions in stories by William Faulkner. An essay by E. L. Doctorow, writing in the NY Review of Books, 24May2012, considered Faulkner's "As I Lay Dying." In basic outline the novel is the story of the Bundren family, including a bitter, worn-out mother, Addie, who has just died, and describes a journey by her family carrying her coffin in a mule cart across rain soaked, dangerously flooded terrain, to fulfill Addie's wish to be buried among her own people in a distant county. Her wily, self-serving husband, Anse, enlists his four sons and a young, pregnant daughter for the task, using the occasion to seize the few material possessions they possess to buy things for himself while on the journey. On the way Anse has to leave one of his sons, suspected of being a little mental, at an asylum, to save the family some legal trouble. Well, so be it, no need for everyone to suffer needlessly. For Anse, that would be an affectation of no value in this world.

Doctorow, a wonderful author of novels himself, has some valuable observations about Faulkner's style of writing:

> Faulkner does a number of things in this novel that all together account for its unusual dimensions. Nothing is explained, scenes are not set, background information is not supplied, characters' CVs are not given. From the first line, the book is in medias res (*in the midst of things*): "Jewel and I come up from the field, following the path in single file." Who these people are, and the situation they are dealing with, the reader will work out in

the lag: the people in the book will always know more than the reader, who is dependent upon just what they choose to reveal. And at moments of crisis and impending disaster, what is happening is described incompletely by different characters so as to create in the reader a state of knowing and not knowing at the same time--a fracturing of the experience that has the uncanny effect of affirming its reality.

Surely an effective way of engaging the reader's attention and piquing his interest in following along on the story's unfolding journey. Often times writers spend many beginning pages of a novel attempting to give a complete exposition of who the characters are, how they arrived at this point in the story, and the problems they have to overcome.

Doctorow gives one more paragraph that illustrates these main points:

Of course Faulkner was not alone in his disdain of exposition. Though he didn't begin to write screenplays for Hollywood until some years after this novel was written, film had been around all his life and it was film that taught him and other early-twentieth-century writers that they no longer needed to explain anything--that it was preferable to incorporate all necessary information in the action, to carry it along in the current of the narrative, as is done in the movies. This way of working supposes a compact between writer and reader--that everything will become clear eventually.

Excellent essay, and valuable strategies to be considered by any writer.

Pinocchio, Themes from Classic Fables

Pinocchio, like many of the classic fables, seems to have numerous layers of symbolic meaning, much like the more studied, often darker, fairy tales of the Brothers Grimm. Perhaps the staying power of such stories owes something to our subconscious resonance to the embedded symbolism.

Tim Parks, writing for NYRB (30Apr2009), penned an interesting review for the new translation of the classic, "The Adventures of Pinocchio," by Carlo Collodi, translated by G. Brock. Collodi had a formative background that may well have colored his story of Pinocchio. Born in 1826, the first of ten children in a poor Florentine family, where six of his siblings died in childhood, Collodi knew the hardscrabble life he sets for Pinocchio and the puppet's creator/father, Geppetto. Collodi was educated in a seminary, but in 1848 and 1859 volunteered in two unsuccessful revolutionary wars fought to unify Italy and free it of foreign powers. By the late 1860s the country had been unified, and Collodi began his writing career working for the new Ministry of Education, where he was invited to write for children. As Parks tells it:

> The success of his children's books was welcome but Collodi's ambition had been to write adult literature. Here, however, his work was criticized for failing to deliver realistic character and incident, and for its underlying pessimism about both the new Italy and human nature in general.

Though given an exuberant, feel-good treatment by the Disney movie version of 1940, the original story told the adventures of a brash, gullible, and easily manipulated Pinocchio. Collodi's cynicism about human nature inhabits the puppet's disregard for his poor father's efforts to shelter and educate him, and is palpable in concocting the guileful, unsavory schemes of Cat and Fox for hoodwinking the puppet. Parks opines that Collodi's "…irritation at writing in a genre he thought secondary may have contributed to the story's extraordinary mood swings and unusually cavalier approach to such matters as narrative consistency," but which nevertheless contributed to the story's vitality.

Parks relates how Collodi tired of his story and wanted to end it at the point where Cat and Fox, unable to prise Pinocchio's mouth open to get at his hidden gold coins, hang him in a tree, and plan to return for the coins the following morning. However, the publishers prevailed on Collodi to continue, and he presses on with the following remarkable scene:

"Oh, if only you were here, Daddy!" calls Pinocchio. "His eyes closed, his mouth opened, his legs straightened, and then, after a tremendous shudder, he went completely limp."

Parks notes the scene appears suspiciously like an allusion to the Crucifixion. Yes, astonishing, but credible, considering the profane cynicism of the ex-seminarian, turned anti-cleric, and revolutionary soldier, who fought against Papal armies and their foreign allies opposed to unification of Italy.

Other religious symbolism may be ascribed to the character of the blue fairy, a girl with "sky-blue hair," and "her face white as a waxen image," iconography suggestive of Mary, the Blessed Mother figure in the Church. The blue fairy in the story is a recurring figure of solace and comfort to the beleaguered Pinocchio. Here, Collodi seems not so cynical, and perhaps somewhat wistful for the Italian archetypal figure of the ever-caring mother, exemplified by Mary.

In the end, Collodi tells us Pinocchio becomes a boy like other boys. Are we then elated, or are we rather nostalgic for the loss of Pinocchio's former individuality and freedom? But he never showed anything like individuality or enjoyed much freedom as a puppet, and had only ever been a victim of internal whim and external manipulation. Collodi loved such enigmas, and broke lots of conventional fiction writing rules to spin his magical, compelling tale. Perhaps that might be an invitation to writers not to adhere too slavishly to the so called *rules* for writing fiction.

The God Theme in Literature

Poetry and prose writers through the ages have produced some epic creative works with their visions of the immortal God(s), as conceived at particular times in history. Think of the Greek plays and epic poems, the Hindu epics, and the Middle Eastern and European pagan mythologies. The gods and superheroes in these may be immortal beings endowed with supernatural powers, but they generally resemble or approximate human form, and have familiar human appetites.

The rise of the later monotheistic religions, beginning with Judaism and proceeding through Christianity and Islam, present a more mysterious God, but either through revelation or inspiration, the later writers retain some anthropomorphic qualities for the one God. For example, He occasionally speaks in a familiar language; He's concerned with interpersonal relationships between Himself and humans, and between humans; and He has given some laws which are to govern these relationships.

The descriptive qualities and characteristics of God given by these three dominant monotheistic religions have not changed much, if at all, in the last 1500 to 2000 years, and seem somewhat frozen in the language and conceptual abilities of the authors who committed them to writing. The stasis became reason enough for some philosophers to declare God was now dead. Further modern scholarship, scriptural criticism, and science, have continued to bump up against the traditional, dogmatic views of God. Indeed, there now seems a plethora of books by modern writers promoting the atheist view: *God is not*

Great, by Christopher Hitchens; *The God Delusion*, by Richard Dawkins; and others. None of the atheists seem, however, to adequately address a resulting, fundamental issue of why then is there something instead of nothing?

Religious authorities have often frustrated progressive-minded theologians with a fear of heresy in exploring the questions and nature of a revealed God. Perhaps a lot more insights might otherwise have been gained in all these years.

Even literary fiction might happen onto some useful insights to God, through imaginative storytelling, guided by human experience and psyche. Think of *Moby Dick*, and consider an article in the NY Review of Books (Oct. 13, 2011), in which the writer, Robert Pogue Harrison, makes reference to remarks by Kafka:

> In his conversations with Gustav Jaknouch, Kafka reportedly remarked,
>
> "God dwells in darkness. And that is a good thing, because without the protecting darkness, we should try to overcome God. That is man's nature."
>
> These are the words of a modern individual speaking in the wake of what Nietzsche called the death of God. Something similar could be said of Shakespeare. Like Kafka's *Deus absconditus*, he withdraws into a protective darkness that prevents us from getting a secure handle on him, hence from overthrowing him.

These are extraordinary reflections by Kafka and Harrison.The God theme in literature can certainly be a powerful one for imaginative writers, though fraught with difficulties in not offending sensitive readers.

Cutting Ties

The books chosen for discussion are, *A Story of a Girl,* by Sara Zarr, a 2007 novel, and *The Member of the Wedding*, by Carson McCullers, 1946, an old classic. The two novels are very different in tone, mood, and style of writing, but a similar, elemental theme threads through both stories: an urgency, as a maturing main character senses the approaching time to leave home.

In 'Story,' Deanna's father had discovered her having sex with an older boy in his car when she was barely a teen. Not only does it undermine her relationship with her father, the boy spreads the story around their high school and Deanna's reputation suffers over the next several years. To complicate family dynamics, Deanna's older brother has had to marry early, after getting his girlfriend pregnant, and he and his wife and child live in the parents' basement. Chalk up another defeat for dad's shaky morale. Deanna dreams of finishing high school and then escaping her situation by teaming up with her brother and his family to get a house together. However, the brother realizes he's got his own growing up to do, and plans for he and his wife to move out on their own, without Deanna.

The story has strong emotional content, but the father, and mother, come close to being 'flat,' barely sympathetic figures. That's a hard writing obstacle to overcome, because with Deanna as first person narrator, we can't really get inside dad's or mom's head to build sympathy for any pain they might truly be feeling .

"Member..." is a wonderful read, almost Faulkner in mood and tone. It describes the awful loneliness and anxieties of Frankie, a twelve-year old girl, and her obsessive decision that she's going to leave the house of her widower father after the wedding of her brother, recently home from the Army. She conjures up immature images of the adventures she and the newlyweds will have as they travel the world together. As the wedding date approaches, Frankie raises the tension level of the story when she wanders into town, meets a boozy on-leave soldier, and naively accompanies him back to his hotel room. We are aghast as the situation deteriorates for the inexperienced Frankie.

In other scenes, long conversations Frankie has in her kitchen with her father's black servant woman, Berenice, and elsewhere with Berenice's friends in their homes, reveal the tenuous relations between races in the old South. The moods and anxieties of Frankie are everywhere so well portrayed.

A deeply satisfying classic story.Both stories are good models for the 'Leaving Home' theme.

I

Islands in the Sea

Author Michael Parker was interviewed on National Public Radio about his new book of short stories, *Don't make me stop now.* One of the stories was about an elderly black man and two elderly white sisters hanging on and living out their days on one of the Outer Bank Islands off the east coast. They're the last ones on the island. The man's son is trying to get him to leave, telling him those sisters don't mean anything to him, but there's some sort of relationship and he's adamant about staying. A good theme of people trying to hang onto a disappearing way of life, near a rugged sea coast.

There are two other memorable books on our theme. They are memoirs about the near-last inhabitants of the austere, wind-swept, Great Blasket Islands, off the southwest coast of Ireland: *Peig,* by Peig Sayersk, and *The Islandman,* by Tomás O'Crohan. The island people ultimately grow weary of their hard existence and petition the government to resettle them on the mainland, in about the late Thirties. The memoirs are written in Gaelic, and translated into English. Good reading and a great theme.

Fictional Truth

An essay by Frederick Reiken in *The Writer's Chronicle,* Mar./ Apr. 2007, titled *What is True?—Thoughts on Fictional 'Truth,' Unconscious Metaphor, and Celery,* had many cogent thoughts on our theme.

One of the ideas is that a 'fictional truth' needs to rise above the ordinary, factual, black-and-white happenings of real life if we want it to support a literary work. We've often heard, in workshops and such, 'just because it happened doesn't make it interesting.' Reiken's essay used an excerpt from a short piece titled "How to Tell a True War Story," included in Tim O'Brien's Vietnam fiction work, *The Things They Carried*:

> You can tell a true war story by the questions you ask. Somebody tells a story, let's say, and afterward you ask "Is it true?" and if the answer matters, you've got your answer.

> For example, we've all heard this one. Four guys go down a trail. A grenade sails out. One guy jumps on the grenade and takes the blast and saves his three buddies.

> Is it true?

> You'd feel cheated if it never happened.

> Without the grounding reality, it's just a trite bit of puffery, pure Hollywood, untrue in the way all such stories are untrue. Yet even if it did happen—and maybe it did,

anything's possible—even then you know it can't be true, because a true war story does not depend on that kind of truth. Absolute occurrence is irrelevant. A thing may happen and be a total lie; another thing may not happen and be truer than the truth. For example: Four guys go down a trail. A grenade sails out. One guy jumps on it and takes the blast, but it's a killer grenade and everybody dies anyway. Before they die though, one of the dead guys says, "The fuck you do that for?" and the jumper says "Story of my life, man," and the other guy starts to smile but he's dead.

That's a true war story that never happened.

Which provides a great illustration of literary, fictional truth. Another idea in the essay touched on a fiction writer's use of story ambiguity. Quoting work by author John Berger, Reiken says, "Authentic writing depends primarily on a writer's willingness to stay faithful to the fundamental ambiguity of experience." Also, "a writer who attempts to close too many ambiguities at once without opening others will run into a problem…"

The idea of keeping ambiguities afloat during a fictional work seems so important, to extend the suspense of events, and to keep the reader turning the pages. One of my favorite creative writing mentors, John Gardner, also gets some play in Reiken's essay. He uses topics from Gardner's book entitled, "On Moral Fiction," and it resonates a lot with the 'metaphors' of our essay title. In sum, this is an essay to read over a couple of times—good stuff.

Thoughts on a genre label

Out Stealing Horses by Tor Petterson was listed in the NY Times as one of the 10 Best Books of 2007. The book encompasses the coming-of-age story of a Norwegian boy, Trond, beginning with a summer in 1948 when he lived with his father in a rustic cabin near the border between Norway and Sweden. The title derives from the boy and a local friend stealing rides on a neighboring farmer's horses at night. Other accounts of Trond's subsequent summer experiences at the cabin are given as reflections when Trond returns to the cabin to live out his final days as an old man. We learn that Trond's father was part of the Norwegian Resistance against the occupying Nazi forces, and of an occasion when Trond accompanies his father on one of his risky trips into neutral Sweden. As Trond becomes an older teen, he helps his father float timber logs, cut from their cabin property, down the river to a sawmill in Sweden. The quiet, ending days of Trond in the wintery cabin have a poetic simplicity.

How should a writer best pitch this novel for publication, as a YA, coming-of-age, or general literary fiction novel? Would it have been any easier to market as one or the other? Would It have been as successful if marketed as a YA novel? Would the declining arc of Trond's life, no matter how beautifully written, engage a young reader, and perhaps weigh on the decision?

Boys' Tribalism, and Rites-of-Passage

In all strata of life, in every neighborhood, and every ethnicity, there seem to be common rites of passage that boys must navigate in one way or another. Girls will have their own rites of passage, in some ways similar, other ways not. Such rites endure, though the threats change with times. A pensive mood and reflections may arise after reading a YA novel, *Sins of the Fathers*, by Chris Lynch. Lynch is such a memorable writer in YA literature.

The three boys of the novel form a tightly knit tribe unto themselves: Drew, the narrator and most expressive, Skitz, the fatherless clown, and Hector, seemingly the strong, silent force. Drew's dialog, flowing smoothly from inner to outer expression, draws the reader into almost inhabiting his physical character. The setting is a parochial school in Boston, and rough as they are, or would like to see themselves, they respect the sisters who teach there and the three parish priests who oversee the school. One of the priests is a newly assigned, young, hippie-like Jesuit, who tries to befriend the boys, and continually uses bad judgment, drinking on outings with the boys to a Bruin's hockey game, rolling a joint in Drew's presence—immature conduct, and ultimately damaging to him. The boys have some destructive habits themselves: popping St. Joseph aspirin with RC cola to get a buzz, and one of them experiments with sniffing glue.

A deeper, darker theme emerges toward the end of the novel. The abuse of minors by some clergy has been all too common in the newspapers, but it is unfailingly wrenching with each new disclosure. One of the boys has probably endured such a betrayal, and the reader will hope his tribe will be able to keep him from falling into an abyss of remorse and substance abuse, and that the three friends will help carry each other forward.

A difficult theme to work with, but Lynch does a good job.

Gene Robbers

Recently our local Grange held a benefit for Percy Schmeiser, a visiting Canadian, who owns an organic farm raising canola (rapeseed) plants. Percy's farm is located near other farmers who use Monsanto's genetically modified canola seed. Percy's crop became contaminated with the modified genetic strain (wind, birds, footprints, who knows?). When it was discovered, Monsanto ordered Percy to pay for a license or to have his crop destroyed, otherwise, he would face legal action. The Grange benefit was to help Percy with his legal costs contesting Monsanto's action.

It seemed a case of intellectual property and patent rights gone amok. In another case, an article in a newspaper discussed how patents may be awarded to researchers of human genes they discover to be markers of certain genetic traits, especially genetic disorders. Consequently, the researcher might actually own the rights to genes some people have in their bodies, presumably making them intellectual property rights pirates.

If such were discovered in routine medical exams, would a person be required to pay a fee to license their own genes? Or, perhaps somehow remove them? Just thinking. Might be a sci-fi story hidden in this modern theme.

Free Will—a Story Theme?

A Jan. 2, 2007 issue of the NY Times says "a bevy of experiments in recent years suggest that the conscious mind is like a monkey riding a tiger of subconscious decisions and actions in progress, frantically making up stories about being in control." Free willers generally hold that whatever choice you make is unforced and could have been otherwise, but it is not random. "That strikes many people as incoherent," a Dr. Silberstein said. Every physical system that has been investigated has turned out to be either deterministic, or random. "Both are bad news for free will," he said. There's a story, just waiting to be developed.

Sci-fi Underpinnings

It can be enjoyable to explore the use of real, philosophical underpinnings in writing sci-fi, but also important to make it seamless and unobtrusive when used in a story plot. We've seen story characters, even young ones, toss off allusions to concepts of Teilhard de Chardin, a Jesuit geologist who did exploration in China in the early Twentieth Century (he discovered the remains of Peking Man). In a sense, Teilhard felt that all matter in the universe had a level of consciousness-- even rocks. Young readers have liked that idea. In another sense, all components of creation become more complex as time advances. Think of man as a complex molecule, becoming ever more complex with time. A good underpinning for sci-fi, but needs to be kept subsumed in an interesting, dramatic storyline.

Wilderness Survival

A youth struggling to survive in the wilderness makes for compelling reading, and *Touching Spirit Bear*, by Ben Mikaelsen, 2001, is another addition to the genre, with an interesting twist. The wilderness struggle is set up as a juvenile justice experiment. This sort of rehabilitation has been applied in Native American justice, and in this MG/YA novel it is portrayed as being tried for a non-Native American youth offender in Minnesota.

Cole, a violent tempered high school student has badly mauled a classmate in a fight. A chance to avert a jail sentence is offered to him by an experimental Circle Justice Council brought in by the court. The Council offers Cole a chance to spend a year in isolation on a deserted island, somewhere in Minnesota, as a means of applying justice and healing for the criminal offender, the victim, and the community. Cole is interested only in escaping a prison sentence and accepts, though inwardly mocking those trying to help him. While on the island, he destroys the shelter and food he was provided with, and tries to escape, but fails. His rage is directed at a white bear that ventures near his camp, a bear known to Indians in the region as the spirit bear, and he is badly mauled by the bear. After he is found by his Tlingit Indian supervisor who visits the island periodically, he is nursed back to health and elects to return to the island to try and complete his trial.

The story is interesting, with compelling wilderness aspects, though the character of Cole, the violent young boy who was beaten by his alcoholic father while growing up, and the father, could have been better developed.

A good theme that can be developed into many different settings and character types to amplify the theme

Reading Ease of YA Novels

The Astonishing Life of Octavian Nothing — Traitor to the Nation, by M. T. Anderson is a challenging read on many accounts. It took many pages to get grounded in the story: is it a futuristic, or fantasy novel? People who are members of a curious enterprise called *The Novanglian College of Lucidity*, 'devoted to divining the secrets of the universe,' and called only by digital identification, 03-01, 07-04 — that give some measure of a person's social standing and his profession. What's going on here? What period of time are we in?

A first clue, or not, is that the language seems a sort of archaic English. Gradually the reader learns the setting is colonial times, and near Boston. At the beginning of the story, the main character is an African boy, named Octavian Nothing. The college purchased him and his mother, an African Princess, in the slave market, to be studied for the characteristics of their race. Can they learn Western music? How much of what they eat is converted to energy, to waste? These and other seemingly banal quests for knowledge leave the reader questioning the mental capacity of the college intellects.

Gradually, possible story themes emerge, of how unenlightened the social, philosophical, and scientific thought might have been in some circles of Revolutionary-era America, and particularly how unenlightened it was toward African slaves. It might not have been as harsh as in the more agrarian South, but seemed just as degrading.

The complete story of Octavian Nothing will be published in at least two volumes, reportedly, and this volume carries us up to Octavian's participation in some early Revolutionary War clashes, where slaves were "loaned" by their owners to the patriots for some of the heavy work of war, and to 'excuse' their own lack of participation.

Anderson has set in motion an ambitious story, which is not an easy read, but seems to have all the hallmarks of intensive research—from the language of the times, to the previously little known attitude of colonial New England toward slavery. Apparently it has received favorable attention from young readers, and that it renews confidence in youth's abilities to wrestle with a difficult literary work, if it encompasses a good story.

To point out what is meant by difficult reading, a sample was taken at random, p.54, and analyzed with WORD's grammar check, to find the following interesting statistics:

Words per sentence—40
Flesch Reading Ease—55 %
Flesch Kincaid Reading Level—11th Grade

Contrast these data with the scores for some bestselling authors, and a Pulitzer Prize winner, in a study that shows a Reading Level—Grade 6, and Reading Ease—80 Percent for the study group.. Perhaps Octavian's reception is welcome news for writers of young people's literature who might like to use more difficult language, and intricate plot development, but were held back by assumptions about youths' reading abilities.

STRUCTURE

Elements of Choice for how to start

E. L. Doctorow was noted for creating fiction in a historical setting and mingling real persons of the period along with his fictional characters. For example, in his novel, *Ragtime*, he has a fictional episode with Sigmund Freud and Carl Jung, sharing a ride at Coney Island. NPR aired an earlier radio interview with Doctorow in which he said he preferred to think of such writing as 'national' fiction, instead of historical fiction. Perhaps because he veers more widely from the known historical script for his characters and period, though he captures the true characters and place settings of the era all the same.

In the radio interview, Doctorow discussed his writing of *Billy Bathgate*. He had spent a lot of time thinking out the character of *Billy* and the elements of plot and motif, but was having a difficult time getting started with the actual writing. It wasn't until he wrote out the first line of Billy *himself* telling us who he was, that Doctorow knew where he was heading and what *Billy* was to be about. From there on it was a process of learning from his characters what had to follow, and how best to get there. The method strongly suggests a process of listening to some inner muse, or the author's subconscious, to commune with the characters in writing the most authentic, compelling fiction.

This process is at the other end of a writing spectrum for starting a work of fiction, wherein it has been suggested to first develop a written outline of the novel before beginning to write, and maybe even a preliminary storyboard (a graphic, sequential display of the principal plot elements). The hazard of starting a new work without a well developed outline can lead beginning writers to "spaghetti-ing," a term coined by Jon Franklin, a two-time Pulitzer Prize winner, in his book, *Writing for Story*.

Franklin's book is honed toward creative non-fiction writers, but he stresses his advice is meant as well for fiction writers, too. His point being that as any story moves along more and more complications can arise; precedents that have been established seem to be falling by the wayside; motivations seem to be clashing; and so, the flow "is taking on the consistency of horse-hoof glue." Seems like an apt description for a manuscript in trouble, nonetheless, one can allow that a writer as gifted as Doctorow may more readily avoid such calamities, even without an outline, by being truly in communion with his characters and practiced enough to consult his muse at key points about where the ongoing plot may be leading. It may take a little more experience and courage to dare taking Doctorow's approach, even if just occasionally. It certainly seems a bit more exciting and may be more creative—In skilled hands.

So, we have Doctorow's example of how he began a specific, highly acclaimed novel (which led to a movie of the same name, featuring Dustin Hoffman); Doctorow had his character tell us who he was and what he was about. This also presented an early opportunity to establish a unique *voice* for Billy, an eventual 'must' for any character in a compelling piece of literature.

Another often used and competing motif is to start with a description of time and place setting for the story. The thought being these are usually principal screening criteria for many readers while trying to decide whether to go any further before choosing a book. Recalling another frequent advisory, there are usually only three to five pages to capture the interest of a reader, agent, or editor. Although place can indeed be an important element in a story, almost as compelling in stature as to be a 'character' in itself, this choice might also easily devolve into some static, overly wrought descriptive language for opening the story.

A closing thought on choosing a beginning motif is to consider the use of *in medias res* (into the middle of a narrative, into the midst of things.) It might also provide a good opportunity for incorporating voice and place setting together, and right up front. Select some dramatic scene that was visualized for later in the story and bring it forward, perhaps a scene that shows the principal character in action and speaking in his own, unique voice. Keep in mind, only three-to-five pages, at most, before your reader might make a choice whether to add the book to his cart and proceed to checkout.

Starting the story in medias res—into the midst of things

A river becomes a thing of substance *in medias res*, long after its headwaters take form, and not yet to the ocean estuary. Sometimes an author's story has advanced to substantial sections of vivid, suspenseful, engaging material, but such sections now lie buried somewhere in the midst of the story. The author may have chosen to first introduce his cast of characters, perhaps fixes them somewhere in the social hierarchy of a place, and dramatizes a few of their strengths and weaknesses, before revealing the main obstacles or tension they must overcome.

It may be that if the introductory material has characters of unique personalities, and the special quality of 'voice' so often stressed in writing classes and conferences, the reader may stick around long enough to reach those compelling sections of our book.

Alternately, perhaps the better strategy for structuring the book is to consider the technique of *in medias res (into the midst of things)*, and find a way to bring the best material forward to the beginning. Capture the reader early on, and fill in details as needed for the progression of the story toward a final resolution.

A Manual for Cleaning Women, by Lucia Berlin, is a collection of short stories that mostly begin *in medias res*. The stories are first person narration, but since the action starts almost immediately we don't get to learn much about whom our narrator is, or her relationship to other named characters, until

Berlin drops the appropriate links which tie the characters and events together without interrupting the trajectory of her story. Berlin often writes in an abbreviated, urgent syntax, sometimes inserting independent observational clauses that surprise us but increase our interest, and she uses stream of consciousness thoughts on the unfolding action.

Taking a few excerpts from the first two pages of her story, "Emergency Room Notebook, 1977:

> You never hear sirens in the emergency room--the drivers turn them off on Webster Street...If it is Code Three, where life is in critical danger, the doctor and nurses wait outside, chatting in anticipation. Inside, in room 6, the trauma room, is the Code Blue team. EKG, X-ray technicians respiratory therapists, cardiac nurses. In most Code Blues, though, the EMT drivers or firemen are too busy to call in. Piedmont Fire Department never does, and they have the worst. Rich massive coronaries, matronly phenobarbital suicides, children in swimming pools...

> Madame Y is the most beautiful woman I have ever seen. She looks dead, actually, her skin translucent blue-white, her exquisitely boned Oriental face serene and ageless. She wears black slacks and boots, mandarin-collared jackets cut and trimmed in Asia? France? The Vatican, maybe--they have the weight of a bishop's cassock--or an X-ray robe. The piping has been done by hand in rich fuchsia, magentas, oranges. Her Bentley drives up at nine, driven by a flippant

Filipino who chain-smokes Shermans in the parking lot. Her two sons, tall, in suits made in Hong Kong, escort her from the car to the entrance of radiation therapy...

She is dead now. Not sure when it happened, on one of my days off. She always seemed dead anyway, but nicely so, like an illustration or advertisement.

So we're two pages in and we know almost nothing about our narrator but we see lots of activity through her eyes, and the style of writing and quirky observational detail promise interesting reading ahead. A writer can learn some useful structuring and elements of style from Berlin.

Backstory in This Volume or Next?

We sometimes begin our stories *in medias res*, in the midst of things, with no preamble as to who these characters are, or how this situation developed. It's often a good strategy, and can help capture a reader in the crucial early pages of a book.

A competing strategy for a writer is to first spend some time characterizing the protagonist(s), the principal problem(s) he faces, and the obstacles or opponents he must overcome. In this strategy, a tendency exists for the writer to load the development of a story with too much detail, before a reader might even have had a chance to become invested in the characters or the problem of the story.

Depending on our chosen writing strategy, if we need to reveal some important facet of the character's life, or the development of the problem, before the time of the narrative, the writer will often resort to a 'flashback.' The flashback can be as short as a few sentences, or it might encompass an entire chapter embedded within the narrative of the current story. Regardless, an effective flashback can be difficult to use without disturbing the '*fictional dream*' (John Gardner, *The Art of Fiction*) for the reader, and possibly losing our reader.

It was interesting to note how author Marilynne Robinson handled the absence of any backstory for an otherwise quite interesting character, Lila, who appeared in *Gilead*, her 2005 Pulitzer Prize winning novel. Lila was an intriguing young woman who appeared out of nowhere to marry a much older preacher, as related in this spare, beautifully written story set in the mid-nineteenth century Iowa plains. Nevertheless, she was not to be the focus of the *Gilead* story. It was enough to just have her appear on the scene as a secondary character, and with an air of mystery.

Robinson then devoted the subsequent novel, *Lila*, to expand on this unique woman. It deepens our sympathies with and understanding of Lila's character, but could not have been accommodated any further than what was done within the theme and structure of the earlier *Gilead* novel.

Serial Novels

The NY Times (11/21/2011) reported that the writer, Mark Z. Danielewski planned a 27 volume novel, titled "The Familiar." The novel was planned to be released with one new volume every three months, beginning in 2014. Knopf Doubleday was reported to have paid one million dollars for the first ten books.

Danielewski had an optimistic view that a huge, long-running, serial release like his would generate perhaps daily, or at least ongoing, buzz about the characters and storyline. He hoped for something similar to what unfolds in newspaper columns, radio talk shows, and public conversations during a season of popular TV episodes, like the "Sopranos," or the "Mad Men."

"Literature is capable of being a subject that people want to catch up on or discuss, whether at a coffee shop or a watercooler," Mr. Danielewski said. "It can become an intrinsic part of their dialogue." His editor said the books would be an attempt to create a "serial relationship" with the readers.

Well, certainly J. K. Rowling had epic success with serial releases (7) of her Harry Potter fantasy novels over about 10 years. According to Wikipedia, her book series has sold about 450 million copies.

Another greatly successful novel series was the eight books, beginning with "Anne of Green Gables," written by Canadian author Lucy Maude Montgomery, and published between 1908 and 1921. The books track the life of Anne, beginning when she arrives as a precocious 11-year old orphan at a farm on Prince

Edward Island in Canada, up until she is a teacher there in her early fifties. The books have sold about 50 million copies, according to Wikipedia, and are included in school curriculums all over the world.

An example of success in serial novel publication in a different genre is Patrick O'Brian's Aubrey-Maturin seafaring adventures, which included 20 novels published between 1969 and 1999. Jack Aubrey is a British Royal Navy officer, and Stephen Maturin is the ship's surgeon, who serve together at sea during the French Revolutionary and Napoleonic Wars. This series sold over 2 million copies, according to Wikipedia.

A more common serial novel enterprise is, perhaps, the more manageable trilogy. A good example of a well-done trilogy is the "Hunger Games," by Suzanne Collins. It is a young adult, science fiction series set at some time in what could be a not too distant future, in which the surviving sociopolitical structure of North America has been reduced by internal wars to a despotic capitol and twelve outlying districts--a thirteenth was assumed to have already been annihilated--and wherein the districts serve all the economic needs of the capitol. Annual 'Hunger Games,' gladiatorial contests organized by the capitol, in which a male and female from each district are selected by lottery to fight until the death of all but one, serve to keep the masses sufficiently traumatized, and entertained. Each of the books in this series were on best-seller lists, and were critically acclaimed.

It is interesting to note in Wikipedia the structure adopted by Collins for each of her books in the series. Each book in *The*

Hunger Games trilogy has 27 chapters and is further divided into 3 sections of 9 chapters each. Collins says that this format comes from her playwriting background, which taught her to write in three acts. Her previous series, *The Underland Chronicles,* was written in the same way, as Collins is "very comfortable" with this structure. She sees each group of nine chapters as a separate part of the story, and comments that she still calls those divisions "act breaks".

It seems interesting to organize the structure of a story, as Collins has done here. It is reminiscent of the very organized and focused method advocated by Jon Franklin in his "Writing for Story." Franklin is a two-time Pulitzer Prize winning author. His craft has been honed on creative non-fiction short stories, but his writing advice seems equally valuable for fiction writers. A good reference for lean, taut writing.

Stoker's Dracula, and the Annotator's Twist

The classic story of *Dracula*, by Bram Stoker, originally published in 1897, has had a long, and continuing run with readers of fiction--or was it even fiction? In the 2008 special edition by W. W. Norton, with an introduction by Neil Gaiman, and annotated by Leslie S. Klinger, we read in the preface by Klinger:

> *My principal aim...has been to restore a sense of wonder, excitement, and sheer fun to this great work. To that end, perhaps for the first time, I examine Stoker's published compilation of letters, journals, and recordings as Stoker wished: I employ a gentle fiction here, as I did in The New Annotated Sherlock Holmes, that the events described in Dracula "really took place" and that the work presents the recollections of real persons, whom Stoker has renamed and whose papers (termed the "Harker Papers" in my notes) he has recast, ostensibly to conceal their identities.*

As Stoker wished. We wonder what Klinger meant?

Some readers may remember the Bela Lugosi movie of *Dracula* from many years ago, and some may be more than a little surprised by the resurgent popular interest in all things 'vampire' over the past decade--Anne Rice's books, TV series like "Buffy the Vampire Slayer," lots of YA novels, etc. Norton's new, annotated version is a new look at the Dracula story, and also contains Stoker's originally published manuscript. The writing is good and the story engages the reader. The numerous annotations made by Klinger on almost every page may be distracting at first, but when one pauses to read them they are usually quite informative. The story flows well and is suitably mysterious. However, as the plot unfolds within the Transylvania region, the earnest annotations arguing for and against the veracity of certain events and geography seemed forced. It began to appear that perhaps Klinger was too invested in pointing out physical or historic facts and circumstances that matched a real, but little known history of the vampire, Dracula.

As the story progresses, and Dracula makes his way to England, his depredations become more ghoulish. Klinger's notes begin to compare the attacks of the vampire, and the countering strategies employed by the story's four men and one woman opposing Dracula, contrasted with previously known folklore, or testaments as to the powers and habits of vampires. The reader begins to be seduced into believing there might be a quasi-historical foundation for such vampirism. However, the 'fictional dream' state necessary to sustain good fiction suffers somewhat whenever the reader's attention is drawn from the flow and suspense of the storyline to check on what Klinger has to say about events. Sometimes what he has to say has a strong rational basis, as when Professor Van Helsing makes on-the-spot transfusions of blood to one of Dracula's victims on three separate mornings, using different volunteer donors each time from among the men. A Klinger annotation remarks how 'fortunate' that these transfusions were all successful:

> *Truly remarkable doctoring. Although the science of blood transfusing was still in its infancy, there was some understanding that compatibility of donor and recipient was important. Having transfused Lucy twice successfully (by blind luck), Van Helsing rolls the dice a third time, risking serious problems, rather than fall back on a tested donor.*

Klinger's point seems valid, but it seems risky to disrupt a continuity of the 'fictional dream' with such a disconcerting observation. Other critical annotations seemed to question distances traveled in elapsed time periods, conflicting dates of diary entries, etc., unethical legal behavior of the solicitor, Jonathan Harker, the credulousness of Professor Van Helsing, criticisms of Helsing's dialect (remotely Teutonic) etc. However, many such items were not likely to cause the reader too much difficulty in staying with the story. There were a few items pointing out an inconsistency in the powers available to the vampire which might have given the reader some pause, even without the annotation.

For the most enjoyment one should probably read the story through completely before looking at any annotations. However, rereading while pausing to go over the annotations, or just skimming back over the story to study the annotations, can be quite enjoyable. The annotations refer repeatedly to differences or agreements with the "Harker Papers," which are a fictional construct of Klinger.

The actual documentation left by Stoker for his conceptualization and writing of the Dracula novel are a collection of *Notes*, prepared circa 1890-1896, and held by the Rosenbach Museum and Library in Philadelphia, Pennsylvania, and an interim manuscript prepared sometime prior to the published version of 1897. The interim manuscript is currently held by a private owner, Mr. Paul G. Allen. Klinger had reviewed all of these documents for the annotated volume published by Norton. It appears the "Harker Papers" are a label used by Klinger for the interviews we are to presume were made by Stoker with real people, and who were involved in real events described in *Dracula*. Klinger suggests that the existing *Notes* were subsequently prepared from those interviews, after changing names to protect identities of the real people. An original set of "Harker Papers" that predate Stoker's Notes are thus Klinger's "gentle fiction."

The idea of the interviews suggested by Klinger are not so far-fetched, however. The creative process followed by Bram Stoker employs typical elements that some, if not most, writers might consider in developing such a novel. The concept is the usual first step, followed perhaps by an outline. Not all writers will employ the outline, preferring to give the first draft free rein without any such constraint. However, before starting a first draft, some writers will conduct a written interview, as if it actually happened, with one or more of their main characters. Such a process can help a writer find a unique 'voice' and personality for a character, and how they might be disposed to act, given the tensions anticipated in playing out the concept of the story. Thus, the idea proposed by Klinger that a collection of interviews of real people by Stoker actually fits in as a conceivable step in the writing of *Dracula*.

It is recommended to read the story through at least once without reference to the annotations, to enjoy the full mystery and atmosphere of Stoker's compelling story, and then enjoy reading it again with reference to the annotations by Klinger. Many are rich in content, others perhaps a little carping, but writers will appreciate both Stoker's, and Klinger's, feats of imagination; first in the original creation, and secondly in the annotated heightening of the mystery of *Dracula*.

Creative nonfiction, synchronous with storytelling

Who hasn't been inspired by the historic photographs of stoic and enduring men and women, poor by birthright, and struggling to survive the additional economic calamities of the Great Depression, and the Dust Bowl. Many Americans will recall the famous photograph, taken by Dorothea Lange, showing a migrant mother of two children in a camp for the homeless during the Great Depression. Another famous photographer known for his work in that era was Walker Evans, chosen as the partner of a writer, James Agee, in a reporting team sent by *Fortune* magazine in 1936 to document living conditions of cotton tenant farmers in the Deep South.

Agee wrote the resulting article about the lives of three farm families he observed during two months in which he lived with one of the families. However, his article was never published by *Fortune*, and no reason was given by the magazine. It was fairly long, about 30,000 words, but tabling the article was perhaps in no small measure due to the descriptions of desperate, marginal living conditions documented by Agee for those poverty stricken families.

The sometimes overwrought language, and often scandalous opinions written by Agee on the character of the tenant farmer or sharecropper families could presumably have been reworked by his editors, but perhaps the editors of a magazine extolling the virtues of capitalism and free market enterprise to achieve an upward mobility of workers might have seemed to be in bitter contrast to what was actually documented in the draft article.

Agee was fresh out of Harvard when he went to work for the magazine. He so impressed his bosses with his work over the next four years that he was chosen to do the feature story on the lives of cotton farm tenants in the summer of 1936. There seems little doubt from his original manuscript that his heart was with the tenant farmer. However, his point-of-view (POV) as a writer seemed that of an omniscient narrator, imparting thoughts and motivations of individuals that were at best subjective, and often had a scandalous effect. He must have known that if his story was published much of what he wrote might be seen as a sort of betrayal by the people he had lived among.

The publisher released the original manuscript back to Agee after declining to publish it. Agee worked the raw material for another several years and he published a novel from it in 1941, "Let Us Now Praise Famous Men," (an ironic title, taken from Ecclesiastes). It sold only 600 copies when first published, but became a bestseller when it was reissued in 1960.

The typescript for the article written for Fortune was found by his daughter while going through her father's effects in the house he left to her. The rediscovered material was published in May, 2013, as "Cotton Tenants: Three Families," with selected photographs taken by Walker Evans during their field assignment. Follow-ups of the story first told in "Famous

Men" were done by other reporters in July, and August, of 1986, fifty years after Agee and Evans did their original field work. The book that resulted, "And Their Children After Them," by David Maharidge and Michael Williamson, won the Pulitzer Prize for non-fiction in 1990.

Of the surviving cotton tenant farm adults, and their children, some were offended by their story as told in "Famous Men," and others weren't. In any case Agee died of alcoholism in 1955, at age 45, long before he might have had to face up to any in the tenant families who had felt betrayed. As one of the tenant families daughters related in her journal, speaking of Agee's book,

> There's a whole lot in there that's true, and a whole lot that isn't true. He was a mess. My goodness, I could turn around and write a book on him.

The story, the descriptions, and the photographs of "Cotton Tenants: Three Families," are mesmerizing, though some of Agee's subjective assessments and over-the-top language may be insensitive to the telling of a crushing way of life. By the late forties, things had changed significantly in the Deep South Cotton farming was fast disappearing as an important economic activity in the region, and the ordinary life of country folk, removed now from the penury of marginal existence imposed and maintained by the old tenancy or sharecropping system, had many things to admire.

Some still ate biscuits and gravy with eye-watering salt pork for breakfast, drank chicory coffee, and perhaps had a simple, crumbled cornbread in fresh-churned buttermilk, eaten from a goblet with a spoon for their evening meal. You might describe the earlier tenant's diet as a greasy, fat-laden mess, destroying everyone's teeth, as Agee does, or you could see some similarities to the modern Atkins high fat diet. A little levity here, to lighten the heavy sledding through Agee's hard-edged but powerful prose.

A review of "Cotton Tenants: Three Families," appears in the Nov. 7, 2013 issue of NY Review of Books, written by Ian Frazier.

Think with the story

The title is a spin on some advice that Ezra Pound was reported to have given poets: *think with the poem*. Contrary advice is sometimes given to fiction writers who have been taught they must be completely aware of every facet of their characters' likes, dislikes, past life, foibles, strengths, and, above all, what it is they want in the story, their desire, and the obstacles to achieving that desire, before setting the pen to paper (or fingers to keyboard).

Some may recall instructors who advocated sitting down with a few pages of prepared questions (or an entire notebook) to familiarize themselves with the earlier life experiences and a physiological genome of the fictional character. This might include her Briggs-Meyers psychological profile, and enough physical appearance detail that might suffice for a modeling agency photo-op, spec sheet.

David Jauss, writing in the magazine, The Writer's Chronicle, Mar/Apr 2013, in "Homo Sapiens vs. Homo Fictus," gives some formidable arguments against such all-encompassing prep work, preferring something for character definition more along the lines of Ezra: *think with the story*. "If compiling a list of traits and attributes isn't the way to create a character, what is?" posits Jauss. "A more effective way, I'd argue, is to let the imagination supply the details as the needs of the story arise-- and during the actual composition of the story, not in advance."

Jauss suggests that developing reams of preconceived data about our character may put us at risk of wanting to use a lot of it and "in danger of proving that Voltaire was right when he said, *The secret of being a bore is to tell everything*." The point being, a writer can deaden his character by weighing him down with too much revelation and detail. Jauss uses Salinger's character, Holden Caulfield, to illustrate the point: "he consists of a handful of physical details, a couple of days of conversations and interactions with fewer than a dozen characters, and snippets of memories of three or four past events (principally, the death of his brother, Allie)."

Jauss says Salinger gave only seven descriptive details about Holden, and all served to reveal the essence of his character. Here are the details (Jauss's page citations from *Catcher in the Rye* have been omitted):

1. he has a deep voice
2. he's unusually tall for a 16-year-old
3. he's had "millions of gray hairs" on one side of his head since he was a kid
4. he wears a crew cut even though it's out of date and girls encourage him to grow his hair longer
5. he wears a red hunting hat backwards
6. he has a sore on the inside of his lip
7. he's unable to make a fist with his right hand because he broke it while knocking out all the windows in his family's garage after his brother died

It's amazing to see such a brief list when so many readers are usually able to conjure up fairly vivid memories of this irascible character. Still, we remember Holden promised that he wasn't going to give us *all that David Copperfield kind of crap* about himself.

The other points we started out to discuss for our fiction characters was the need for determining what it is they want in the story, e.g. their motivation, or their desire, and the obstacles to achieving that desire. Such strictures have usually been the principal focus, often the only focus, for creative writing workshops and critiques. They might be called the Hammurabi Code for Writers, after the famous 1750 B.C.E., Middle-Eastern legal code:

> If a builder build a house for some one, and does not construct it properly, and the house which he build fall in and kill its owner, then that builder shall be put to death.

Substitute author for builder, story for house, and publisher for owner, and you get an idea of the moral charge some would impose on a writer for settling on a character's want, or desire, before beginning their story.

Jauss says "The desire-based theory of character implies characters actually *do* know what they desire, that their motivation is clear, and that each effect has a definable, understandable cause. Interestingly, the most intriguing characters in literature don't know why they do what they do, and neither do we." He goes on to discuss with us that most famous of indecisive characters in literature, Hamlet. "I suspect that even those who claim we need to know our characters' motives inside and out find Hamlet a more compelling and believable character precisely because they don't understand his motivation."

Jauss cites other authors on contemporary fiction about characters who lack a clearly defined desire to motivate their behavior, who want something he or she can't define, and includes some favorite short story writers, Alice Munro, Flannery O'Connor, and Raymond Carver. He also pays homage to the mastery of Chekov, whose stories frequently comment on the inscrutability of human motivation.

Mythic Energies to Enhance Fiction

Mythic energy in fiction may be hard to define in words, but we usually recognize its presence when we engage it in a work of fiction, whether as a reader, or a writer. When a fiction writer recognizes his story has mythic undercurrents, he would probably do well to sharpen the plot to exploit such material. Fiction that lasts generally touches on universal themes, stuff that excites emotional resonance in our DNA, and the stuff of myths typically does this for everyone.

Take a classic in YA literature, *Tuck Everlasting,* by Natalie Babbitt. The story tells of the Tuck family, in rural, early America, where family members share the secret of a spring that contributes to their immortality. Another myth of the fountain of youth, tells of a search for it in Florida by an earlier, Spanish explorer, Ponce de Leon. *Tuck Everlasting* is beautifully written, with wonderful pastoral scenes, but it was the mythical undercurrents of immortality, aging, and related secrets, that gave the story its power.

A contemporary bestseller that exploits the mythic energy theme is *The Thousand Autumns of Jacob de Zoet,* by David Mitchell. In this story of Dutch traders in 1700s Japan, a Japanese woman, a midwife, whom Jacob has fallen in love with, is abducted by a powerful noble, and is forcibly confined in a secluded temple under his control. Ostensibly, the temple mission is to rescue destitute, often disfigured, women, and provide a place of refuge for them. However, under the trappings of goddess worship, the women are made to bear children for the monks. The children are soon removed from the women, presumably to be given to good families on the outside, but actually the children suffer a terrible fate in the quest for the immortality of the noble and his monks. Again, an interesting background story of the Dutch East India Trading Co. activities and its people in early post-Edo era Japan, but with a bizarrely fascinating overlay of a search for immortality.

The yearning for immortality also comes to mind as a theme in Wagner's cycle of *The Ring*, a series of four operas based on Norse mythology. In the complete cycle, Wotan seeks to avert the twilight of the gods and preserve their immortality within a newer, and more resplendent Valhalla. In doing so he inadvertently entwines the fate of the gods with the heroic deeds of mortals. The music, staging, and drama are superlative, suggesting that not only Norse mythology, but Greek and Roman mythology may be sources of similar mythic energy for fiction writing with universal, mythological underpinnings, for breathing life into a contemporary work of fiction.

Stories and Memorials for Tragedies

A powerful example of our theme is "The Graves are Walking,"
by John Kelley, a story of the death by starvation of over one
million people over a couple years period in mid-nineteenth
century Ireland, due to failure of the potato crop. The resulting
famine caused another two million people (in a total population
of only five million) to flee the country to escape such a death.
There have been greater total losses in other famines, including
35 million deaths in China in the 1950s, but the memory of the
Irish famine has been most memorable for the fact that there
are so many of the descendants of those who fled the famine
that are living in America today..

Since Ireland had been conquered and was ruled by Britain at
the time of the famine, there were bitter recriminations by the
Irish over the enabling role of the British in magnifying the
effects of the famine, bordering on charges of willful genocide.
Probably more likely, the tragedy reflected a cold-hearted
indifference toward the plight of a conquered alien people, and
their supposed low morals, indolence and superstitions.

Though the price was high, people survived the tragedy. There
have been recent efforts in Irish study programs at universities,
and with public sculptures, monuments, and memorial parks, in
both Ireland and the U.S., to commemorate that catastrophe,
referred to in Irish as *An Gorta Mor*, The Great Hunger. That
seems well and good, but it also raises some concern about
commemorating tragedy. The remembrance of *An Gorta Mor*

might better be of the endurance and courage that helped many to survive. However, the artistic dramatization seems sometimes focused on people as victims and the magnitude of the lives lost.

Think of the museums, artifacts, and memorials dedicated to the Jewish Holocaust, to the Armenian massacre, to our own Twin Towers and Oklahoma City terrorist events. These were massacres of non-combatants, civilians who were sacrificed to some megalomania. Nonetheless, throughout history, populations were sometimes able to resist and eventually overcome imperialist invaders, even if it took centuries, as in India, South America, Ireland, and Africa, or people had the good fortune and resilience to pick up to a new place and start over.

The drama of passionate memorials honoring courage and resistance might provide more resonance and inspiration for storytelling. Any inspiring memorials might better focus on the heroic battles waged against oppression, and not on passive victimhood. Nonetheless, simple, quiet groves of prayer or reflection for mourning peaceful victims of atrocities who did not have the opportunity or means to fight back can always be of solace. Or, stories written of the historic dramas.

First Pages

Fiction writers quickly learn how critical the first pages of any submittal are for moving a manuscript from an editor's slush pile toward serious consideration for publication. If the first several pages, usually mentioned as less than five, do not grab the editor's interest, most likely the submittal will be declined. That doesn't leave much slack for building the fictional dream, so eloquently described by John Gardner. At the minimum, the writer must quickly produce a character(s) of interest; a tension or suspense that moves the action along; and a competent, narrative voice; all of which combine to capture a reader's commitment to finishing the story.

The driftwood shelter sketch above can set our scene. Here's the first draft pages of a possible short story:

> The brown, sandy beach extended a mile south of their driftwood shelter, sweeping a gentle arc, cut off by a rocky peninsula stretched out into the ocean at the far end of the beach. A tall, white lighthouse tower rose from the knobby end of the peninsula, where breaking waves threw up plumes of spray.
>
> "You never even mentioned getting an ocean-going kayak," Teresa said. "And how could you have just left it stashed out here in the dune grass. Weren't you worried someone might steal it?"
>
> Tom leaned back against the ocean polished driftwood of the shelter. They'd built it two months ago, and the

storms still hadn't swept it away. He took another toke from his joint. Medical marijuana, to use the new, compassionate term for legal, old-fashioned pot. In his case compassionate was accurate enough. He'd be dead in six months. He passed the joint to Teresa.

"I didn't have the energy to drag it back and forth to the trailer park," he said. "Anyhow, it's ready now for a maiden voyage."

"Oh, no. Why don't you just take it out a little ways for your first day and come back in, while I watch out for you. If all goes well, okay then, you can paddle down the coast to see your son tomorrow."

"I'll be fine. It'll just be a little strenuous paddling through the surf."

"Did you tell Brad I need to drive you to the city for your doctor's appointment next Monday?" Teresa said.

Tom nodded, took the joint back from her and pulled another toke. He hadn't told her he'd quit the experimental program. He'd thought a lot about the remaining options: this, or enter the hospice program. If he took this route, it wasn't really a suicide. There was a theoretical chance he'd make it to Hawaii. No sin involved.

"I need to get started if I'm going," Tom said. "Help me drag the kayak down to the beach."

They climbed the sand bank and trudged through thick dune grass to where he had concealed the kayak. The cockpit was covered with a tarp. They removed it, and Tom stowed it inside. When they lifted from both ends, Teresa gasped. "What have you got in here? It weighs a ton," she said.

"Well, you know, foul weather gear, radio set, GPS, all the stuff you need even for a twenty mile jaunt. Better to be safe."

Well, we've introduced the characters, a physical and moral problem faced by one, created a place setting, and a third person point-of-view narration in our first couple of pages. Maybe there will need to be some taut backstory and a bit more characterization in the next few pages, and the story is launched.

Story Inspiration and Narration

First, there needs to be an interesting idea or concept for a story. An image, and it often is in the form of imagery, of some idea, person, or concept springs from the subconscious mind, and depending on the energy the image conveys, we may have a possible storyline.

Perhaps in the solitary quietness of a walk along a deserted beach, the sight of a delicately assembled structure like the teepee fort built of driftwood can't fail to arrest one's attention. What sort of person constructed this? Extrovert rather than introvert, likely; young, probably; feelings of insecurity, maybe; building sense, surely. Of course it would make for a neat twist in a story if the builder was someone completely unexpected, like an older woman, who lives nearby in her own home, on a small but adequate pension from her share of community property she got when she divorced her boring husband of thirty years. So why did she erect this teepee?

Let's explore the selection of elements needed to write the story a bit further. Some good guidelines are available in, *Letters to a Young Novelist*, by the 2010 Nobel Prize winner for Literature, Mario Vargas LIhosa. He describes elements one needs to decide on when setting out to write a story:

- narrator
- space
- time
- level of reality

His first three criteria are not so different than those discussed by other authors, but Llhosa's eloquence and fresh ways of describing them are worth reading. Narrator and space, as discussed by Llhosa, are intertwined, and are often discussed by other writers as the Point of View (POV) to be used in narrating the story. In choosing a narrator the writer can employ a character from within his story, i.e., someone who occupies the 'space' of the story, and who tells the story in his own words, such that the operative pronoun used throughout the narration is "I."

Of course the narrator can also be a plural narrator, such as an entire classroom of students observing the new kid arriving in class (Llhosa's "*Madam Bovary*" example), in which the operative pronoun in the narration will be "We." His examples of the use of the collective (plural) pronoun in literature is worth reading.

The story narrator can also, of course, be someone outside the story space, i.e., an omniscient narrator. Nothing new about that, but again, the examples he uses from literature are marvelous and prompts one to think of this potential choice in new ways. A third category of narrator he discusses is the 'ambiguous narrator,' one concealed behind the second person, and who talks directly to the reader. Good examples are given here, too, such as Victor Hugo and *Les Miserables*.

Starting a Story

Perhaps one of the most pivotal points in laying out a short story is where to begin. According to Michael Kardos in his excellent article, "In Defense of Starting Early," (Writer's Chronicle, Feb. 2009), much of the contemporary advice is to start at, or immediately following, a conflict, and proceed efficiently to the resolution. He quotes Vonnegut: "Start as close to the end as possible."

Many stories will include initial settings of time and place, and character development, that may not be needed to engage the important question of, "what is this story really about?" In some of these cases the story might easily have started a little closer to the end. Whether it would improve that particular story would have to be seen. However, Kardos, whose job was reading several thousand manuscripts for three literary magazines over the previous seven years, had come to see how frequently the story that starts late fails to develop an engaging plot.

He says that, typically, the late-starting manuscript begins in the aftermath of some accident or tragedy (twenty percent of the stories received at his literary magazine assignments) and moves forward from there, depicting how a character deals, or doesn't deal, with the accident or tragedy. Often the story doesn't work because the accident or tragedy seems to exist mainly to add gravity to the work. If the backstory were cut, the events of the dramatic present that follow wouldn't change at all. Other times, even if the accident or tragedy is directly relevant to a story told in the dramatic present, we are shown characters moving from place to place, making observations, having conversations, etc., but very little in the way of plot. This is because the important story—the gripping story—is already over. The most dramatic event in these characters' lives has already happened.

Kardos mentions the "Ur-text" or foundation of narrative theory, Aristotle's "Poetics," in which the beginning of a plot is said not to follow anything by causal necessity. Rather, the beginning is, by definition, that from which events of causal necessity follow. Kardos thus concludes that "after-the-accident" stories are:

> "unconventional, especially when the accident is not actually an accident at all, but rather, as is often the case, the tragic result of causal factors. Often these causal factors, if rendered in the dramatic present, might make for a more compelling and satisfying story than the one actually written."

Why is this unconventional structure so often used now in contemporary fiction? Kardos hypothesizes it has to do with the dominant aesthetic virtues of subtlety and restraint, as seen in the continuing relevance of Hemingway's "iceberg principle," such that "if fiction were an iceberg, then seven-eighths of the iceberg ought to remain hidden underwater." Another example given is Raymond Carver: "Most of my stories start pretty near the end of the arc of the dramatic conflict." Kardos says that "Given Carver's tendency to avoid flashback and backstory, we are typically denied knowledge of the events that have gotten his characters to where they are now, at the start of their narratives....One of the effects that Carver achieves by starting late, and skipping these earlier, character-shaping events, is the downplaying of causality—action and reaction, or problem and decision—in favor of a brief, shimmering moment in a character's life, the exact significance of which is difficult for either the character or the reader to articulate."

Kardos makes a thoughtful case for being wary of starting too late in our story.

Coming-Of-Age Inside a Mystery

"Edenville Owls," by Robert Parker, is a MG/YA novel about an *Indie* club of Middle School basketball players who take on local JV school teams. It tells a story of the team leader's journey toward discovering his first girlfriend, and of a diabolical figure threatening their eighth grade teacher. The author has published over fifty bestselling adult detective stories before this book, his first book for young readers. The story is set right after WWII, and some readers will relate to the boy's descriptions of his favorite radio stories and other background for the era. The mystery part of "Owls" is a little bizarre, but the story holds up.

For older readers, as well as young adults, the nostalgic asides of the narrator, who is our protagonist, talking about radio shows he liked—those dated adventure and detective stories— even the commercial jingles mentioned, may strike a memory chord, as well as the double-feature "B" movies appearing at the local theater on weekends. Parker inserted some of these nostalgia trips into the story as two-page chapters, in italics, which set them off from the ongoing plot line. That was an interesting technique to enhance background, place and time, without intruding on the plot. It was interesting to revisit that era, and the story has many poignant moments. The standalone brief chapters of nostalgia might be a good addition to a writer's techniques for structuring certain novels.

Notes on T.C. Boyle's Process

T. C. Boyle had one of his vintage short stories published in the New Yorker magazine, entitled "Sin Dolor." It is the story of a young boy who was born with some sort of genetic mutation that causes him to feel no pain. The doctor who examines him for numerous burns and lacerations when he is a child at first suspects child abuse by the parents, though he's at a loss as to why the boy feels no pain. The doctor becomes interested in doing long-term medical observations, and since the boy is from a poor family, he is able to have the boy spend a great deal of time at his house, providing meals and teaching the boy, and generally taking a paternal interest in him.

However, the father appears at the house one day, removes his boy, and leaves the village with him. After a long period the boy and his father return to the village and the doctor comes upon the spectacle of the boy performing on stage, putting red hot blades to his flesh, and piercing his cheeks, while the father is taking up donations. The father has made a sideshow of his son to earn money. The doctor manages to speak with the boy, but he is resigned to his fate of earning money to support his family. He dies shortly after.

This is the sort of wrenching story in which Boyle is so effective. Language, style, drama is always good, but there seems always a hard psychological and visceral toll on the reader. Another of Boyle's stories that will illustrate this: a young couple in a new home in southern California, where the high crime rate is of concern, engages a home security firm. They provide the couple with a sign for their lawn warning that intruders will face armed response. This enrages one of the crazies who lives in the area. Boyle has already convincingly portrayed this man being interviewed by a woman real estate agent, and we note his bizarre behavior. The man subsequently invades the home of the young couple firing a gun and demanding armed response from the owner, as advertised. He locates the cowering couple in the house and kills both of them.

One can marvel at the power and craft of such writing, but also get a sense of hopelessness from the theme and denouement. It was interesting to read an interview of Boyle by Diana Bishop, published in *The Writer's Chronicle*. In some selective excerpts, Boyle says he is "fascinated with these other guys to see how they've ruined their lives. Maybe writing about them provides a cautionary tale for me." He also says: "the theme of man as animal often plays a part" in his stories. "I don't want my readers to do anything. I'm not imposing anything on them. They come to me because they like to communicate…I am simply an artist. I'm disturbed by things, amused by things, love things, am horrified by things. I want to constantly address this mystery of the world and so that's why I'm creating art. If it communicates to people then I'm very gratified."

Boyle is currently interested in identity theft—his recent novel, "Talk Talk," takes up this theme. "What is identity, who are you, how do you find out?" The reader had better be ready for powerful, though disturbing elements.

What about his drive, and process? He says, "(F)or me the thrill of producing fiction, of pursuing and discovering something ineffable, is enough…because it's such a rush for me to explore something and see where it will go." As you might also infer from this, Boyle is someone who doesn't write to an outline. Bishop also asked, "When you start to write a short story or novel do you know the ending or do you like the exploration?" Boyle says, "I know nothing at all. Nothing. The first line comes and I start…I begin by seeing something and then it's translated into a voice talking to me and then I follow it and see where it will go." Bishop asks him how he revises? "Constantly, as I go along." Revisions after the first draft is completed? "It is, with minor exceptions, exactly as it evolved on the keyboard," and apparently Boyle's manuscript does not need much more before going to the agent.

Bishop asks, "While you may begin writing short stories or novels with a question, you may not end up with the answer? "No." When Bishop asks can art save the world, so to speak? "Well, the world is unsavable to begin with. Art illuminates you. It makes you feel that somebody else is feeling the same thing that you are so you're not alone. But it doesn't have a political agenda; it can't. Because an agenda destroys the aesthetic impulse of the discovery and the exploration of what you're doing. You're doing it because you have no answer. That's why you do it."

Inventiveness in Writing

To illustrate our topic we will start with *Just in Case*, by Meg Rosoff. She's also the author of *How I Live Now,* last years Michael L. Printz" award (for a book that exemplifies literary excellence in young adult literature). *How I Live...* is an interesting book, with a 15-yr. old American girl visiting her cousins in England at a time when some shadowy guerrilla force has risen all over the countryside. She and her cousins are left to fend for themselves while the adults of the household are gone. The character and voice of the girl is compelling, and the book was a little daring in that she becomes involved in a relationship with her same-aged first cousin.

The title of Rosoff's new book, *Just in Case,* is a play on words, as the protagonist, a 15-yr. old who has a doomed outlook on life, changes his name from David Case to Justin Case, not recognizing the irony. As he's in a clothing store looking for a set of threads to go with his new persona, he meets a girl who's decided to help him dress tastefully. Here's an excerpt:

> "Justin turned slowly. The voice belonged to a girl of perhaps nineteen who peered at him through a heavy, clipped pink fringe. Her eyes were thickly rimmed with kohl, her mouth neatly outlined in a vivid shade of orange that clashed perfectly with her hair. She wore four-inch platform boots in pale green snakeskin, wildly patterned tights, a very short skirt, and a tight see-through shirt printed with Japanese cartoons over which was squeezed a 1950s-style long-line beige elastic bra. A camera bag hung from her shoulder.
> Even Justin recognized that her dress sense was unusual."

The inventiveness in using language, is typical of Rosoff. How can the reader not keep turning the page to see what kind of person we have here? The age difference intrigues, too; what's the author going to do with this? Agnes is obviously a lot more extroverted than the doom-struck Justin. Rosoff goes on with her inventiveness, and it all flows nicely without seeming contrived at all. It's entirely engaging and an inventive way to write.

Young People's Literature

Bridge to Terabithia, by Katherine Paterson, (1977), has been adapted as a movie (also in 1985). BTT is a moving, sensitive story about an anxious, artistic boy named Jesse, and an athletic tomboy named Leslie. Leslie is the 'new kid on the block' having moved into the locale with her New Age, intellectual parents--lots of books, no TV, no formal religion— and she easily wins a school race, for which Jesse has long trained. Nevertheless, they become good friends and create their own mythical world, Terabithia, in the woods near their home.

The book created a shock in its day because of the tragic death of a young character. Such an attitude might seem too protective, today. It may be thought an overwrought response even for back then, considering the older, classical favorite, "Grimm's Fairy Tales," had plenty of young deaths. Other young people's literature taboos were also supposedly crossed by BTT --Leslie's parent's New Age spirituality, and a sexual content. If sex was there it was only inferred, and yet BTT was on ALA's "Ten Most Challenged Books of 2002"...for "offensive language, sexual content, and references to the occult and Satanism." Well, it seemed only an emotionally moving, sensitive story. Nowadays many of those young readers' literature taboos have fallen—although not always to the benefit of a good story. Still, the more liberal attitudes have generally been rewarding for young readers on the whole.

Contemplating Don Quixote

Our discussion book is Cervantes's "Don Quixote," translated by Edith Grossman. There are other, earlier translations, but this is both scholarly and a handsome edition, replete with footnotes about Cervantes's story references, and the manuscript history. A jacket blurb by Lionel Trilling suggests: "It can be said that all prose fiction is a variation on the theme of "Don Quixote.".

The theme of an addled but learned man coming centuries late to the call of knightly chivalry, and setting out in comical, makeshift knight's regalia to seek adventure, has all the ingredients of a farce, and yet, it never admits to anything like tongue-in-cheek comedy. We groan and shake our heads at Quixote's foibles, sometimes smile, ruefully, but the language, and often the wisdom, sweep us along. Another jacket blurb by Milan Kundera says it well, "Don Quixote is practically unthinkable as a living being, and yet, in our memory, what character is more alive?"

There are many story variations on this hero's journey, or quest, from the crossing of the threshold from our world into the story world, to the trials the hero must face along the journey, the winning (or losing) of some treasure, and the return—richer or poorer, in wealth or spirit. Perhaps none have, or will, make the journey quite like Don Quixote.

Repaving Route 66

Some YA authors are able to construct stories that will keep a reader turning pages even though the conflict situation and structure may be somewhat familiar. Laurie Halse Anderson's "Twisted" is like that, and though the protagonist, a high school senior named Tyler, has had to work off a minor vandalism rap at his high school, he's not really serious 'Gangsta' material. He and his younger sister, Hannah, do have some problems with a psychologically abusive, work-driven father, who's been shaped by his own father-abused childhood. Predictably, the mother at times retreats into the solace of a drink or two rather than confront her over-controlling husband. Tyler falls for an airhead rich girl at his school, and endures the hostility and finally a violent encounter with her brother, another classmate.

It could be an all too familiar scenario and characters, but Anderson's writing is good and she injects the right amount of tension to keep moving the story along. A good secondary character, Hannah, Tyler's younger sister, just starting her freshman year at Tyler's school, enhances the story. She metamorphoses from a dutiful, homebound girl into an exuberant, confident, breakout personality, eager to set Tyler and herself onto the popular track in school life—though there's still the grinding problem of dad.

Previously toured routes can still reverberate in the hands of good writers.

Three Levels of Story

J. M. Coetzee's novel, *Diary of a Bad Year,* is an example of interesting, major tinkering with the typical form of the novel. His credentials for experimenting include winning the Nobel and two Booker prizes. The reviews are somewhat mixed as to whether the experiment is a complete success. The idea, nevertheless, remains interesting. A principal protagonist, Señor C, like Coetzee himself, is a South African writer transplanted to Australia, and he is compiling a collection of his "Strong Opinions" for a German publisher representing philosophical, political, and literary positions.

Señor C enlists the help of a young Filipina woman named Anya to type a manuscript from his voice recordings. The printed novel's format consists of three, subdivided sections on each page. The topmost section is given over to the transcribed essays on the "Strong Opinions" Señor C holds (similar to actual essays Coetzee has himself previously published). The middle section of the page contains Señor C's thoughts on how and why he has come to hold such opinions, speculations on how Anya might interpret them, and views on how that might reflect on him. The bottom section is in Anya's point-of-view, her observations, personal reflections, and a narrative of the unfolding relationship between her and Señor C.

The page's arrangement seems representative of three stages of consciousness in the writer. Whether we refer to him as Coetzee or Señor C, the analogy is the same. The topmost section is in Señor C's fully conscious mode, with all the writer's normal strategies of academic rigor, sophistication, propriety, and political correctness at work. Too often this can lead to uninspired, stilted writing. In the middle section Señor C steps back from some of his "Strong Opinions" and thinks critically of how and why he might hold such views. It seems reminiscent to an old, current affairs radio program, called "T-U-C; Time of Useful Consciousness," described as a brief flash of time before losing consciousness when a pilot has to react to save his aircraft after his mind is subjected to acrobatic, super-G forces. Similarly, for Señor C, the wrappings of erudition and neat philosophical packaging fall away from his "Strong Opinions" and the raw instinctual elements of his subconscious shout to him. In the bottom section of the page we have the complete submergence of the writer's thoughts into a pure story level, in the POV of a fictional person, Anya, giving her own thoughts on the "Strong Opinions" she is typing, and her thoughts on the developing situation between her and Señor C.

It's interesting to think of such new forms for the novel, and Coetzee has given a unique and interesting model.

An Artful Novel

A Caldecott Medal was awarded for *The Invention of Hugo Cabret,* by Brian Selznick. The book is an artful arrangement of text and graphics. Interestingly, it was a candidate both for the Newbery Medal, for a written novel, and also the Caldecott, for a graphic illustration book. It demonstrated a new interest by readers in a blending of the two mediums for telling a story. Unlike a graphic novel, with its steady progression of graphic panels, or the typical illustrated novel with perhaps only a graphic plate introducing each chapter, 'Hugo' is interspersed with multiple pages of text followed by one and two page spreads of artistic, shaded, black and white drawings. Sometimes the drawings taken together illustrate only fleeting seconds in the action of the storyline, like successive still frames of a motion picture. Indeed, part of the storyline deals with the lost career of a French cinematographer, dating from the early years of motion pictures.

Hugo, a young boy, lives in the apartment of his uncle, which is buried in the labyrinthine inner passages of the massive central train station in Paris. Hugo's father has died in a fire at a museum where he worked, and Hugo has been taken in and trained by his uncle to assist him in keeping all the clocks in the train station in a good, accurate condition. However, the uncle has mysteriously disappeared, and Hugo struggles to keep the clocks running. He does not want to report his uncle's disappearance for fear he'll be turned out of the station. However, this means he has to pilfer his food from shop owners in the station just to survive. In addition to his timekeeper duties, the mechanically talented Hugo is trying to restore a mechanical man, an automaton, that his father had found in museum discards and gave to him. The automaton, a gear-driven marvel that can write and draw pictures, becomes the key to the mystery surrounding Georges Melies, a famous cinematographer, now a poor, novelty shop owner in the train station, and his adopted daughter, Isabelle, Hugo's newfound friend.

A structured five hundred pages of story and art that go together seamlessly. and only needs a couple of evenings of intriguing reading.

Subconscious Underpinnings for Fiction Writing

Many of us experience a rich relevance of certain place settings we may encounter on local excursions, or on distant travels. Such encounters may set in motion a sort of subconscious connection to the scene, even though having little or no direct memory of any physical connection with the place. We're not speaking of the 'déjà vu ', or, 'I've been here before' feeling, but rather one more specifically targeted to the writer: 'this place expresses something that I would like to deal with in my fiction.'

Such thoughts came to mind when sorting through photographs of an old, now largely empty dairy ranch property, circa 1880-1940, located nearby. One was of a Victorian-style tree house, seated within the twisted trunks of a gigantic, ancient cypress tree. The mysterious doorway conveys something of a magical portal into fictional space. Inside are carved figures representing the Garden of Eden: Adam, Eve, the animals. Intriguing, especially after reading the recent novel, "Infinity in the Palm of Her Hand," by Gioconda Belli, a story about the expulsion from the Garden of Eden. Other photos were taken going away from the tree house on a walk through lush, overgrown vegetation to the now abandoned, original ranch house, slowly subsiding into the black earth beneath. It brought such a sense of loneliness and mortality, that were somehow linked to the tree house diorama. Such are the germs of inspiration for new stories.

Cherry Blossoms and Butoh Dance

The emotional impact of any story can largely depend on our own life experiences, and where we now stand on that unfolding journey. A German film, "Cherry Blossoms," besides the good acting and visual gems, has a powerful theme that will be useful to discuss from a story writing viewpoint.

First, a summary of the film story: a married couple lives in a small German town, and the man is nearing retirement from his civil service office job. Trudi's doctors reveal the results of her recent medical exam; she has a fatal illness. They suggest she break the news gently to her husband, perhaps while they are off on some adventure together, a change of scenery. Trudi is very dejected; she tells them Rudi doesn't like changes or travel. Nonetheless, she coaxes Rudi to take a vacation with her to visit their three adult children. Trudi had studied Japanese Butoh dancing (modern Japanese dance form in which the dancers apply white paint on their bodies) before marrying, and would love now to visit their youngest son, Karl, who lives and works in Tokyo. However, not knowing of her illness, Rudi protests that it would be cheaper for Karl to come here, and so they go instead to visit their other son and daughter in Berlin. The visit was unexpected, and the son and his family have little time to entertain their parents, nor does the daughter. The daughter's lesbian partner is persuaded to drive the parents around town for sightseeing, and to a Butoh dance performance. The expressionist dance intertwines graceful movements with the grotesque, the light and shadows of coming into being, and the ceasing to exist. Rudi, who has no taste for Butoh, sits on a bench outside the performance area.

The parents soon realize their busy children have no time for them, and leave Berlin to visit a lake resort. While there, Trudi dies, and Rudi is plunged into despair. He has depended on his wife all his married life for his happiness. The children return to their parents' home for the funeral. They have a dubious, even distasteful, expectation for Rudi's ability to fend for himself without their mother, but are fearful that he will become dependent on them.

After some reflection on the Butoh keepsakes and Japanese travel literature his wife had left behind, Rudi travels to Japan to visit Karl, and to come to terms with his loss of Trudi. Like his siblings, Karl is busy with his work and wary of his father's despondent and dependent-like intrusion into his life. Rudi wanders the seamy side of Tokyo, in and out of strip joints and massage parlors, but all in grief. Often he wears his wife's clothing beneath his topcoat. Rudi overhears Karl on the telephone with his sister describing his wanderings and cross-dressing, and complaining that it is her turn to be a host to their father. The next day Rudi wanders into a park, where he watches a young Butoh dancer perform in a remote, sylvan location. He starts up a conversation with her, and she tells him how dancing Butoh helps her keep contact with her deceased mother. Rudi returns to the park each day to watch her dance, and she befriends him and helps him find his way around Tokyo. One day he follows her home, to discover she lives in a tent in a wooded outskirt of the city.

Rudi asks the girl to accompany him to visit Mt. Fuji, a long cherished ambition of Trudi. The girl cautions him that Mt. Fuji is very shy, and is often lost to misty cover for days at a time. They go and stay together at a resort near Mt. Fuji, and indeed, one day leads to another as the mountain stays hidden in mists. During this time in the resort their friendship deepens; he shows her his wife's clothing which he carries in his luggage, along with the mementoes of her Butoh period. After some days at the resort, however, Rudi becomes weaker, and grows ill. One night he steals outside and discovers that the mists have lifted to reveal Mt. Fuji in the moonlight. He quickly dresses in his wife's kimono and Butoh makeup, and hurries to the side of a lake beneath the mountain. There, he dances his own interpretation of Butoh, and is joined in the dance by an apparition of his wife. The next morning the girl awakens to find Rudi gone and she hurries outside, only to find him dead by the lakeside. Returning to their room, she finds he has left her a large amount of money in an envelope. Together, she and Karl participate in the cremation ceremony for Rudi, and afterward each walks off on their own way back into the city.

A powerful theme of life, death, aesthetics, and a beautifully structured story. How one might draw on an aesthetic art form to dramatise the plot of such a moving story is a great lesson.

Encountering Distant Relations

What is left unsaid by the author can sometimes provide an ultimate, satisfying epiphany in a work of fiction. *Distant Relations*, by Orhan Pamuk, is a short story appearing in the Sep. 7, 2009 edition of *The New Yorker*. Pamuk was the 2006 winner of the Nobel Prize in Literature. His short story is a gem, and well suited to gaining a better understanding of the art of storytelling.

The story is about a young, cosmopolitan Turkish man, who has finished his degree in America, and is being groomed as a manager in his father's prosperous business in Istanbul. Kemal is due to be engaged to a girl from one of the wealthy, Westernized families of the city, girls who are beginning to break the old taboos, and, occasionally, are bold enough to sleep with their boyfriends before marriage. Here is Kemal, summing up his relationship with Sybil:

> Believing myself a decent and responsible person, I had every intention of marrying her; but, even if I hadn't wished to, there was no question of my having a choice now that she had 'given me her virginity.' Before long, this burden cast a shadow over the common ground between us, which we were so proud of—the illusion of being 'free and modern' (though, of course, we would never have used such words for ourselves), on account of having made love before marriage—and in a way this, too, brought us closer.

However, early in the story, he goes to a shop where Sybil had pointed out a handbag to him that she had admired. He is startled to find he knows the store clerk from his childhood; she is a younger, distant relation, and very beautiful. Fusun stretches into the window display to fetch the bag from a mannequin, and Kemal is mesmerized by the too-short, lacy yellow skirt, and the yellow pump she kicks off while reaching. They make small talk, and Fusan, a blonde, tells him the cost of the handbag, but she is sure the shop owner, a close relative of Kemal, will offer him a discount when she returns from lunch. "It's not important," he says, and takes out his wallet, "a clumsy gesture that, later, Fusun often mimicked..." he tells us.

Well, we have some foreshadowing here, and expect perhaps later we will observe a more intimate relationship, where Fusun grows to affectionately mimic him.

Meanwhile, Kemal seems to wrestle with his vision of himself as "a decent and responsible person," and his yearning toward perhaps a more modern, uninhibited sexual freedom. He suggests to Sybil that instead of meeting in his office for their trysts, they meet in an unused flat his mother owns in the Merhamet Apartments. However, Sybil doesn't want to sneak around in secret apartments as if she were his mistress. "Where did you get this idea from, to meet in that apartment?" "Never mind," Kemal says. We feel the tension developing in Kemal's two states of mind.

Sybil points out to Kemal that the 'Jenny Colon' handbag is a fake, and suggests he "return the bag, get his money back, and run,' because the shop has cheated him. Kemal reluctantly goes back to the shop for a refund, but faced with the wounded pride of Fusun, and his continued enchantment with her, he is soon consoling the weeping girl with tender hugs. She can't return the money to him because the shop owner has gone home and the register is locked--another humiliation for Fusun. Kemal struggles to get out a reply: she can drop it off at the Merhamet Apartments, where he goes afternoons to catch up on office paperwork.

We seem now to be heading toward the denouement of our story; will Kemal shed Sybil and take up with Fusun, or perhaps he will break loose of his old-fashioned inhibitions and carry on with both simultaneously? He leaves the shop in a state of shame and guilt, mixed with images of bliss, on his way home to his parents' house. Enroute, he notices a yellow jug in a shop and impulsively stops in and buys it. The symbolism of the yellow equates, of course, as it does throughout, with Fusun, the blond.

The story, (related by Kemal in a distant past tense), hurtles toward a conclusion. When Kemal reaches home he asks his mother for the key to her Merhamet Apartments, and it becomes obvious it has been unused for years. Kemal tells us the "yellow jug drew no comment from anyone during the twenty years that it sat on the table, where my mother and father and later my mother and I, ate our meals. Every time I touched the handle of that jug, I would remember those days when I first felt the misery that was to turn me in on myself, leaving my mother to watch me in silence at dinner, her eyes filled half with sadness, half with reproach."

The story has a masterful construction. It forces the reader to return to key encounters and dialog to satisfy himself that he, at last, understands Kemal, and the resolution of the story. The author laid out all the foreshadowing and clues that successfully engage the reader, and lead to the conclusion that Kemal attempted to continue a double life with the two women, and ended up with neither, a saddened and lonely man in his later life.

Not many short stories with such veiled endings are as well done.

Negative Space in Writing Scenes

The concept of negative space might be as useful to writing as it is to art. Negative space is a basic concept to make a watercolor painting come alive. It involves many of the same challenges as making a scene in fiction writing come alive.

In painting a nude figure and some minor background in watercolor, we might start with a pencil drawing on a white sheet of paper, paint a light, neutral value color wash over the entire paper, followed with a flesh-color wash that covers and extends out from the nude drawing. Before these washes are fully dry, another medium value flesh color might be brushed over shadowed parts of the figure and slightly overlapping into surrounding areas. A limited range of hues and values are now established, but it's a hodgepodge of color without any real focus. Perhaps like a scene in the beginning of a story, where several characters, objects, or activities may be vying equally on the page for the reader's attention.

To "pop" the figure forward in our painting, we can apply a medium value (darker) color to the "negative space" surrounding the nude figure. The lighter, flesh-colored figure now begins to emerge and draw the viewer's attention. But perhaps the effect is too strong, and the figure now seems too remote from the background, so we wash over part of the figure with the same, medium value color of the background. The lighter, flesh tone of the figure can still be seen through the added darker wash, and the overlapped part of the figure is now partly subsumed or merged into the background. The painting has become more integrated, but maybe we're concerned that we've lost some needed focus where we've blurred sharp edges of the figure. We go back in and apply a still darker value to the negative space outside selected parts of the subsumed figure. That's better; and the figure emerges more dramatically. The figure has become the main focus of the painting, and the related flow of washes surrounding the figure adds interest to the viewing experience.

To explore the idea of negative space in writing, here's an opening to a story:

> *Geronimo and Corky, shirtless and wearing sweatbands, edge forward, swatting a handball against the red brick wall, —pocketa-pocketa-pocketa.*
>
> *Greg, a slender, dark-haired boy, sits on the sidewalk curb and watches the game. He's wearing an eyeglasses frame without any lenses, and has a burnt cork mustache. He turns and looks as a city bus hisses to a stop at the curb. Luke gets off the bus, gripping a backpack over one shoulder, and comes over to watch the game.*

Okay, we've got some initial light color washes over the complete scene; a couple of areas of interest, but nothing too focused. Let's pop a main character forward by brushing some dark color washes in the negative (empty) space surrounding him. We want Luke to stand out as our focal point.

> *Corky hits the ball to the sweet spot in the corner, and it rolls back across the sidewalk, unplayable. Point and*

game—Corky throws up his arms and lets out a whoop. Geronimo pulls off his sweatband, curses, squats next to Greg and puts an arm around his shoulder. He holds the struggling boy in an arm lock, kisses him on the forehead, and glances up at Luke.

"He's mine; go get one of your own," Geronimo says, smiling. "I hear they got lots of these little darlings up at that school of yours."

"Yeah, ease up on him; Greg's maybe a little weird, but he's all right," Luke says. "He grew up with Corky and me and you don't think about that, but maybe you need to."

That silhouettes Luke against the negative background, but we don't want too much contrast so we'll brush a bit of the darker wash from the background over part of Luke, and make him merge more with the background.

"Maybe you're not one of us anymore," Geronimo says. "Maybe you've gotten too good for us."

"Nah, cool it," Corky says, sweeping up a gray tee-shirt from the sidewalk and mopping sweat from his face and torso. "As long as the cops are still looking for who did the kid at our Grover Heights rumble, we've all gotta stick

together. Luke is in it as much as any of us. We're each other's alibi."

Luke has been shown as part of the darker background, but emerges as a figure of greater interest, with character qualities of education and sensitivity.

Two art forms, writing and painting, and maybe each has some similar scene development techniques.

Bolting From the Rez'

Only Sherman Alexie could have written "The Absolutely True Diary of a Part-time Indian" and to have carried along the reader so effortlessly, and intriguingly. It's not that a good writer couldn't imagine the hard situation and trapped circumstances described for life on the Reservation, but perhaps an outsider would have much greater difficulties in plumbing the depths of such a story. So it's been a boon to have Alexi's *Diary...* with all its courage, and warts, and sorrows, and the resilient hopes, of a boy who's been there, done that, and can talk of it in gallows humor, as well as with a great affection for the parents who tried their best to do the right thing by him.

The story gets underway with 'Junior,' or Arnold Spirit, nearing the end of his time in middle school on the Rez, and feeling like he's going to die soon if he doesn't get off the Rez. Alcoholism and unemployment are rampant, and life expectancy is mean and short. Junior thinks of attending high school off campus, at a nearby town called Reardon. Of course, this is going to be interpreted by his best friend, Rowdy, and most of the other boys on the Rez, as becoming a traitor. Regardless, he's too sensitive and hungry for life to let such worries dissuade him, and he makes the leap.

The boys at Reardon are at first skeptical about this kid from the Rez, but Junior has one good thing going for him. He's pretty good at basketball. And he manages to swallow his fears enough to give a good account of himself in a scuffle with one of the strapping big players on Reardon's team. Junior also acquires a serious crush on one of the Reardon girls, and it's good for a little humorous tension. Through it all he's still living on the Rez', commuting back and forth, and his audacity is gradually accepted by the other Indian youths. We continue to get a glimpse of the existential life on the Rez, or the untimely demise of it for some, and we're glad that a promising boy has started his journey to more hopeful things.

A good coming-of-age story with a classic structure for a writer's playbook.

Chabon's Yiddish Mystery

Michael Chabon's *The Yiddish Policemen's Union* is a very imaginative story, and a good one to study for structure. The U.S. government has temporarily settled Jews, driven from Palestine in the 1948 war (a *'what-if'* fabrication), into their own, self-governing enclave in Alaska. However, the land is soon to revert back to the State of Alaska, and the Jews will then have to leave. There is a plan to this madness, and Chabon weaves it well. Meanwhile, Detective Meyer Landsman of the Yiddish Police Department has a murder to solve, involving a Messiah; a fundamentalist, "black hat" Jewish sect; and loads of intriguing Yiddish lore, all of which are intricately threaded into the plot.

Chabon's writing style is often remarkable, with his choice of similes, and metaphors, and descriptive detail. Sometimes the similes are stretched a bit, but they're so entertaining you forgive him. A really good writer to emulate.

Writing Antarctica

The White Darkness, by Geraldine McCaughrean, is the story of Sym Wates, a 14-yr. old British girl, and her Uncle Victor—just an honorary title—and their journey across Antarctica to find the legendary *Symms's Hole,* a portal to a hollow Earth.

When Sym was a child, her father was a business partner of Victor, and Victor's obsession with finding *Symms's Hole* became the father's own dream, to the point of giving over his life savings and property to help finance a future discovery expedition. Victor even persuaded her father to place Sym on a regular regimen of antibiotics, to ensure her health and protect any inhabitants of Earth's interior against contamination when they would explore the interior. This drug regimen has probably caused Sym's near-deafness, requiring her to wear hearing aids. Victor also sees to Sym's education in all things pertaining to Antarctica. It is during her lonely, introspective period of study that she has conversations with a Captain Lawrence Titus Oates, who perished ninety years before on Scott's expedition to the South Pole. When Sym's father dies, Victor dupes Sym away from her mother to begin the portal search in Antarctica. He has enlisted the services of a Norwegian writer, who has located a probable location for *Symms's Hole* using satellite imagery, and who is accompanied by his son. Thus far Victor seems a somewhat sinister figure who appears to have an alarming interest in Sym. We wonder if he is serious about this expedition?

In Antarctica, the situation becomes even more bizarre. Victor manages to drug the other members of their commercial sightseeing tour, and commandeers the tour's tracked vehicle to transport himself, Sym, the Norwegian and son, in a mad dash across Antarctica to the reputed portal location. Without giving up too much of the story, it can be said that the writer and his son aren't who we thought them to be, and Victor becomes ever more possessed. It may only be because of her voluminous reading of the historical Antarctica expeditions and scientific lore that Sym is able to help navigate their journey as they endure countless hardships. It is also a tribute to McCaughrean's writing that she is able to spin such a plot and give voice to characters that can absorb us in a wasteland of nothingness. Worth a read and a consideration of plot, structure, and magic realism. The latter being Sym's conversations with the long-dead Captain Oates.

POINT OF VIEW NARRATION

Point of View Narration Makes All the Difference

We shall refer to Robert Roper's book on Vladimir Nabokov, *Nabokov in America--on the road to Lolita*. Reading it gave occasion to reflect on Nabokov's writing of *Lolita*, one of the most widely known novels in contemporary American literature. Lolita is the story of a middle-aged man who pursues an obsessive love relationship with a twelve-year old girl, a stunningly controversial theme for mainstream literature at the time. Early editions came out in Europe in the mid-fifties, and by 1958, a first edition in America. Many of Nabokov's academic circle and some editors warned him it would not be well received; nevertheless, it proved a literary and financial success.

Although this first-person narrative seemed moderately engaging, it did not exert as powerful an influence as some critics have ascribed to it. Humbert is a unique, sophisticated though demented character, who is also a blundering assassin. The reader may find some sympathy for his character, but it gets harder and harder to sustain as Humbert reveals his near murder of Lolita's mother, and toward the end his actual murder of a rival for Lolita's favors. As for Lolita, she remains almost a cipher to the end, regarding her inner emotions or hopes, or the level of comprehension she may have regarding the two men who dominate her life.

In contrast, we have the third-person limited, simple but powerful novella length book, *Member Of the Wedding*, by Carson McCullers, 1946, which tells the story of another twelve-year old girl, Frankie, coming into a growing awareness of an inner, vaguely sensual nature, a coming-of-age anxiety, which eventually leads her into a harrowing, near-rape experience with a drunken serviceman in her hometown.

The first-person narrative of Humbert doesn't really allow us to reach into the consciousness of Lolita, and how could we believe much of what this demented person tells us about Lolita, anyway? We can observe how Lolita physically acts in various scenes—sometimes she initiates the intimacies—but that doesn't help us to know her very deeply, or on what level we sympathize with her.

In *Member*, the writer easily moves us into and out of the consciousness of Frankie, without the many constraints and prejudices potentially imposed on a first-person narrator. In consequence, we get to know Frankie more deeply than her counterpart Lolita, and become more moved by her story.

No doubt there were many considerations Nabokov weighed in choosing to write his story as a first-person narrative, including the writing strategies of a rambling journey across the American landscape of sterile motels, a chance for him to use stream-of-consciousness Joycean dialog, chances for literary allusions, and other perks that appealed to his imagination and writing powers. His story was well received by many readers.

Multiple Perspective or Point of View Constructions

Point of view, or POV, the perspective from which a narrator describes a story as it unfolds, can make all the difference in capturing a reader with shifting perspectives and accompanying dramatic tension.

"The Partial Glimpse--Perspective and Dynamic Plotting," by Catherine Brady (*Writer's Chronicle*, May/Summer, 2013) describes some interesting facets in POV:

> Multiple POV, with all the attendant unreliability and partial knowledge, prejudices of each POV character, can enhance the tensions in an unfolding plot...a device used for destabilizing the reader's take on the dramatic situation."

Brady makes the point that we are often advised to choose as the perspective character the one who has the most compelling desire to tell the story, and yet desire by itself is not enough to carry a story. For any chosen perspective character you're yoked to that character's limitations, and if you have multiple perspective characters, figuring out how to get information to the reader behind the character's back means you get to play with every possible permutation of the wavering sympathetic connection between character and reader. She continues,

> A perspective character's limitations are a veritable gold mine of dramatic tension. His uncertain reliability provides the key...Most perspective characters fall into a gray area in which they sometimes have the reader's sympathy and agreement and at other times do not. This is the engine that drives dramatic tension.

Brady uses an Alice Munro story, "Love of a Good Woman," to discuss some of her salient points of multiple perspective construction. This Munro story keeps a reader guessing as to where the story is going, as her stories often do, right up to the epiphany of discovery, or has there been a discovery? The reader has often to re-examine clues to the reliability or unreliability of the multiple perspective characters that contribute to the story. The dramatic tension of any Munro story is almost always compellingly resolved.

The construction of our Munro story is memorable in that some perspective characters that contribute to the epiphany never actually meet or interact within the time frame of their narration. For example, a third person omniscient narrator tells of three boys who discover a drowned body in a creek bed at the beginning of the story; the boys and their families, after some discussion of their home life, are not heard from again.

Next, a third person limited narrator tells of a virtuous nurse, Enid, assisting a dying woman and her husband who live in a rural countryside. This is interrupted by a third person limited narrator describing a confession to Enid, by the possibly now-deranged wife she is caring for, concerning a past infidelity with the drowned man, and the husband's role in the impassioned killing and hiding of the man's body.

The story concludes with a third person limited narration of

Enid's quandary of whether to bring the wife's confession to the attention of the police, or consider a prospect of staying on and maybe even marrying the otherwise decent widower and taking care of him.

Although the story has widely divergent elements, they all piece together in a coherent whole. The reader is perhaps uneasy about the quandary faced by Enid at the end, but then the dying wife's state of mind might have led to her fantasizing the confession, or perhaps, recognizing a potential attraction between her husband and Enid, she wished to poison Enid's mind against him.

What of the role of the boys? They set our mystery in motion, but was it also useful to describe the circumstances of their lives and their families? As Brady points out, perhaps so. Two of the families had difficult circumstances of life, but as country folk, they were attuned to how social conventions shield both the good and the bad, and how good people might have to make compromises in order to get by.

Writers may appreciate the dramatic tensions raised by multiple and shifting perspectives in this story.

Point of View, Multiple Characters

Deciding on the best point of view, or narrator's perspective(s), to unfold your story on the page can be an important step toward achieving success with the cast of characters and thematic material at hand. The point of view (POV) consideration used to be loaded with rules for the writer, and any disregard of those rules was regarded as a sign of the amateur writer, or if published so, usually the sign of a well-known writer who could sit above the fray.

An article by Liz Radford in Writer's Chronicle (May, 2013) featured an interview with author Audrey Niffenegger, focused on POV. Niffenegger has authored two best-seller novels that make highly effective, and instructive use of multiple POV structures. *The Time Traveler's Wife* (2003; 3 million copies sold internationally, and followed by a movie) has two principal narrators, and *Her Fearful Symmetry* (2009) has eight or ten narrators, including ghosts.

Niffenegger says:

> With first person point of view, you have all the advantages of being very close to that character, and you have more or less unlimited access to them, insofar as they have access to themselves. This certainly has its charms. But you're experiencing every other character through the narrator's biases. The writer has to work extra hard if the reader's understanding is going to be larger than the character's.

Those final two sentences are well worth thinking about for any writer.

To further consider Niffenegger's POV philosophy:

> With third person point of view you have many more options. Sometimes you can be very close, sometimes farther away, and you don't have to stick with a permanent vantage point. As long as you practice consistency and signal clearly about what you're doing, you can create many possible combinations of distance and closeness. The narrator is allowed to add whatever information needs adding that the characters may not be observing, so you have more scope.

In discussing her POV concerns while writing *Her Fearful Symmetry,* and facing an expanding cast of characters with no one character she could follow all the time, Niffenegger recalls, "I'd been reading *War and Peace* in which Tolstoy skims along and changes point of view, sometimes within the paragraph. If he wants to just look at something for a second, he'll pop into somebody's head and then pop out again. It's quite nice. I wanted to do that." Similarly, in another place she says, "There's no reason why, for a sentence or two, I can't just wander into someone's head, even if they're not going to be a major part of it. That's something I really love about *Mrs. Dalloway*. Virginia Woolf just briefly strolls into peoples' minds and then wanders away. You never see them again, and that's fine."

Radford remarks, "In *Her Fearful Symmetry*, there are instances during which we are privy to four characters' thoughts on a single page. This happens seamlessly, without distracting the reader. Any tips and tricks you can share for accomplishing fluidity like this?" Niffenegger replies:

> You want to keep voices differentiated so that you're signaling the reader when you change characters. Also, there's no point in leaving someone's head just to get an identical viewpoint from somebody else. Signaling is nuts and bolts. I italicize thoughts. I constantly tag "Robert thought," "Elspeth said." Simple mechanicals.

The complete article has a wealth of information. Niffenegger has a buoyant personality and some excellent advice, and Radford did a fine job of exploring the author's approach to POV and related matters.

Point of View and an Observant Use of Distance

Point of View, or POV, is often a dominant factor in creating a compelling story on paper. The POV a writer chooses to tell his story, and a decision whether to use only one, or multiple POVs, can make all the difference in whether a writer fully exploits the opportunities presented by the choice of characters, the place setting of the story, and the drama of the plot. After deciding POV, at first perhaps tentatively, the next aspect of writing strategy to be kept in mind is maintaining the most effective psychological distance in narration.

A reader might be observing at an objective, fly-on-the-wall distance as a third-person objective narrator leads the way through a story. At some point the narrator describes a meeting between our protagonist, Allen, and his friend, James, downtown on a street corner. The POV might shift to the first-person inner thoughts of Allen, thinking of some earlier dispute he's had with James and how to respond to their chance meeting. The POV might then shift to the first-person inner thoughts of James, about the bad luck of meeting Allen here today. The POV might finally shift back to third-person omniscient to describe the continued dialog and visible signs of tensions between the two friends.

This passage of a story not only shows shifts in POV, but also shifts in perceptive distance between the reader and the character he observes. However, it is important for a proper use of distancing, that the writer should be wary of introducing disruptive distancing effects in his narration which could tend to jar a reader's sense of a continuous, fictional dream (see "The Art of Fiction," by John Gardner).

Some misuses of disruptive distancing are recalled from a writers' workshop, occurring when the author was in a third-person, objective point of view, and introduced a descriptive passage beginning "There was," or some variation of it. The workshop recommendation was that, on the first revision of any completed draft, get rid of all such disruptive distancing. Just describe what the POV character is observing, without stepping back as if committing the scene to some recording document, or journal entry.

In the novel, "Return to Oakpine," by Ron Carlson, some pages seemed to move at a dawdling pace, with lots of single line, he said and she said, volleys of idle dialog. That effect is a sort of distancing too. Bear in mind that the book has enjoyed some good critical review, and any successful novel might have things other writers could quibble about. However, sometimes it's simply a question of whether we might make a good book better.

> The Pronghorn had been a little tavern three miles south of Gillette, a place the roughnecks could stop on the way back to town. Over the years it had grown, first with a room on one side for four pool tables and then a large quonset in the rear with a hardwood floor for dancing. This area was lined with tables behind a low, wooden corral. There were neon beer signs everywhere, red, and

blue, and green, so the general glow added to the odd effect of having three ceilings of different heights in the gerrymandered room. Tonight all the tables were full, two and three pitchers of beer on each, four, and the dance floor, too, was packed with a fluid, partisan crowd, groups of people churning forward, cheering their friends, under a glacial slip of cigarette smoke that drifted toward the high center.

First we might notice the use of historical exposition, which is a bit distancing from the story at hand; perhaps a POV character could just say what he sees, and then move briefly into his thoughts on things he's noticed. Observe, too, that we have an instance of the journaling phrase,"There were...," and perhaps a few writers might choose to examine whether some stretched or odd adjectives like gerrymandered, fluid partisan, and glacial slip, are suitable for this rural Wyoming crowd. If not, remember, any such 'flags' interrupting the fictional dream tend to introduce some distancing effect for the reader.

Let's look at an old favorite, James Joyce, and see how he handled some of his intensely descriptive scenes in the famous short story, "The Dead," without any seeming to be forced, or notably distancing. Here's a paragraph describing the Christmas banquet of an upper class Dublin crowd:

A fat brown goose lay at one end of the table and at the other end, on a bed of creased paper strewn with sprigs of parsley, lay a great ham, stripped of its outer skin and peppered over with crust crumbs, a neat paper frill round its shin and beside this was a round of spiced beef. Between these rival ends ran parallel lines of side-dishes: two little minsters of jelly, red and yellow; a shallow dish full of blocks of blancmange and red jam, a large green leaf-shaped dish with a stalk-shaped handle, on which lay bunches of purple raisins and peeled almonds, a companion dish on which lay a solid rectangle of Smyrna figs, a dish of custard topped with grated nutmeg, a small bowl of chocolates and sweets wrapped in gold and silver papers and a glass vase in which stood some tall celery stalks. In the center of the table there stood, as sentries to a fruit-stand which upheld a pyramid of oranges and American apples, two squat old-fashioned decanters of cut glass, one containing port and the other dark sherry. On the closed square piano a pudding in a huge yellow dish lay in waiting and behind it were three squads of bottles of stout and ale and minerals, drawn up according to the colors of their uniforms, the first two black, with brown and red labels, the third and smallest squad white, with transverse green sashes.

The entire paragraph has an immediate presence to it. Joyce makes it seem as if you, the reader, are right there at the table, looking down the length of the table and marveling at the numbers and luxury of food and dessert items, without any noticeable authorial presence interposing distancing effects to interrupt a marvelous fictional dream (though I might have gotten rid of one 'there' and have written 'In the center of the table stood'). Some of the more emotional scenes elsewhere, when Joyce moves deeply into the minds of his characters, are enormously effective and memorable.

POV, Age Level, and Other Gems

Francine Prose's book *Reading Like a Writer* is interesting enough to read straight through in daily sessions, though it might be better to take it slow and intersperse such craft reading with a good fiction book. It can give your subconscious a little more time to dwell on the writing strategies presented. Another good overview on craft is in an interview of Prose by Andrea Dupree in the *Writer's Chronicle*, Sept. 2007, and touches on many of the topics included in her crafts book.

One of the topics Prose discusses deals with the voice and Point-of-View of a young person. Sometimes authors use a wiser, more mature narrative voice than a first-person YA protagonist would likely use. Prose says "I've been writing a novel from the point of view of a fourteen-year-old girl, and I was tormented by the question of adult consciousness versus child consciousness, adult language versus child language— you know, that stupid statement: I don't think a fourteen year old would say that." Nonetheless, Prose goes on to discuss a story by Leonard Michaels where a seemingly adult consciousness works for a kid at times. "And when I read the Lenny Michaels story, I found things in the story that clearly come from the pre-adolescent kid, and things that clearly come from the adult looking back... It's first person, but sometimes it's a first-person twelve-year-old, and sometimes it's the first person forty-year-old, and it really works..." It's somehow freeing for a writer to read that, but of course if one is an unknown writer it might be a riskier business.

Along that line, Dupree says to Prose, "In 'Reading Like a Writer,' you encourage people to disregard the typical rules that are trotted out in writing classes. At the same time, do you feel that writers who are transgressive in their writing have as good a shot of breaking in as others who are more conventionally polished?" Prose allows that it may set a higher hurdle to overcome in selling the book, but, "I don't think there's any choice. If somebody is talented, they're not going to be able to write for what they think the market wants." Proust sounds about right, or ought to be right.

Another kernel that Prose tosses out, "...the better the writer is, the greater the degree of self-doubt. I've had students who really think they're Tolstoy, and they're not the best students I've ever had. Whereas my friends, whose work I respect enormously, whose work I feel lucky to read, are tormented by self-doubt."

There's a certain thrill in reading any good crafts book. One usually concludes that, armed with such insights, their next book is going to be written better than the last.

Unreliable Narrators

The writing strategy for a story told by an 'unreliable narrator' presents an interesting challenge to an author, and a short story in The New Yorker, *Gravel,* by Alice Munro, is an excellent example of a winning strategy.

The narrator in *Gravel* is never obviously unreliable, as is the narrator in "Catcher in the Rye," by J. D. Salinger. However, a question of reliability in *Gravel* surfaces as we realize the events leading up to and surrounding a childhood tragedy are being told by a grown woman drawing on her earlier memories as a kindergartner.

It takes just a column or two for Munro to develop her principal characters and a problem or complication that the story will deal with. The story switches between the Point-of-View (POV) of a child, and the POV of her grownup self, recalling. The back-and-forth is relatively seamless as Monroe moves between the consciousness of each. There's never any question of who.

The younger sister, the kindergartner, is not named; her older sister, Caro, attends grade school. The father, a kind, educated, but gray sort of insurance agent, travels a lot.

The mother "had got busy with various fund-raising schemes for the theater and donated her services as an usher. She was good-looking and young enough to be mistaken for an actress. She'd begun to dress like an actress, too, in shawls and long skirts and dangling necklaces. She'd left her hair wild and stopped wearing makeup. Of course, I had not understood or particularly noticed these things at the time. My mother was my mother."

This passage kind of suggests the seamless way the mother and daughter each inhabit the consciousness of the narration. The kindergartner couldn't possibly have taken in all the earlier comprehensive detail, but her rudimentary observations are being fleshed out by an older self, looking back.

A little later: "Well, then came a development that could have been foreseen, and probably was, but not by my father...She told him that the baby was Neal's."

"Was she sure?"

"Absolutely. She had been keeping track."

"What happened then?"

Neal is one of the amateur actors in the theater. The play-by-play commentary later seems to be the sort of breathless commentary of the bewildered child, looking at astounding events unfolding. It works so well.

Neal is an idealistic liberal, a drop-out and turn-on sort of guy. The pregnant mother (she's never named), Neal, and the two girls, move into an old trailer beside a gravel pit outside of the town. One snowy morning the mother spies what she believes to be a wolf, and wants Neal to get a gun and shoot it. They argue.

"Easy. Easy. Let's just think a bit. Guns are a terrible thing. If I went and got a gun, then what would I be saying? That Vietnam was O.K.? That I might as well have gone to Vietnam?"

"You're not an American."

"You're not going to rile me."

It's the kind of laid-back guy he is. He usually smokes pot on weekends, and one time he lets Caro try one, but tells her not to tell her mother.

"I was there, though, and I told. There was alarm, but not quite a row."

"'You know he'd have those kids out of here like a shot,' our mother said."

The father begins to pick the girls up for visits with him on Saturdays, but becomes ill with recurring flu and stops coming for a while. It seems to have an effect on Caro, and she repeatedly sneaks their dog onto the school bus to leave it off at her father's house near her school. Meanwhile the mother begins acting more like a mother than a free spirit as the birth of her new child approaches, and warns the girls about playing at the rain-filled gravel pit near the trailer. Nevertheless the girls wander over to the pit with the dog one day. At one point the younger girl realizes her sister has given her some instructions:

"I was to go back to the trailer and tell Neal and our mother something.

That the dog had fallen into the water and Caro was afraid she'd be drowned.

Blitzee. Drownded.

Drowned.

But Blitzee wasn't in the water.

She could be. And Caro could jump in to save her."

She watches Caro leap into the water with the dog and runs to tell. But there's an odd interval of delay when she gets to the trailer.

The events at the trailer, and the recollections over the years haunt the woman. She's now a professor teaching at a college when Neal notices an article about her in an Alumni annual from his town, where she'd done her undergraduate work, and he writes her. She's reluctant, but agrees to meet him.

Neil tries to reassure her about the events of the past with his be-happy philosophy.

"I see what he meant. It really is the right thing to do. But, in my mind, Caro keeps running at the water and throwing herself, as if in triumph, and I'm still caught, waiting for her to explain to me, waiting for the splash."

Is it a case of the unreliable narrator? Did it really happen as the memories suggest? We can't really know. Great writing, though.

Unreliable Narrator 2

Our discussion on 'unreliable narrators' includes reflections on the writing strategy found in *Gone Girl*, a NY Times best selling novel by Gillian Flynn. The novel has been variously described by the critics as a literary mystery novel; a frightening tale of psychopathy in a failing marriage; a love story wrapped in a mystery—suspenseful, funny, and chilling, and sometimes all of these at once. At each turn in the plot, it gradually dawns on the reader that there's something amiss, and going through the remaining chapters is like downing successive boilermakers lined up on the countertop.

Reading up to the denouement, the chapters alternate between the husband, Nick, who narrates in first person and gives a chronological progression of the story line from the day his wife, Amy, has disappeared, and the diary entries of Amy during an earlier time period leading up to the day of her disappearance. It is essentially the story of a failing marriage.

Nick has lost his job as a writer for a magazine publisher in NY, is unable to get another job, and has burned through all of his savings. He decides to return to his midwestern hometown to help his twin sister care for their cancer-stricken mother, and maybe get another career start. He borrows money from Amy, drawing down her trust fund, and partners with his sister to open a bar in town. To keep up his credentials as a writer, he also teaches a journalism class at the local community college.

From Amy's diary entries we notice she is unrelentingly optimistic and supportive of Nick, even as he seems to decline into a narcissistic, self-centered and immature man. Why Amy, an attractive daughter of a wealthy family, well educated, and clever, should remain so supportive of Nick seems a mystery to us.

(spoiler alert): Suddenly, Nick's narrative startles the reader. During the police investigation of his wife's disappearance, he admits to having an affair with one of his young students. At this point, if the reader has only limited patience with typical, modern romance plots, he's hoping Nick will quickly be convicted and possibly executed for 'disappearing' his wife. We suspect Nick has proven himself to be an unreliable narrator about what was going on. However. we might notice we're only half-through the book, so we may decide to continue a bit to see if the author has any other surprises (it should be said all the author's surprises are well earned and fit the plot).

Abruptly, Amy's diary entries end, and she begins narrating what has been occurring to her since the day of her disappearance. The diary, discovered by police investigators as she had planned, was prefabricated by her to point suspicion toward Nick. She is actually in hiding now while the police investigation into her disappearance draws a tighter noose around Nick. Amy is revealed to the reader as a psychotically unreliable narrator, and further story events are stunning. In the story denouement, Amy checkmates Nick into continuing their marriage, but on her terms.

144

Nick's example of an unreliable narrator lies in his omission of key information that would have led us to form a different view of his character, up until he makes the disclosure of his infidelity. This is one of the more common signs of unreliable narrators, where the narrator hides essential truths, mainly through evasion, omission, and obfuscation, without ever overtly lying. Other common types include contradicting oneself, or explicitly lying to other characters. Holden Caulfield, in *Catcher in the Rye*, signals his unreliable narrator's role with various instances of evasion, obfuscation, and lying. In Holden's case, it all seems to work agreeably well in the story as the bravado of a sensitive, confused youth, facing entry into an adult world. Nick Carraway, the narrator of *The Great Gatsby*, occasionally falls into a role of unreliable narrator as he reports events he couldn't have known about, and obfuscates other narratives with intentional fantasy.

Another memorable story of an unreliable narrator was in *I am the Cheese*, by Robert Cormier. It is a very dark and discomforting novel in which we think we're accompanying a boy, Adam, riding his bicycle from Massachusetts to Vermont, to visit his father in a hospital. The family had been in a witness protection program as a result of his father being a whistle-blower on some sort of government corruption scheme. A subsequent auto accident involving the family killed the mother and injured Adam and his father. During his bicycle trip Adam meets with various spooky events and people, and a sort of deja vu prevails along the way; he oddly recalls seeing some of the places before. When he arrives to the hospital and is being interviewed by a doctor, we realize Adam has some sort of psychiatric condition and is actually a patient there, as are some of the people he has reported meeting on his trip. In fact, the entire bicycle trip has been occurring on the hospital grounds.

However, none of the stories of these unreliable narrators quite compare to the psychopathic performance of Amy as an unreliable narrator in *Gone Girl*.

Psychological Aspects of POV

A fiction writer is commonly faced at the outset with the decision of choosing a theme and the POV that will be used to tell the story. Various considerations enter into the choices, including whether a first-person or third-person narrative might achieve the desired closeness with the reader, and whether the POV can adequately dramatize the envisioned scope of story.

Often the story theme may be based on a personal life experience. That experience may offer some sort of hidden meaning the writer wants to explore, and then it seems there should be some best POV for the cast of characters and the type of story being considered. However, it may be that the POV choice actually takes over and steers the story into directions and choices that are driven by it, and which more closely relate to the writer's own psychological makeup than the fictional story he starts out to tell.

In a NY Times article, "This is Your Life, and How You Tell It: In Storytelling, Deep Clues to the Self" (by Benedict Carey, 22May07), some recent research looked at ways people narrated their life stories. Those with mood problems had many good memories, but the scenes were often tainted with some dark detail. By contrast, those individuals who scored more positive, "generative" personalities on psychological tests might recall the same sorts of life problems in a reverse way, and as linked by themes of redemption. "They flunked sixth grade but met a wonderful counselor and made honor roll in the seventh." In other words, their understanding of their life's story drove their narrative themes. That might be a useful observation to keep in mind when choosing the experience and setting out to write.

The research then seemed to offer other useful insights to the fiction writing process, and the retelling and reinterpreting of experiences from our own life stories. How do we recall the most vivid scenes from our experiences? An important factor was the perspective people in the study were told to take when revisiting a life experience—whether in first-person, or third person. The investigators found that revisiting a bad experience —an argument, say, or a failed exam—was significantly less upsetting when viewed in the third person, as compared to first person; and, a shift in perspective to third-person allowed the storyteller to deepen and even reshape the event instead of being immersed in it.

Which POV is going to create the stronger fiction story? If the event is compelling enough, and focused, total immersion in a first-person narrator might work okay. If the event is still not clearly understood in the author's own mind, using third-person narration to explore a deepening and reshaping of the personal event might lead to a better fictional story.

Writing in First Person POV and other perils

Has there been an overwhelming tendency in contemporary times for authors to favor writing in first person point-of-view? Cris Mazza, an author and professor of writing, thinks so, and discusses results of her informal surveys in "Too Much of Moi?" published in <u>The Writer's Chronicle</u>, Oct/Nov 2009. Mazza surveyed literary magazines and story anthologies, including about 150 stories within each category, and 123 novels. She generally found first person story narratives to be on the order of 60% to 70%, but with up to 80% in some individual magazines. For the novels, about 66% of the total, and 87% of thirty-one first novels, were in first person.

Mazza makes a point that: "While 65% may not seem overwhelming, it would be considered a landslide in a primary election that offered more than two choices on a ballot." Our authors' ballot, would of course, include first, second, and third person candidates, with at least several variations of the latter: typically called omniscient, objective, and limited third person. Not many enduring stories have been written in second person. Generally, fiction written more than a few decades ago favored limited third person, and older classic fiction favored omniscient third person.

Various motives are given for writing in first person. Some authors believe it to provide a more intimate story, one that feels more 'real' to a reader, and, in view of the current market popularity of memoirs and 'chick-lit' stories, may provide a narrative style of obvious appeal to a wider share of the reading public. Good first person stories have been, and will continue to be, written; but an author should have a good understanding of the potential weaknesses. Mazza says "Really effective first person should be like viewing the story's events through a clouded, scratched, nicked, warped, or otherwise marred piece of glass, or plastic." Otherwise, one of the pitfalls may be that it becomes all too easy to slip into a mode of narrowly relating a character's emotional and physical responses to a series of obstacles placed in the way of the character getting what she wants. A straightforward, major problem, multiple sub-problems, and final resolution, constitute the road map of the story. It becomes difficult to include perceptions of irony, nuance, and character complexity that can raise the story to the level of a literary work. Another potentially draining situation is when the first person author and the story protagonist become the same character, probably a common problem.

Some good, in-depth material on the advantages and disadvantages of the several point of view narrative styles are given in *The Art of Fiction,* by John Gardner, and *Creating Fiction,* edited by Julie Checkoway.

Looking at Second Person POV

There are not many stories written in second-person point of view, at least not many well-known. In books on writing a handful of examples are given that are often repeated among discussions, but from time to time a new use of the mode will be undertaken by a fresh, contemporary fiction writer.

A good example of second-person writing (and an excellent work of fiction) is given in a recent short story, "The Rhett Butlers," by Katherine Heiny (*The Atlantic*, Oct. 2014). Second-person writing is sometimes described as simply substituting 'you' for ' I ' in what would otherwise be first-person writing. That's largely true, but just that switch can have a major effect on how the reader responds to a story. Moreover, there are many other nuances that also can be called into play with the second-person technique. Let's just shorten the terminology to POV-2, and for first-person writing, POV-1, etc., for our following discussion.

Heiny's story is about a seventeen-year old girl student who becomes involved with her 40-yr. old history teacher. It's a story that might be attempted in POV-1, but how reliable would the girl character be in revealing her motivations and emotional state? She might easily be expected to prevaricate about such things. By using POV-2 we might be able to challenge her views, and allow her some sidestepping or irony in revealing her motivations. The POV-2 can also be useful in having the second-person narrator reveal some backstory or exposition that might seem unnatural or forced if left to the girl to furnish to the reader. It will be useful to examine a few excerpts from the story to show the style and nuances that Heiny employs. Here is one of the early paragraphs that will help set up the story as well as show the POV-2 style she so deftly uses:

YOU AND MR. EAGLETON are becoming regulars at the Starlite Motel. The first time you stayed in the car while Mr. Eagleton checked in, but now you go in with him to see what name he uses when he signs the register. He always chooses characters from your favorite novels: Mr. and Mrs. Gatsby, Mr. and Mrs. Caulfield, Mr. and Mrs. Finch, Mr. and Mrs. Twist. This idea seems very romantic to you, even though you would never change your name, and certainly not to Eagleton.

The woman behind the counter seems to like Mr. and Mrs. Butler best. "Ah, the Rhett Butlers," she says every time. "Welcome back."

She is a large, motherly woman, who looks a lot like Mrs. Harrison, the woman who drives the Children's Bookmobile. She always has the TV on, and always on a channel showing *Wheel of Fortune*. She's unbelievably good--you once saw her guess "*Apocalypse Now*" just from the letter C.

This woman makes you feel a lot better. Nothing bad can happen to you here.

Notice how the narrator can fill in the reader on the prior frequency of visits, and show an equanimity of the girl, as well as her naïveté, and other background things that would have been a lot more awkward in first-person exposition. Here is another, later example from Heiny that illustrates the nuanced values of POV-2:

MARCY TELLS HER PARENTS that she's sleeping at your home. This way she can stay out past her curfew or even all night. She's going over to Jeff Lipencott's house; his parents are out of town.
You agree. Of course you do--think of all the times Marcy has covered for you. You sit in the TV room, wearing sweats and your glasses and eating cold Pop-Tarts. You wish only the very best for Marcy, but you feel forlorn picturing her at Jeff Lippencott's, maybe lying in his parent's bed, leading a real life.

Marcy knocks on the window a little after 11. You open it and she steps over the window ledge, shaking little diamonds of cold rain from her hair, and says, "Oh my God, he's such an asshole! He spent the whole time doing handstands with his friends, and I didn't know anyone and wound up helping his little sister weave pot holders."

This story should make you feel lots better. It should make you happy to be you again. But it doesn't.

The choice of POV-2 for this story seemed right. Check out the full story in *The Atlantic*.   Another interesting story in POV-2, a novel actually, is Chris Lynch's, *Freewill*, a Printz Honor Award book. Lynch has a long list of good YA titles, and is such a fine writer that it was inevitable he'd take up the challenge to write an intriguing POV-2 classic.

Further explorations of Second Person POV

Another POV-2 article from <u>Writer's Chronicle</u>, by James Chesbro, was titled: "Notes to You--Second Person in Creative Nonfiction." Chesbro's examples are taken from essay and memoir writers, but the techniques will be the same for fiction writers. His article is sometimes a bit complex and difficult to follow, but can further our understanding of POV-2.

In many, perhaps most cases, the persona or real identity of the protagonist addressed by the "you" of POV-2 is actually the narrator of the story. For example, in the case of a memoir the person "you" addresses is often the narrator himself at some earlier age. However, intermittently, and sometimes in the same paragraph, the "you" being addressed may be the reader. This slipperiness might be used to good effect in conflating the tensions felt by the protagonist with those felt by the reader. When the reader is cast in the role of "you," he or she becomes more intimately associated with the protagonist. He or she becomes the protagonist.

Let's look at an example given by Chesbro, from the essay, "Swimming With Canoes," by John McPhee:

> The canoe rocks, slaps the lake, moves forward. Sooner or later, you lose your balance and fall into the water, because the gunwales are slender rails and the stern deck is somewhat smaller than a pennant. From waters

deeper than you were tall, you climbed back into your canoe. If you think that's easy, try it.

In the early part of the paragraph the narrator's "you" is self referring, in a scene that took place when he was a young boy. The reader may be gripped by the risks and dangers faced by the boy, but can keep some distance from what is happening. However, in the last sentence of the paragraph, Chesbro suggests a slippery switch by the author from self address to direct address of the reader.

This construction can trick the mind of the reader into placing himself on the gunwales of the canoe, and to slip, just as the boy character does. The conflation of direct and self-address is a purposeful strategy of McPhee's multi-faceted utilization of second person construction. "If you think that's easy, try it," does indeed have an effect of causing the reader to more directly imagine just what he might have done in that same incident.

Let's move now to another example from Chesbro, a beautifully straightforward example of POV-2: "If You Should Want Flowers for Your Table (Advice to a Daughter)," a 565 word essay by Marsha McGregor. The second person construction allows a direct address to the narrator's daughter. The mother's voice is part of what makes this undemanding use of second person work so well. Ostensibly, the mother is advising her daughter on how to care for flowers, and it is a gorgeous POV-2 example:

A small garden patch to call your own is lovely, but even a sad, weed-choked spot near the highway will yield plenty...Last week I veered off the road near that custard stand you loved, parked the car on the shoulder and waded into a riotous patch of wild sweet peas, all tangled tendrils and wiry stems, reminding me of the way you looked as a child when you slept...If you pursue the wild things, love, look out for bad drivers and poison ivy. Be careful.

Multiple POV

The Disreputable History of Frankie Landau-Banks, by E. Lockhart, is a YA novel with a prep-school setting, prompting a little expectation it might be like an old favorite, *Tom Brown's School Days*, by Thomas Hughes. The Disreputable History has nowhere near the tension and drama of Tom Brown, but it has some nice writing, character development, and harmless, if not sophomoric, pranks carried out by a males-only, secret society. Frankie, a spunky young woman, newly endowed with a terrific body over the previous summer, falls in love with one of the boys in the society. She manages to penetrate the secrets and inner workings of the society, and uses phony email messages to commandeer their programs.

The story is narrated generally in third-person omniscient, though at times Lockhart projects the reader into the mind of Frankie in long passages, where it temporarily assumes a first-person narrative. Frankie, and a less affluent, scholarship student at the school, a friend of Frankie's boyfriend, Matthew, comprise the better developed characters in the story. Frankie might be maddening to some readers with her urgent need to know everything Matthew thinks, or she'll assume her relationship is going nowhere. Still, she's engaging, and inventive. She goes a little overboard on her use of 'neglected positives,' like describing someone as ept, her presumptive opposite of inept. Frankie tells us in several places she's Jewish, which held some expectation of somehow enriching her character, but Lockhart leaves it to us to imagine how. Writers will find the story informative in handling multiple point of view usage, and a good read as well.

More Point of View Thoughts

Point of View is a writing concept and in which it can be easy to err. One of the foremost instructors of creative writing, as well as being a first-rate author, was John Gardner. His book, *The Art of Fiction,* (1984), is an outstanding craft book. One of Gardner's comments on POV was:

"We may go along for years without ever noticing that the third-person-limited point of view is essentially sappy...the third person limited point of view forces the writer into phony suspense."

Gardner sets up a story situation in third person omniscient where a man named Alex Strugatsky is taking his Saturday morning ballet class when his mistress, the wife of the local Chief of Police, comes in to stand watching. Alex is distressed —he does not want their affair known, lest the police chief shoot him, but he does not want to be impolite, either, because his mistress, Genevieve Rochelle, is a beauty.

Gardner shows that if we start off this story in the omniscient point of view, as Checkhov would, we can get the important facts in right away and get on to what's really interesting, such as: What will Alex do? But if the writer starts off in third-person-limited, where, Gardner says, ", Alex's story quickly becomes sappy. The sappiness occurs because the writer has no other way of showing what happens except by somehow putting it into Alex's head.

To overcome this constraint, some writrs may qualify the rules. Gardner's non-omniscient, third person POV, wants to be broken down into <u>two separate categories</u> by Lynna Williams in her chapter, "And Eyes to See: The Art of Third Person," included in the book, *Creating Fiction,* edited by Julie Chekoway. The 'sappy' construct of third person limited given by Gardner is Williams' 'third person unified,' in which "everything, even the "telling" that goes on in exposition, is filtered through the point-of-view character's consciousness (as in the bold passage in Gardner). However, in Williams third person limited, the POV character:

> "will continue to be our angle of vision on events, and we'll still have access to her thoughts. But in this use of third person, we'll also be able to take advantage of objective narration; that is, neutral exposition that is not tied to the character's consciousness."

Perhaps it's the latter type of third person limited that most contemporary writers follow, rather than the bold-marked, third person limited version discussed negatively in Gardner's discussion.

In general, omniscient POV seems a best choice.

CHARACTERIZATION

Constructing Characters

An interesting writer's article appeared in the Jan/Feb issue of the Society of Children's Book Writers and Illustrators, SCBWI, Bulletin, entitled "Character Building," by Louise B. Wyly. Wyly discussed using the Myers-Briggs personality test groupings, to construct interesting characters that logically support or conflict with each other. For example, you want a boy or girl who places high value on cooperation from others—a born leader—one who takes for granted that he or she would be followed. For this, Wylie selects an ENFJ type individual. The test assigns four dominant personality traits for any individual:

E or I; Extrovert or Introvert
N or S; Innovative or Sensation/Practical
T or F; Thinking or Feeling
P or J; Perceptive or Judgmental

Once you've selected perhaps two dominant traits you're looking for in a character, you might complete the character's personality with two other tentative traits, and try to stay aware throughout your story how that character would logically react in each conflict or problem situation. Any grouping of four traits has a certain frequency of occurrence in the population as a whole, and this has been borne out in decades of M-B testing. That's not to say that a fiction writer couldn't have a character switch traits in a stressful situation, but it doesn't run true to form, and the reader might need extra convincing.

Experience with M-B shows people, however, can gradually change their grouping over time, but usually as a result of changing life experiences. The book Wyly gives as a reference for her article is *Please Understand Me*, by David Keirsey and Marilyn Bates. The M-B might be a useful idea for a writer to think about.

Finding the Character's Virtual Reality

"We all live in a virtual reality, and the brain is the final arbiter." The quote, taken from a newspaper interview (NYTimes, 11/26) with Dr. M. Samuels, a neurologist at a Harvard hospital, teaching affiliate, was a cautious response to a colleague's best-selling book on a near-death experience and its accompanying visions *(Proof of Heaven,* by Dr. Eben Alexander III).

The quote also relates to an essay by Pablo Medina, titled "Lunacy and Longing: Don Quixote and Adventures of Huckleberry Finn (Writer's Chronicle, v.45, 2012). Medina discusses related scenes and connections between the two fiction classics, which are interesting to think about in relation to the concept of virtual reality (VR).

For example, there is the scene where Tom Sawyer persuades his friend Huck to accompany him on the ambush of a company of Arabs camped nearby with an entourage of elephants, camels, mules, and a rich treasure trove. After the raid, Huck points out that it was just a Sunday-school picnic that they broke up. Tom retorts that if Huck weren't so ignorant he'd have read Don Quixote, and would have known that the company of Arabs had been turned into Sunday-school kids by their enemies, the magicians. We recall from a reading of Don Quixote's adventures that Tom may indeed be acting out a borrowed VR, while Huck's VR mirrors a down-to-earth, simple life realism of Sancho Panza.

Medina suggests other parallels between the two books, some dealing with class distinctions and social mores of the two eras, but the idea of the brain interpreting the same scene as different realities for different characters is intriguing (and as Medina suggests, poses problems for a well-ordered society). Nonetheless, it has always been a classical, philosophical challenge to define any reality as 'truth.' If you deviate too far from a contemporary norm of conduct, however, and do not have the mental capacity to recognize it, you may be in for difficulties.

The author of a fictional work, though he may strive to narrate his story in a omniscient, strictly objective point-of-view, will usually introduce some sort of VR for each of his characters, scenes and actions in the story. And if his protagonist's VR is very unusual, like Don Quixote's, it may be well to have one or two characters with a more grounded VR, like Pancho's or Huck's. Recognizing at least one character with a VR not too different from a norm might give the reader a little more confidence in staying around to see where an unusual story is going.

To explore these ideas further, we could consider "Moby Dick," by Herman Melville. Ahab's interpretation of a VR built up from his own experience is that it is possible for a brute force of nature, the great white whale, Moby Dick, to embody supernatural forces of evil. He is outraged that this evil force has violated him by ripping his leg away in a past encounter, and so he has vowed to find and destroy Moby Dick. Indeed, if God were to insult him, he would strike God, himself. Such is Ahab's VR that he perceives himself to be an equal to God.

Ahab is intriguing, but his VR is so different than most reader's VR that it becomes difficult to find ways to sympathize with his character. To that end, Melville also gives us a more grounded character, Starbuck, a brave and admirable ship's officer, who has a down-to-earth VR, and so gives opportunities to contrast the mind and character of Ahab during their shipboard discussions. Starbuck is the Sancho Panza of the story, who sees Ahab's misfortune as simply another accident in a dangerous trade, and it is time to drop this Moby Dick obsession and get on with the business of hunting any and all whales, and filling the ship's holds with whale oil.

Mythic Characters 2

An interesting article, "The Absence of Their Presence: Mythic Characters in Fiction," by Steven Schwartz, appears in The Writer's Chronicle, Dec. 2011. Schwartz shows how developing a mythic character in a fiction piece requires some attention to the use of the point of view (POV) chosen to narrate the story. A basic concept is a need to stay out of the head of the mythic character. The reader gets to know him or her only through dialog and action, and through reports of the story narrator. Even in a third-person, omniscient POV, the narrator should not move into the head of the mythic character to show any of his feelings or thought process.

> "What might seem less than more at first—an external perspective versus an internal view—turns out to be the necessary narrative device for creating their unique myths."

Using *Moby Dick* Schwartz illustrates his point:

"With more conventional characters we may feel cheated when their motivations remain opaque, and their psyches, like Ahab's, ultimately unknowable. But we do not make the same demands of mythic characters, often because the prearranged audience in the story reflects our own bafflement. By their surrogate reactions and scrutiny, they preempt our silent protests. That is, we need (the POV narrator) to act as our agent of disbelief..." and, "...we may clearly see what (the mythic character) do(es), but not why, and it's the why that creates a chilling gap of suspense."

Of course the mythic character has to present actions and dialog that elicit a tension and bafflement which grow to suspense. Often appearing as an outsider, with abnormal behavior, the writer should avoid having the observer-narrator explain away the mythic character's motivations, and "never minimize the complexity nor the significance of the strange."

Schwartz explores the mythic dimensions of Jay Gatsby, in Fitzgerald's *The Great Gatsby*, and of Bartleby, in Melville's *Bartleby the Scrivener*.:

It may seem odd to think of Gatsby as a mythic character. Still, we are never invited into Gatsby's head to discover what he really feels about his experience, and we have only Nick Carraway's first-person POV for a subjective opinion on Gatsby and his motivations. Gatsby is shown to be an outsider in his society, but doesn't seem to show a particularly strange or abnormal behavior. The Bartleby character, however, does show such behavior, and in abundance.

Schwartz uses a Steven Millhauser short story, "The Knife Thrower," to illustrate other points about writing the mythical character:

Interestingly, Millhauser uses the plural first-person, we, to serve as both narrator and audience watching the controversial knife thrower, Hensch, as he visits their town for a one-time performance. The narrator alludes to rumors that Hensch, in his early carnival days, had badly wounded an assistant. Now, the narrative leaves open a possibility that Hensch, in his present performance, mortally wounds an audience volunteer, a girl, who had wished to be marked by him.

All of which makes for a strangely normative viewpoint that in its plurality gives additional weight to its judgment of Hensch. On the other hand, this impersonal "we" relies on rumor and hearsay and is even more incapable of penetrating Hensch''s mystery than an individual observer-narrator such as Nick Carraway ... would be in gaining confidences, creating an extra layer of insulation from the subject. And Millhauser clearly wants it that way to promote the morally ambiguous atmosphere and mythic tone...

At the conclusion of "The Knife Thrower," illustrating the elusive nature of the mythic, the collective viewpoint voices its frustration. The more we thought about it, the more uneasy we became, and in the nights that followed, when we woke from troubling dreams, we remembered the traveling knife thrower with agitation and dismay. This could well stand as a summary of all mythic characters. Fascinatingly inconclusive, they trick us into remembering them by the absence of their presence.

It all rings true; nonetheless, creating a mythic character may be
quite a challenge to the writer.

Wishing for Sympathetic Characters

The Goldfinch, by Donna Tartt, had a good popular reception.
The standard font size edition clocked in at over 800 pages,
and the large type book, was over 1200 pages long! At first the
story seems to have promise. Scenes of a slightly selfish boy
(think of *This Boy's Life*, by Tobias Wolff) and his art-loving
mother, struggling to get by to live in New York City, and their
hurried visit one day to an art museum, culminate in a terrorist
bombing of the museum and death of the mother. A
compelling plot, thus far.

Gradually, however, some overwrought language begins to
make itself noticeable, in the form of catchy metaphors and
weird similes which don't seem to fit anything. Not to be too
quick to make negative judgments, we may press on with
reading.

After his mother's death, the Children's Protective Society gives
the boy temporary refuge. He then is made the ward of a
schoolmate's family, who are upper-class socialites. Things
look promising, but his deadbeat father, who'd abandoned his
family years before, shows up with a druggie girlfriend and
assumes custody of his son. Dad and girlfriend take the son
back with them to Las Vegas and a weirdly sterile world of
McMansions, spacious buildings in various states of arrested
development after the bursting of the subprime mortgage
bubble. One of these semi-finished buildings is their rented
home.

Dad is pursuing some sort of numerical scheme to beat the odds at the gambling casinos, and does well at it for a while — until he doesn't. Meanwhile, the boy hooks up with a streetwise, multi-lingual Russian kid, who introduces him to an astonishing assortment of pills and opiates. They rarely seem to go to school, and their biggest problem is keeping food in the house. The downtown pizza bakery refuses to deliver out to this wasteland.

The father is killed, either a suicide or was murdered, when he is unable to pay his gambling debts. The boy returns to New York, and pursues a brief, unrequited love for a girl his age that had lost her guardian in the same terrorist bombing at the museum. However, the promising girl character disappears into the custody of an Aunt, to be raised in Europe. A weird plot turn. Flash forward, and the boy is a young man. He is a success in the antiques business through highly dishonest dealings, and is still a heavy consumer of illegal drugs.

All things considered, the overwrought, bombastic language, unsatisfying plot turns, and shallow personality of the main character, may defeat any attempts to stay engaged to the end of the book. A similarly critical review of the book by Francine Proust appeared in the NY Review of Books (Jan. 9, 2014).

Some of the problems may be stylistic, but the biggest problem with this book was the total inability to find any sympathetic characters to care about. Something we need in any good book.

Evoking Sympathetic Characters

Every so often one picks up a novel in which the protagonist has been given some demoralizing physical affliction, but which is not his main obstacle in getting what he wants in the story. It seems to have been factored in by the author, either to create added sympathy for the character, or perhaps to provide an interesting, additional tension. But does it work?

On one end of the scale, arguably, we might have the overweight character, whose romantic horizon is consequently more constricted, or who suffers numerous barbs and indignities as a result of his weight. Does the overweight condition add much to the story? Several YA novels in this category might be useful to discuss.

Skim, by cousins, Mariko (author) and Jillian (illustrator) Tamaki, is the story of Kimberly Keiko Cameron, attending a private, girls' school in Toronto. Kim and her small group of friends practice an eclectic mix of Goth and Wiccan lifestyles, which sets them off from the majority, the more affluent and conventional girls. Kim, who lives with her divorced mother, is a very lonely girl to begin with, and her overweight condition intensifies this. She develops a crush on her English teacher, a young, hippie-like, New Age woman. The graphics are quite effective in showing how Kim's fantasies sometimes mix with the realities of her infatuation. The teacher abruptly transfers away from the school, and Kim is despondent. She compensates a little by eating more frequently, and resists attempts by her girlfriend to hook them up with college boy dates. The story has its tender moments and story interest, but the overweight factor, and eating compulsion, are ultimately a little off-putting. Kim's lonely nature, her search for identity and meaning through Wiccan ritual, and through a fantasy love, seemed enough for the story without the added unresolvable tension of her body weight.

Overweight may or may not have a genetic basis, but cerebral palsy definitely does, and we'd really be loading down our character with this while he's on his search for what he wants in the story. *Stoner and Spaz*, a YA novel by Ron Koertge, does just that. Ben is a conservative, strait-laced, generally ignored student with a CP disability, a spaz in cruel juvenile slang, who escapes his loneliness with a heavy dosage of movies at the local arts theater—until he meets Colleen there, another lonely student, but a rebel who'll do any drug, and take any dare. She doesn't ignore his disability; she teases him about it, and thrillingly they're on some sort of high wire together. He doesn't even smoke cigarettes, but she has him try a joint, and takes him to all the swinging clubs with her. She challenges him to direct his own movie, and he challenges her to give up the drugs. We get the feeling Ben will have the strength he needs for his challenge, but our heart goes out to Colleen who just doesn't seem like she'll make it. So, does the affliction make for a better story? It probably would have worked fine if he were just the lonely, movie-addicted, introverted young man he was, without the CP complication. However, the CP seemed to have a reasonably good fit, wasn't overly clinical, and the story didn't strain to send any message about disabilities. Koertge continues to be a favorite YA author.

The Curious Incident of the Dog in the Night-Time, by Mark Haddon, demonstrates a deeper end of the scale in discussion of an affliction borne by the character. Christopher, an autistic 15-yr. old, narrates our story. Here, the affliction is the dominant theme, though Haddon weaves the autistic child's own view of the world into a light mystery plot concerning who killed a neighbor's dog. Christopher utilizes his love of reading Sherlock Holmes mysteries and an acute, deductive logic, to pursue the mystery. He is handicapped by an inability to 'read' the moods and behaviors signaled by other people, and though he cannot tell or understand jokes, he is often ironically funny. Other times, he is maddeningly irritating with his idiosyncrasies, and petulance toward his beleaguered father. Haddon had job training in social work, and he probably understands his character's affliction well. In the case of this novel, the affliction, and the writing, are compelling reasons for reading the novel through, but the reading experience finally seems less rich when the mental process of the character is so far removed from most readers.

States of Becoming

What kind of insights did we get from the literary fiction we can recall or the movies or plays we saw in those early formative years, the years spent urgently trying to become who we are now--for better or worse? Some stories that jump to mind might simply have been good, escapist fare transporting us to another place or time, or featuring especially interesting characters. We might have thought those characters' exploits seemed exciting, or fun-laden, or sad; however, perhaps in only a few cases a character really touched something deeply profound in the ongoing search for who we were, or were trying to become.

Some of the books remembered from our formative years might have included works of Charles Dickens, Robert Louis Stevenson, Herman Melville, Mark Twain, Booth Tarkington, Rudyard Kipling, and an assortment of other classic authors. These are not meant to be any universal, all inclusive reading list, but a takeoff point for reflections on a few perhaps lesser known books and interesting to discuss.

For example, *Tom Brown's School Days,* by Thomas Hughes. Most likely our school choices today bear little or no resemblance to the nineteenth century English public school that Tom is sent off to attend. We admire his sense of honor and bravery while there, and the hardships he came through in that difficult, sometimes brutal environment, to become a leader among his school peers. When we scan those pages today, it's a wonder how we admired Hughes' Victorian ethos of 'Rule, Britannia!' and its code of the manly virtues, but the story was somehow appealing in our own days of youth.

An odd one next, *The Amboy Dukes,* by Irving Shulman, read while attending a NYC public high school in the late Forties. The old neighborhoods in south Queens were changing, with more of the inner city tough youth culture beginning to appear in our far out reaches of the city. Initially the story was a bit exciting, and of course girls were becoming a big interest at that age. *The Amboy Dukes* story dramatized this new era, but ultimately, the story seemed disheartening with its random savagery, sex, and betrayals.

Finally, "How Green Was My Valley," by Richard Llewellyn. The closeness of the story's large family of young men and their one sister and loving parents, was appealing. The setting was in a coal mining community in Wales around the turn of the century. The narrator was the youngest son of the family, and described his coming of age trials in the harsh school system of that time and place, and the rough-and-tumble world of the youths his age. His father and all his brothers were miners, and if they did have a cheerful, song-filled approach to life, living was nonetheless hard, given the wages and labor unrest of the time. The father had hoped his youngest son, a bright lad, would go on to a higher education than any of the rest of the brothers had attained. It was not to be. As his brothers were discharged from the mine and left one-by-one for a better life in America, the boy passes up a chance for higher schooling and goes down into the mines to work alongside his beloved father. The sentiment and courage shown in the story was almost overwhelming.

The formative power of books during our coming-of-age period, and going through our rites of passage into adulthood, will always be with us, and can be great material for one of our own stories..

Boys Bonding

Author Meg Rosoff has a thoughtful YA novel, *What I Was.*
Typically, boys are not known for intensity of emotional
relationships with other boys, except perhaps in a story of a
gay boy. "What I Was" never commits to identifying the
protagonist Hilary's attraction to a mysterious boy, Finn, as gay,
neither in Hilary's mind, nor in their experiences. But it is an
underlying tension in the plot and keeps the reader wondering
throughout, even into the epilogue, where Hilary reminisces, as
an old, never-married bachelor, on his experiences as a boy at
St. Oswald's.

Rosoff chooses an intriguing setting for her story, St. Oswald's
School on the southeast coast of England, one of the austere,
ancient boarding schools that seem to dot the country, and it
contributes to the mood and dynamics that propel the story
along. Finn, about fourteen, lives alone in a fishing shack along
the periodically almost submerged headlands, and it is his
grace, simple lifestyle and taciturn manner that intrigues Hilary,
about sixteen, son of a wealthy family, who has been expelled
from several boarding schools before St. Oswald's. Hilary is
one of those boys who are recognized as 'different' by other
boys, and his roommates delight in tormenting him. Meeting
Finn, who does not go to school but has somehow escaped the
notice of any authorities, makes life more tolerable, even
interesting, for Hilary. He cuts school as often as he can to
spend time with Finn. Finn becomes alarmingly ill at one point,
and the story makes a revelation that adds a layer of
complexity to what the reader may think about the nature of the
special relationship that has been cherished by Hilary. Their

relationship is perhaps fundamentally unknowable, but invites some thought.

The skill of a writer in withholding a sensitive, key element of his character's psyche throughout a story and its denouement can make a work all the more memorable.

The Quiet American or The Great Gatsby

Writers generally know that in addition to writing every day one needs also to continue reading regularly, including the best of the classics and acclaimed contemporary work. But where to find all the necessary hours in a day? One strategy might be to better leverage the extra-curricula output of a growing number of colleges across the country that have added creative writing programs to their curriculum. Instructors working in these programs, often published writers motivated by a love of the writing craft and perhaps also challenged to share their teaching skills with a large student body, have made available some excellent learning materials on the Internet and in periodicals published especially for writers. Much of the Internet material is free, accessible on the authors' blogs and home pages, and an access to author interviews and topical essays in periodicals is usually at only nominal cost. A good choice among the periodicals, The Writer's Chronicle,' is published by a professional association of nationwide writing programs.

The great thing about most of the topical essays one finds in the periodicals is the critical spotlighting of material taken from the literature to illustrate the topic of an article. Writers might want to read such an essay, let's say, "On the Use of Epiphanies in Fiction," because they've been interested in examples of how this has been done successfully. If it's a good essay, one can learn a few things about epiphanies, and become interested in a new author, or a book listed in the references given by the writer for his article. In this way a writer can add to a focused reading list for material that meets his current interests and needs.

For example, a past issue of the Chronicle discussed "*The Quiet American*," by Graham Greene. His fiction often has an engaging mix of political, spiritual, philosophical, and even comic elements. "*The Quiet American*" has all but the comical. Greene uses a direct, linear style of storytelling, and doesn't load an otherwise complex story with any more exposition than is necessary up to each stage of events.

The story is set against a backdrop of the twilight of French colonial rule in Vietnam, and the struggles of a communist-dominated Vietminh insurgency to overthrow the French. The United States, critical of French imperialism but fearful of a communist victory in southeast Asia, seeks to undermine the communist power in the insurgency by supporting rival warlord factions.

The core tension of the story is about the efforts of an aging, British journalist, Thomas Fowler, to hold on to his relationship with the young, Vietnamese girl he loves, Phuong. A young, American diplomat, Alden Pyle, has met Phuong and and has fallen in love with her and asks to marry her. Pyle can promise Phuong a security she'd love to have. Fowler, however, cannot promise her any kind of future security. He already has a wife in Britain who won't give him a divorce, and he can't marry Phuong. Consequently, he's fearful of losing her to Pyle, and of dying alone and pitiful.

Here are some random passages that are revealing of Greene's writing style:

> (Priest) ...It's strange what fear does to a man.
> (Fowler) ...It would never do that to me. If I believed in any God at all, I should still hate the idea of confession. Kneeling in one of your boxes. Exposing myself to another man. You must excuse me Father, but to me it seems, morbid--unmanly even.

> (Fowler, on learning his newspaper wants him to return to Britain) ...I had experience to match his (Pyle's) virginity, age was as good a card to play in the sexual game as youth, but now I hadn't even the limited future of twelve more months to offer, and a future was trumps.

> (Fowler)...What are you afraid of? Phuong asked, and I thought, I'm afraid of the loneliness, of the Press Club and the bed-sitting room, I'm afraid of Pyle.

In some ways the story structure puts one in mind of Scott Fitzgerald's *The Great Gatsby*. We learn most of what we know about the protagonist of each story through its narrator: Nick Carraway in *Gatsby*, and Thomas Fowler in *Quiet Man*. Interesting twists lie in the characters of the narrators: Carraway is a well educated, quite moral man, while Pyle is a hard-bitten journalist, rather immoral and solipsistic, and smokes opium. Also, the characters of the protagonists are opposites: Pyle is from a moneyed family and a mannered professional, if naive, man, while Gatsby has humble origins and got his fortune as a bootlegger.

184

Eloquent writing by both authors in terms of characterization.

VOICE

Voice Uncovered

The NY Review of Books had an intriguing review by Wyatt Mason on a book written by David Lipsky, *Although of Course You End Up Becoming Yourself: A Road Trip With David Foster Wallace*. The book encompasses a collection of conversations between Lipsky and Wallace.

Although Wallace's fiction has at times been cited as "excessive, not edited, arbitrary, self indulgent, mad, gibberish, nonsense," such criticism may have owed to his being "an avant-garde writer. He believed that one of fiction's main jobs was to challenge readers, and to find new ways of doing so." A short section of the review analyzed a "spoken casualness" that would become a characteristic quality of Wallace's prose. An excerpt from a Wallace story includes a suicidal-depressive narrator's description of his state of mind when he witnessed the driver of his bus get seriously injured:

> *I felt unbelievably sorry for him and of course the Bad Thing (an euphemism for his depression) very kindly filtered this sadness for me and made it a lot worse. It was weird and irrational but all of a sudden I felt really strongly as though the bus driver were really me. I really felt that way. So I felt just like he must have felt, and it was awful. I wasn't just sorry for him, I was sorry as him, or something like that.*

The reviewer, Mason, suggests:

The mix of registers here is typical of Wallace: intensifiers and qualifiers that ordinarily suggest sloppy writing and thinking ("unbelievably"; "really" used three times in the space of a dozen words; "something like that") coexisting with the correct use of the subjunctive mood ("as though the driver were"). The precision of the subjunctive—which literate people bother with less and less, the simple past tense increasingly and diminishingly being used in its place—is never arbitrary, and its presence suggests that if attention is being paid to a matter of higher-order usage, similar intention lurks behind the clutter of qualifiers. For although one could edit them out of the passage above to the end of producing leaner prose—

I felt sorry for him. It was irrational, but I felt as though the driver were me. I wasn't just sorry for him, I was sorry as him.

—the edit removes more than "flab": it discards the furniture of real speech, which includes the routine repetitions and qualifications that cushion conversation.

The paragraph by Wallace stands out as a unique "voice," that thing we're always being challenged to develop in our fiction writing, while at the same time being advised to tighten-up our prose, weed out all but the necessary adverbs and adjectives, "kill the little darlings," meaning our effusive metaphors, similes, and erudite words, and more often than not the use of any constructs like subjunctive moods. Nonetheless, tightening-up mighty not always be the best approach, as suggested here.

Mason offers many good insights for writers in his review. (As a postscript, it was sad to read in the article that Wallace committed suicide in 2008.)

Dialects

Dialect, "a particular form of a language specific to a certain region or group" as a dictionary has it, can be a strong element for writing a fictional work. It can lend an air of greater embedment of the reader in a story, an immediacy of being among, or of the characters, instead of having a narration that presents the characters' dialog in a grammatically correct syntax--effectively, a translation of their true dialect, and perhaps as translations go, losing some of the native emotive content of a dialect.

For example, a character in our story is a young, partially-disabled vet, working on a northeastern produce farm alongside migrant farm workers from the deep south. They are black, and he is white. The migrants have a rich, rural southern dialect, and the vet has a northern, working class dialect. The dialog includes raucous stories which the migrant workers pitch in conversational tones during the long hours of creeping forward on their knees, harvesting vegetables as they go. The farm owner is working among them and cuts off the storytelling because he feels it interferes with the harvesting work. A tension and silence settles over the field. In the silence the vet's thoughts and reflections, in his own dialect, become submerged in a deja vu experience of crawling forward like this in Vietnam mud, under heavy fire, and ordered on by a demonic platoon leader. Soon, the black workers' storytelling resumes, but in a more subdued manner as they test the farm owner's limits.

The same story can be written in grammatically correct English, but it could lose a lot of the verve and relevance to life that lies in the voice and dialect of the characters.

Every story will have its own pros and cons of using dialect, or even the irregular syntax of some English learners. *Foreign Gods, Inc.,* by Oke Ndibe, a Nigerian-born writer who teaches African and African Diaspora literature in the US. The theme of *Foreign Gods...* involves a Nigerian immigrant to the US who earned an economics degree here, but had been unsuccessful in landing a job in his field. After hearing more than enough criticisms of his *speech*, Ike has given up pursuing that career path and has been driving a taxi in New York for thirteen years. Reading an article about a NY dealer specializing in foreign gods, he visits the establishment, Foreign Gods, Inc. He proposes to sell them an image of an ancient war deity from his village in Nigeria, but the dealer is reluctant to estimate any potential value until he can inspect the actual piece, and see some papers attesting to the provenance of the work. Ike borrows from friends and maxes out his credit card to make the trip back to his village in Nigeria.

A major part of the story following includes a Nigerian dialect, incorporating a local, pidgin English. Often it results in very humorous mashups of Nigerian and American diction. In the story, Ike has neglected for some time to send any money to his mother and sister, and now he Is traveling back to Nigeria to rob his village of their deity, *Ngene*. Such a motive, if they'd known of it, would not matter much to the mother and sister, since they and a large portion of the village have fallen for the new allure of the Christian gospel, as preached by a slick, duplicitous, local minister. The minister views Ike as a probable easy American mark for $50K to build him a new church. A comical, though unsettling bible belt preacher, jousting with a smug religious cynic, seems a sort of opera at times, but holds together well enough. The tension created by Ike's need to purloin the deity from its local temple, presided over by *Ngene's* high priest, Ike's uncle, is almost painful.

Ndibe has written a good story, but the extensive use of such an idiosyncratic dialect might be jarring and tedious to some readers. The dialect is so much more unusual than the common diction and dialog exposures of most American readers.

The use of a true dialect can enhance a story, but needs to be carefully managed by the writer to avoid interrupting or frustrating the fictional dream state of the reader.

The Narrator's Voice

The role played by a character's 'voice' is often stressed in fiction writing. It may be the trait most explored by writers in getting their creations down on paper, but it is tantalizingly hard to capture in a manner that will set a story above the rest. Perhaps just as worthy of a writer's consideration is a compelling voice for the narrator. Sometimes they may be one and the same, as when the story is told in first person.

A few illustrations that spring to mind are "Catcher in the Rye," "How Green Was My Valley," "Lolita," and "The Great Gatsby." They all seem to have had that seamless, enfolding, fictional dream quality in both the character's voice and the narration of the story.

In the case of a third-person story, a great deal more latitude exists for distancing the voice of a character and the voice of an independent narrator who tells the story. Perhaps any of the Charles Dickens stories would do to illustrate this, where the narrator has an educated, intellectual voice, clearly different than the character's own, lower class voice, or that of a criminal and violent class character voice.

In other third-person stories the narrator's voice may closely fit the intellect, mannerisms, and diction of the main characters in the story, and the reader remains generally unaware of the presence or agency of the narrator. This seems to have generally been the case in stories by Alice Munro, or William Trevor, for example.

In the matter of narrator strategy, an author once wrote that he likes to be informed from the beginning how a particular story came into existence--how is it that it came to be written down for himself and others to read. Not many stories try to answer that question; most just take off into the fictional dream. However, some, like *David Copperfield*, or *Moby Dick*, have a go at letting us know how the story we are reading came about. That strategy can make for a compelling narrator presence.

A recent T. C. Boyle story published in The New Yorker, *A Death in Kitchawank,* makes the case for still another strategy, the introduction of a second narrator, who inserts his own observation of the story events, and at a later point in time than the original narrator. The second narrator's asides, included as brief, italicized paragraphs, describe the emotions and responses of one of the secondary characters to the story's events. It doesn't seem to make any dramatic changes to the original telling of events, but provides additional, bittersweet shadings toward a better understanding of the principal character. Like other innovations in fiction writing, this could be a useful tool for a writer to think about.

Techniques of Distancing and Closeup

"Wait for Me," by An Na, is able to summon a good deal of emotional response from a reader. It draws on the powerful, basic need of every youth to adhere to a parent's expectations, but often trying at the same time to find a different life path than the one held out by the parent.

Mina's mother, Uhmma, is intent on her oldest daughter going to a prestigious university, preferably Harvard, and the mother consumes herself, while ignoring her disdained husband, and her youngest child, Suna, in pursuit of her goal for Mina. But Mina has been deceiving her mother for years about her less than adequate grades at school, and has been pocketing money from the receipts at their dry cleaning shop, meant to help support herself when she looks for a job after graduating high school and escaping her difficult home life.

An Na manages to create reader sympathy for hardworking Uhmma, and a mystery is raised early on as to whether Mina may have a different father than Suna. The close relationship between the sisters is lovingly portrayed. A Mexican boy, Ysrael, is hired to work at the cleaners, and a tender relationship grows between him and Mina, though it is kept hidden from Uhmma. The story is brought to a strong resolution point when Mina must choose whether to follow Ysrael when he leaves for San Francisco to study music, or stay at home to nurture Suna until she is strong enough to overcome her dismal lack of acceptance by Uhmma.

The story has a number of points interesting to a writer. Alternating chapters give Mina's first-person POV in immediate past tense, and Suna's third-person POV in present tense. Suna's narration can move rapidly from distancing scenes to close, inner consciousness scenes. Sometimes the portrayal is ethereal, in keeping with her dreamy, sleepwalking nature. Mina's dialogue with Uhmma is sometimes given inside quotations, and sometimes not. Possibly this, too, is done for distancing/close-up effects, but it wasn't always consistent. The writing of scenes between Mina and Ysrael can be deeply emotional, occasionally skirting the romance genre, but An Na, a winner of a Printz Award, remains overall a fine literary writer.

Voices and Alternatives

Voice is such a difficult quality to establish for any main character, and is usually the first task a writer considers in making a story come alive on the page—and to be marketable. Some writers might seize on direct qualities, like a regional dialect, or notable class distinction in the character's diction, to create a unique and interesting voice. Others might use introverted or extroverted modes of expressing their character's speech—hesitant, thoughtful, fearful; or blustering, assertive, combative.

Still others may bag the whole exercise of creating a compelling voice, and instead give their character some challenging trait or condition that will create interest in them as a character. This may be more hazardous to the writer's success than finding a distinctive voice, since the writing must now also avoid any unearned praise, or blame, for the character solely because of their given condition. The writer must be very good to succeed at this type of story, and some have been so. Two YA books that come to mind include:

Stoner & Spaz, by Ron Koertge
A high school boy with Multiple Sclerosis falls in love with a girl who uses and deals drugs. It's an epiphany for the boy, and he also becomes interested in filmmaking. The romance ends, the girl goes back to drugs, but the boy is a better person for the experience.

The curious incident of the dog in the night-time, by Mark HaddonAn autistic teenager decides to find the murderer of a neighbor's dog and discovers his father killed it. This leads to the uncovering of another mystery of why his mother left home. The author inserts lots of graphics and scientific puzzles to dramatize the teenager's inner world and interests.

The challenging condition can be made a lot less severe than in those cases, as in the following YA book:

An Abundance of Katherines, by John Green
The main character is a high school senior who'd grown up as a child prodigy. He doesn't have much of a voice, and his introverted, nerdy condition is definitely an added challenge. Some nineteen girls have dumped him through the years, and all were named Katherine. He goes on a summer road trip with his best friend (he's half-Jewish, the friend is Arab), and through much of the story he works on developing a theorem, shown in mathematical curves, that will predict whether the partner in any relationship will be the dumper, or dumpee. During his road trip he meets an opposite temperament—extroverted— Tennessee girl in a backwater setting, and redemption is at hand.

Voices and Alternatives—consider both equally challenging.

Southern Voices

In the classic short story "A Member of the Wedding," by Carson McCullers, the author develops a strong structure of character voices, sense of place, and a theme of personal change. Frankie Addams is a twelve year-old girl in a small, southern town in the Forties, during WWII. She is still a bit tomboyish, but this spring finds her in a state of heightened awareness and tension, wanting something to happen, to be able to break out of her familiar but suffocating routine. She has been alienated from the society of her former girlfriends and has only the company of her younger first cousin, John Henry, and the doting, but 'tell-it-like-it-is' black maid, Berenice.

In early sections of the story the drama plays out in the kitchen of the Addams house, during evenings of card playing, eating supper, and with Frankie giving voice to her anxieties and frustrations, her vague plans for breaking out of the maddening stasis of her life, only to be brought down to earth time and again by the more sage and practical Berenice, who's had four husbands and has been around the bend a few times. Frankie's diction is forever entertaining, as she reaches for words and expressions of her feelings that belie her young age. The sense of the slow moving rhythm of life in the small town is portrayed in their conversations, and in Frankie's restless pacing around the kitchen, and her sometimes volatile outbreaks. Although there is an underlying bond between Frankie and Berenice, Frankie sometime uses Berenice as a foil for her anger, using aggressive language, but Berenice lets her have it back in style. Sometimes, to work out her pent-up anguish, Frankie practices knife-throwing against the kitchen wall. She alarms us with this.

The indignities and injustices of race relations, more common in that era, come out in some of Berenice's stories and is evident in mannerisms of Berenice's friends, but Frankie doesn't seem much, if at all, tainted by racism. In fact she is a sometimes visitor to Berenice's ancient mother, who tells her fortune, and Frankie is friends with Berenice's foster brother. It's amusing to hear Frankie attempt to give the brother her eloquently phrased version of grownup advice.

In Frankie's attempt to assume a maturity she doesn't have, she roams an unfamiliar side of town and befriends an alcohol-fogged soldier from the nearby army base, and agrees to meet him that night at his hotel to go dancing. Again, it's very amusing to hear her try to converse with this sodden soldier like a grownup, but soon the scene escalates into a trip to his room and Frankie has to almost bite off his tongue and smash him in the head with a pitcher to escape.

Frankie plans to escape her stifling environment by getting her brother and his fiance to take her with them after their upcoming wedding, and they can then have adventures together while roaming the world. It seems her last chance-- and she's devastated when the couple goes off on their honeymoon without her. Her world has collapsed.

In a sort of anti-climax, or epilogue, a couple of months later Frankie has found a very compatible new girlfriend in town, and it looks like life will go on after all. Sadly, Berenice is getting married once more, and has served a notice of quitting to Frankie's father. We'll miss her. It is altogether a good story for a writer to study for structure, voice, setting, and a young passages theme.

Uncovering What Works in Sensory Language

The Writer's Chronicle for May/Summer 2012 includes an article by David Jauss with the title of "Who's Afraid of the Big Bad Abstraction?: Modes of Conveying Emotion." As with most essays and articles by Jauss on the craft of writing, it helps identify strategies for mustering some life into faltering prose.

Jauss is keen to make the point that emotions reside in the senses, and "without some appeal to the senses, ... it is very difficult, if not downright impossible, for us to make our readers experience our character's emotions." He suggests the "primary ways writers can convey emotion through the senses are body language and metaphors." But it can be hard work to convey such emotion on the page, and often the writer will take a shortcut, i.e. just use an abstraction, a sensory bypass, and get on with the story. For example: *Cornell experienced an immense grief.* However, when we abstract like this, Jauss cautions, "we are asking the reader to do the hard work of imagining the physical sensations of the emotion for us, and the readers aren't any less susceptible to laziness than we are ...so she just skips the trip entirely." And maybe also closes the book.

Jauss gives his own examples where, instead of simply naming the character's emotion, as in the sensory bypass naming Cornell's grief, a writer might work a little harder at portraying the emotion in some unexpected way:

In *A Gate at the Stairs*, Lorrie Moore makes Bo Keltjin's grief visible through his unusual use of a handkerchief at his son's funeral. Instead of drying his eyes with it, as we might expect, he 'pressed it completely over his face, like a barber's hot towel.' With a sentence like that, we don't need the word grief; we witness it."

And then we have the gloss.

Whereas a sensory bypass might allude to body language but doesn't actually describe it, a gloss does describe body language--but then proceeds to interpret it for the reader. As in: *Tears of grief wet Cornell's face.* The writer is trying to make sure the reader hasn't missed a turn somewhere and is interpreting those tears correctly.

Another interesting area of enriching sensory language to rescue it from mere gloss or abstraction as discussed by Jauss is to mix the body language with metaphor. To illustrate, he takes another example from Lorrie Moore:

'Here Sarah looked at me mischievously, her look a complicated room one might wander through, exploring for quite some time if there were any time.' If Moore had merely said, 'Here Sarah looked at me mischievously,' she would have been guilty of writing a gloss and the emotion labeled by the abstract evaluation mischievously would have been dead on arrival. The metaphor brings it to life."

Jauss gives many more juxtapositions of body language, abstraction, gloss, metaphor, and action that can bring emotional life to characters, and these examples capsulize some of his good advice to writers.

Using Dialect To Spin a Tale

William Faulkner's *As I Lay Dying*, is especially intriguing with his use of dialect peculiar to rural folk of northern Mississippi in the early twentieth century. However, some teachers of writing caution against a use of dialect in stories. They seem to feel that the use of a proper syntax is the best vehicle for delivering a story of any literary quality. They of course must allow for any exceptions, like Faulkner, but would maintain it's always a hazardous undertaking.

Our reflections may suggest that some hazards probably include being thought of as not politically correct, or PC; that is, of stereotyping people, especially if the writer may not be of the same ethnic or socioeconomic class as his characters. Quite a straitjacket for creativity. Even if some vocabulary Faulkner uses for folks of his famous Yoknapatawpha County is obscure, and the syntax often very irregular, it definitely adds to the mood and moral dimensions of *As I Lay Dying*, as well as others of his novels and short stories.

An example of a short story using dialect and mentioned earlier is about migrant workers at a truck farm on Long Island. Their winter homes were in Florida, and the men worked as farming migrants when the annual growing season started up in the north. Following is an excerpt from the story:

> A field of kneeling, crawling men move forward in the muggy, warm air. The hunched over pickers are strung out along rows of radishes: Wild John, Bama Boy, and Edward, up in front, to Artie, a young man who lives near

the farm, picking way back in the rear. The workers are harvesting four rows each, snatching up small red globes like found money, and twining each bunch with a cord from the bundle tucked beneath their belts. Artie picks from just two rows, slow, hesitant, gauging whether he has enough radishes for a full bunch. He loops his cord around the stems, pulls a double roll knot, and tosses the bunch to a pickup lane beside the bed, then slides ahead on his knees. He uses the back of a dirt-caked hand to wipe away gnats from an earlobe, and right there, he has another of those recurring deja-vu flashes. A sense of having been in a place like this before, last summer, with his platoon slithering through a rice paddy in Korea under heavy fire and pushing a rifle out ahead. Not so long ago, really.

Edward goes on in his laughing, singsong voice. "So Lilly's old man, Chester, he comin' in the front door, still got that postman's suit and hat on, and Lily and me, we just be leaving the bedroom and steppin' into the hall. When I sees Chester, I takes out my pad and pencil and I'm just looking over those sorry walls. 'Yes'm, I think I got all the numbers now, and you be havin' a estimate on your paint job by tomorrow.'"

"Well, you ain't done no such thing," says Bama Boy a couple of yards back, laughing.

Edward turns and grins as he's flying a string around another bunch of radishes. "Sure 'n hell I did, and on the way out I tells Chester he can have his choice, 'get a five year, or ten year warranty on our salmon paint, and the black paint automatic come with fifteen years."

"Salmon 'n black, my, you sure the tasty man for our times," says Bama Boy.

More laughs and inventions on the story from pickers coming up behind . A blizzard of bunches flop into the pickup lane as the men waddle forward on their knees. The farm owner, Mr. Mueller, the only other white picker besides Artie, scowls. He figures this damned nonsense is going too far. He's working just a few feet behind Edward, tight-lipped now, and cinching the knots like he was garroting the bunches of radishes.

Edward has the boys humming now. "That's right, no jive," Edward says, laughing, "The next day I'm layin' low, see, in case Chester do a drop-back to see maybe he getting a paint job or a snow job. But then another day—"

"All right, enough of that," Mueller, says. "We don't need to be listening to all this trash talk—we're here to work. Do it or get out!"

Artie rears back on his haunches and stares ahead toward Mueller. For a brief moment he'd heard only his fanatical platoon leader ordering him ahead. Silence, interrupted only by the flutter of leaves as radish bunches keep looping through the air. Later, a few cautious exchanges test the mood, a baseball score,

209

deal-making on used cars, the right amount of chicory in coffee. The migrants feel the tension, but it always be there. Mueller gets up and walks back along the pickup lane, tossing fresh bundles of strings to pickers as they call out their needs, making a tick mark next to the names on his pad, and he stops beside Artie.

The dialect is from the fifties, and there should probably be more dropped consonants to portray actual speech, but too much of that might impede the reader's flow. Overall, use of the dialect is thought to work effectively to capture the flavor of the incomplete story.

The Holy Clay

Elsewhere we discussed the use of themes taken from myths, and mythical characters, as archetypal elements for the writing of contemporary fiction. This discussion probes some of the elements of transmitted myths.

Some Irish folklore concerns a holy clay, lifted from the grave of a reputed saint buried in an ancient ruined monastery of St. Colmcille on Tory Island, about a mile off the north coast of Ireland. This tale and a few more contemporary folk anecdotes are collected in *Stories from Tory Island,* by Dorothy H. Therman, 1989 (editor clarifications inserted in parentheses and italics, Gaelic words underlined):

> The cliffs along the north coast are penetrated deeply by inlets, or clefts--scoilteann. To the east of the lighthouse, not far from the graveyard (*of a shipwrecked crew of the HMS Wasp, another story of its own*) is Scoilt an Mhuiriseain. Onto its stony beach, in the time of St Colmcille, there drifted a boat carrying seven people. Dr. Edward Maguire quotes Manus O'Donnell, the sixteenth century author of *The Life of St. Columba* (Editor's notes in parentheses):
>
>> The fame of his [St. Colmcille's] wisdom, his knowledge, his faith, his piety, had gone forth throughout the entire world, and the holy children of the King of India had conceived love for him on account of the rumours ... there were six sons (of them) and one sister. The children set sail in

search of him and were not heard from for a long time, until they finally reached the northwest coast of Tory. And on their coming to land, they died in consequence of the fatigue of the sea and of the ocean.

There they were brought across the island and buried together, at a place on the edge of what is now called West Town, and where the foundations of one of St Colmcille's little stone chapels are still visible. Reportedly, for three mornings in a row, the body of the woman was found lying on top of the grave, so she was buried separately and from then on rested peacefully.

Alfred McFarland, who visited Tory in 1849 and wrote *Hours in Vacation,* (Dublin, 1853), believed that the seven were Scandinavian royalty; Mr. T. J. Westropp stated in the "Antiquarian Handbook Series" in 1905 that they were Hollanders. Dan Rodgers of Tory Island says the islanders thought the woman might have been a saint. And it is from the grave site of the 'saint' that the eldest of the Duggan clan retains the prerogative given to him by St. Colmcille to lift 'holy clay', which has the power not only to banish rats, but to protect fishermen from the dangers of the sea. (*Rat control was a life and death matter for farmers on Tory Island needing to protect food storage cribs over the long winters*).

A bit of the holy clay was lifted for the writer one night by the eldest of the Duggan clan living on the island at the time of my visit there. The legend has the elements of a Joseph Campbell myth, from his book, *The Hero With A Thousand Faces,* (3rd ed.

1973). Campbell uses myths taken from cultures around the world, describing a hero's quest for some gift or boon for his people. The quest usually involves a perceived call, often supernatural, a series of trials while on the quest, attainment of the sought-after boon, and a return to the Hero's people.

In a short discourse on the Hero as Saint, Campbell relates how St. Thomas Aquinas reaches a boon of mystical spiritual revelation as he neared the end of writing his major opus of Roman Catholic doctrine, *Summa Theologica*, put down his pen to leave the last chapters to be completed by another hand, and died soon after, in his forty-ninth year. In his case, St. Thomas, unlike, say, the Bodhisattva, does not return to his people, but has:
"stepped away from the realm of forms, into which the incarnation descends ... the realm of the manifest profile of The Great Face. Once the hidden profile has been discovered, myth is the penultimate, silence the ultimate, word."

Did the princess of India and her brothers receive a mystical spiritual revelation like that of St. Thomas upon reaching landfall after the perilous sea voyage? Or did their journey and its fateful conclusion have other meaning? There seems a lot of creative energy available to a writer in the pondering of old myths like this.

Keeping *a bit of the loopy* in the Story

Do some old classics need to be as long as they were when first published? Maybe not, if we agree with British publisher Orion and a new series of "compact editions" of selected nineteenth century classics, including *Moby Dick, Anna Karenina, Vanity Fair,* and *The Mill on the Floss*. Adam Gopnik of the New Yorker (22Oct07) reports they were neatly cut in half, so that they can be taken in quickly and all the more admired. He notes wryly, however, that the names of the abridgers were curiously withheld; perhaps they were alarmed at the magnitude of what they had done. Gopnik says that "Melville's story is intact and immediate; it's just that the long bits about the technical details of whaling are gone, as are most of the mock-Shakespearean interludes, the philosophical meanderings, and the metaphysical huffing and puffing." But wasn't all that half the magic of *Moby Dick*?

Gopnik imagines the soothing letter that Melville might have received from his editor accompanying the suggested cuts, had he been alive to receive it. "Herman: Just a few small trims along the way; myself I find the whaling stuff fascinating, but I fear your reader wants to move along with the story—and frankly the tensile strength of the narrative is being undercut right now by a lot of stray material that takes us way off line." The Orion publisher's editing job is perhaps what a modern critic or professional editor might say about the original book if it arrived over the transom today—"too much digression and sticky stuff and extraneous learning. If he'd cut that out, it would be a better story." A small shudder is in order. Gopnik reflects on how "masterpieces are inherently a little loony…"

but how that often contributes to their originality. He reflects, "What makes writing matter is not a story, cleanly told, but a voice, however odd or ordinary, and a point of view, however strange or sentimental." Although we're often told in the revising process for our fiction, tighten, cut, cut, out with the darlings, kill the adverbs and adjectives, it might be well to remain aware not to lose all loony ambiance and originality.

Language and Translations

A production of Brian Friel's *Translations* was highly acclaimed when it opened on Broadway. Set in rural Ireland in 1833, it tells of the British Army ordnance survey after Ireland's conquest. The British sought to remap the land, changing all Gaelic place names into Anglicized names, which would better speed troop movements and facilitate administrative functions. Overnight, a thousand years and more of local legend and myths associated with the original place names disappeared.

The play's characters include a "hedgemaster," a teacher who instructs locals in the prohibited Gaelic tongue, and also in some of the ancient Greek and Latin classics in their original tongues. He's aging, and one of his sons tries to carry on his father's nationalist tradition, while the other son cooperates with the British in their mapping efforts, thinking it will bring help bring economic progress. A young British Lieutenant in the survey falls in love with one of the hedgemaster's women students and adopts Irish ways, causing problems. The play is so elemental in its problems and conflicts, particularly in the deep roots of language, informing who we are, and who we will become. Good stuff for a writer to ponder.

Voice of a Myth

It can be such a pleasure to read *The Underneath,* by Kathi Appelt. It would be hard to suggest which age group it might best appeal to, perhaps middle grade, but high school, or younger child, or even adults would find lots of appeal. For background structure, it recalls ancient tales of mermaids, and selkies (Celtic), ondines (German), and lamia, which some myths refer to as half-woman, half-serpent. In Underneath, it is a version of the lamia, as a 1000-yr. old cottonmouth snake, a giant water moccasin, which had once assumed the form of a woman, but after being betrayed by a human male, had reverted to her snake form. In Appelt's telling, once the myth creature reverts to its animal form, it can never change back to human. Grandmother moccasin has a sinister presence throughout the story, as she lies imprisoned in a clay jar buried beneath the roots of a loblolly pine in the swamps of East Texas. A thousand years before, a man had taken her lamia daughter, Night Song, from her, and there was a price to be paid. Sssssss, once she was free.

Another character in the story had been an evil young boy, perhaps bent that way by a vicious, abusive father, and who is now a lonely, fearfully evil man, called Gar Face, named after a vicious, ugly fish who lives in the swamp waters. Gar Face figures prominently in the story, but more so does his chained-up, abused bloodhound, called Ranger, and the two kittens, Sabine and Puck. The kitten's mother, a calico cat, had sought refuge beneath Gar Face's cabin, trusting Ranger, and gave birth to her two kittens. The story of the kittens growing up, their games, learning to hunt, but never daring to venture out in sight of Gar Face, is artfully told. Relating their playing and hunting strategies to their big cat ancestors is part of the marvel. Eventually, Gar Face discovers and captures Puck, and also his mother, when she goes to Puck's defense. Gar Face ties them in a sack and throws them into a river. Puck escapes, and the story becomes his struggle to survive in the swamp, and whether he will find his way home to Ranger and Sabine. In the parallel story, we discover in intermittent small chapters how Grandmother moccasin lost her daughter, Night Song, to another magical creature, Hawk Man, after they both had crossed into their human natures, and how they came to have a daughter. Who, of course, is the granddaughter of Grandmother moccasin--and grandmother knows of her and seeks her. How the path of the characters intertwine and ultimately cross makes for an awesome story.

The language of the story provides a good part of the enjoyment; We might imagine reading the suspenseful cadences to our own granddaughter, perhaps in some log-built vacation cabin near a Louisiana bayou:

> "Here then is a hard-edged bitter boy become a man known as Gar Face...Do not cross his angry path. Do not."

> "Do not go into that land between the Bayou Tartine and the little sister, Petite Tartine. Do not step into that shivery place. Do not let it gobble you up. Stay away from the Tartine Sisters.""Grandmother is waking up.

'Ssssoooooonnnnn,' she says, 'my time is coming. Sssssoooonnnn...' Do not look into that mouth of cotton. Do not."

Wonderful material and writing. Think about what you could do in the same vein.

Poems for Enhancing Fiction

Elsewhere, we've discussed the enhancement of written works of fiction with reference to artistic design principles for a good painting: value contrasts, shape arrangements, a balance in complementary spectrum of hues, and the planned arrangement of soft and hard edges, to name a few translatable topics of visual art and fiction.

Here, we'll discuss using brief poems for enhancing fiction, and using the works and writing philosophy of the Irish poet and Nobel laureate, Seamus Heaney, as a guide. Heaney, who died in 2013, was admired for his books of poems in *North*, *Station Island*, and his translation of *Beowulf* from old English, was the subject of a reminiscence by Thomas Sleigh. The article was titled "A Man of Care--Seamus Heaney's Primal Reach into the Physical," *(The Writer's Chronicle, May-Summer, 2015)*. Sleigh is a widely published author of books, has won many literary awards, and who works as a journalist in Syria, Lebanon, Somalia, Kenya, Iraq, and Libya. In other words, some historic hot spots of the world.

Heaney is no stranger to hot spots of the world, himself. His early books of poems, *North*, and *Field Work*, include the poet's agonized, inner response to the *Troubles*, that armed conflict between Republican and Unionist militias in Northern Ireland. In Heaney's words:

> Pure poetry is perfectly justifiable in earshot of the car bomb, and it can imply a politics, depending on the nature of the poetry. A poetry of dramatic wit, of riddles

and flips and self-mocking ironies, may appear culpably miniaturist or fastidious to the activist with his microphone at the street corner, and yet such poetry may be exercising in its inaudible way a fierce disdain of the activist's message or a distressed sympathy with it.

Thankfully, there has now been a lengthy ceasefire in the *Troubles,* but the quoted passage may give some idea as to the temperament of Heaney.

We might now move on to a focus theme, regarding the short poem that could be incorporated into a longer work of fiction to good effect. One of the more basic concepts of Heaney's approach to constructing poems, gleaned from reading some of his works and from the discussions given by Sleigh, is the attention Heaney gives to acute, subjective observations of earth's surfaces, human activities thereon, the meanings they ascribe to what they are doing, the uninterpreted words they use in telling it.

Heaney accomplishes this from his habitual practice of observation, "an activity which is averse to overwhelming phenomena by the exercise of subjectivity, content to remain an assisting presence rather than an overbearing pressure." As he said of Pound's work, which he admired, "Pound's strictures-- the natural object is always the adequate symbol," "Go in fear of abstractions," "don't use phrases like 'dim lands of peace' because it mixes "an abstraction with the concrete... and dulls the image."

Sleigh quotes Heaney about the imaginative powers conferred by sitting in the basalt throne of "the wishing chair" at the Giant's Causeway (*a long line of upraised basaltic columns stretching out from the mainland into the Irish Sea, toward Scotland*), not only should the rock make "solid sense" against the small of your back, it should also freshen "your outlook/ beyond the range you thought you'd settled for." The reader can feel the physical sense of the poetic image, occupying not only the now of time, but the vast, geological age of time, and without any need of more interpretation by the poet. It is perhaps something concrete to strive for.

Following is a poem that the writer used in a preface to *The Young Molly Maguires,* a novel set in the coalfield labor violence of the late nineteenth century in Pennsylvania. It has allusions and similes, but also concrete, non-abstract images most readers' imaginations can readily grasp.

A Lament for the Molly Maguires

God lifted noble man from earth
crowned him lord of all creation
until a stunning fall from grace
banished him to a life of toil and sweat

Impoverished men reentered earth
pillaging black coal so they might live
The miners toiled mightily to earn their bread
How so, earth's new owners demanded more

Till the miners raised up a young prophet, Union,

to lead a way from slavery,
but Union could not strike water from a rock,
and the miners withered in despair

An ancient Joshua rose up to besiege the owners,
when the Molly Maguires entered the fray
and smote the owners' captains from ramparts and wall,
until undone by perfidy of state and church

Who struggle for justice, sing a lament for the Mollies,
though brutal men rode horseback from both camps
it is forever the victor who writes history,
and cartloads of Mollies swung in the air

Writing to Sustain the Fictional Dream

John Gardner, in his classic, *The Art of Fiction - notes on craft for young writers,* Vantage Books ed., 1991, has much to say about the idea of sustaining 'Fiction as Dream.' Gardner suggests as a general rule:

> "Fiction does its work by creating a dream in the reader's mind. We may observe, first, that if the effect of the dream is to be powerful, the dream must probably be vivid and continuous--vivid because if we are not quite clear about what it is that we're dreaming, who and where the characters are, what it is that they're doing or trying to do and why, our emotions and judgments must be confused, dissipated, or blocked; and continuous because a repeatedly interrupted flow of action must necessarily have less force than an action directly carried through from its beginning to its conclusion."

Vivid and continuous. It's well to think of these criteria--and Gardner would be the first to acknowledge there are no rigid rules in fiction. We should try to stay alert to the use of language, or simile, or metaphor, that jumps out, or is jarring, and which may cause the reader to disengage for a moment from the fictional dream, trying to decipher what is going on with this phrase or sentence; would the character really say or think this? Given enough of such distractions, the fictional dream may become harder and harder to maintain, and soon the book leaves the hands of the reader, flies through the air in a triple somersault and half-pike, to land in a corner of the room. That's perhaps an extreme case, but certainly the reading experience will be at least diminished.

"Finding Nouf," a debut novel by Zoë Ferraris, is good to review for fictional dream performance. The American author moved to Saudi Arabia in the aftermath of the first Gulf War to live with her then husband and his extended family of Saudi-Palestinian Bedouins. The novel has been described as a literary detective novel, and it is that, and is also a fascinating glimpse into the severe strictures of social and religious life of men and women, especially the latter, in a fundamentalist Islamic and monarchical society.   On the whole, the novel has good character development, and presents a suspenseful crime plot with many twists and turns.   However, as is probably the case for any first novel, or perhaps even for any established writer's novel, a reader might find a few distractions from a vivid, continuous, fictional dream. Following are a few examples for illustrative purposes:

"The scent of manure lodged in his throat."--

This can disengage the reader from the continuous dream, pondering how the throat might perceive a scent.

"Isn't your escort coming?" Nayir asked. She hesitated. "There's no reason for it. Not while you're with me," she said, although something about the tone of her voice implied Unless I'm mistaken about you.--

The author suggests here how the reader should interpret the character's tone--an intrusion into the reader's fictional dream. Better to have just shown the phrase, 'Unless I'm mistaken about you,' as a simple, declarative sentence. It can then be interpreted by the reader as what Nayir was actually thinking. This writing technique would be termed 'moving into the character's mind.'

> For some reason--perhaps the wind gentled the air around them--her smell drifted into his nose.--

An awkward sentence that calls attention to itself, and an author's presence.

> He felt impossibly dumb and flashed on the idea that people this stupid shouldn't be investigators.--

to flash on an idea seems a Western idiom, and not likely that of a Saudi. An author's presence jumps out.

Some of what is represented as showing an author's presence, or intrusion, into the vivid, continuous, fictional dream of the reader, is subjective to some degree with any individual reader. These are just examples of what interrupted one reader's fictional dream.
And speaking of breaking the rules earlier, an author's presence, or intrusion, can sometimes be used creatively and in an innovative way. David Foster Wallace occasionally uses such a strategy, interrupting his narrative to announce

226

something like: "Hello, author here, ..., " and then goes on to deliver his message about what we are reading. However, that's David Wallace.

PLOT

Plot Twists

Kite Runner, by Khaled Hosseini, opens in Afghanistan just before the Russian invasion in '78. The book is chosen to illustrate a story that is principally grounded in plot. Amir is a middle-class Afghani boy, about thirteen, and his closest friend is a servant boy, Hassan, a Hazara—a minority ethnic group descended from Asian Mongols--who works in Amir's household. Amir and his dad are Pashtuns, a majority ethnic group in Afghanistan, and are Sunni, a dominant Islamic sect in the country. Hassan and his dad are Shia, a minority sect of Islam despised by the Sunnis, and so Hassan suffers a double burden in the boys' daily contacts with other Afghani boys. Though Hassan is devoted to Amir and risks dangers when defending him against other boys, but Amir remains almost indifferent to him.

In one episode, an Afghani boy rapes Hassan for defending Amir, who cowardly watches from hiding. Our sympathies for Amir take a further plunge when Amir later frames Hassan for stealing his watch. He's jealous of his own father's affections for Hassan, and hopes to drive him away from the household. When the Russians invade Afghanistan, Amir and his dad flee to America. There, Amir matures as a better person, aspiring to be a writer, and meets a young Afghani woman and marries her. He regrets many of the weaknesses he'd shown in his boyhood, and when news comes, after the Russians are driven out of Afghanistan, that the victorious Sunni Taliban have slain Hassan along with many other Shia, Amir returns to try and rescue Hassan's surviving eleven-year old son.

In Afghanistan, he learns that Hassan was actually his illegitimate half-brother. In the dangerous search for Hassan's son, he encounters the same man who once abused Hassan has now bought Hassan's son from an orphanage, and is abusing the boy. A horrible plot twist. In some desperate actions, and after suffering brutal injuries, Amir rescues the boy, Sohrab, and flees with him to America. There, Sohrab is a lonely, almost mute boy from his experiences, but Amir and his wife adopt him and wait patiently for him to heal.

The plot skirts close to having too many coincidences, and takes some brutal turns, but it held a lot of suspense and gave the sense of a very different, hard world.

Dystopian Plots

Dystopia is a gripping, palpable presence in some literary works of the past century, and a few of the classics that come to mind include: *Brave New World*, by Aldous Huxley; *Nineteen Eighty-Four*, by George Orwell; *Fahrenheit 451*, by Ray Bradbury; *The Handmaid's Tale*, by Margaret Atwood; *Player Piano*, by Kurt Vonnegut; *The Hunger Games Trilogy*, by Suzanne Collins; and various short stories by F. Kafka, and T. C. Boyle.

The particular dystopia that is the framework of the story might be a societal collapse, and a subsequent rise to power of an elite formed to arrest the decline, but usually at the mind-numbing expense of a majority underclass. In most of these stories the root cause of the societal collapse has been political, leading to brutal, catastrophic conflicts, but the collapse might also be driven by the collapse of an environment.

Powerful dystopian stories seem to be on the rise again. We wonder, can they actually be telling us something? Collins' *Hunger Games* is an example of the political story. The first volume of the *Hunger* trilogy has been made into a Hollywood movie. Another good example of the environmental collapse story has been published as *The Age of Miracles*, by Karen Thompson Walker.

In this story, the earth's rotation has inexplicably slowed, and the days are becoming increasingly longer. As days and nights lengthen, various cultivated foods can no longer be raised in the natural environment. Society separates into two groups of people: the real timers--those who order their lives by the lengths of night and day (the diurnal cycle increases to 72 hours); and the clock timers--those who attempt to work and sleep by the clock, ignoring the presence of light or dark.

Other phenomena accompanying the slowing rotation include the decay of the earth's magnetism. This may be related to the mass beaching of whales on ocean shores, and flocks of birds dropping from the skies. How strong the physical correlations might be sail past us, but they seem plausible and the reader rushes on. The story is narrated by a quiet, sensitive, twelve-yr. old girl, with all the tender, emotional details of her first romance as she tries to navigate a troubled relationship between her parents. The story and sub-plots set amidst this collapsing physical world are well integrated and make for good, solid reading.

If you have a feel for writing a dystopian novel, there's certainly a large audience out there waiting.

Festivals and Banshees

Other books of interest for plotting techniques include *The Festival Of Insignificance*, By Milan Kundera, and *Banshee*, by D. T. Doyle.

An earlier novel, *The Unbearable Lightness of Being, by Kundera,* was adapted into a movie. Kundera was born a Czech, and that novel and all his early novels were written in Czech. *The Unbearable Lightness of Being* won a good deal of critical acclaim when it was published in English.

His later novel, *The Festival of Insignificance,* is a rather slim book of just over 100 pages. The plot is structured around the social lives and party-going camaraderie of a small group of Frenchmen living in Paris. Some of their exploits and conversations are witty and thought provoking, but such a slim volume doesn't allow for much in-depth character development. Nonetheless, some story elements may especially stay with the reader.

Alain's mother, Madeline, did not want his birth. Instead of taking their usual precautions, the husband forcibly completed their intercourse without a condom, and Madeline became pregnant. She is so repulsed and angry that she attempts suicide, which causes the death of a would-be rescuer and lays waste to her plan. Afterward, she goes ahead with the birth, but leaves Paris for America by herself as soon as she is able. This understandably has a lasting effect on Alain later in his life as he pried the facts from his father, and in the present story, from his mother, as she appears riding behind him on his motorcycle in a display of magic realism. Alain's anguish over his mother's rejection of him is poignantly revisited in several places in the novel.

Another thought-provoking setup is in some imagined conferences of Stalin with his cabinet members. The sheer wackiness of the setup captures the reader. How much is based on fact is difficult to know, but apparently Stalin loved to pitch absurdities to his cabinet, and kept them in session for countless hours just because he could. In one marathon session he purposely kept one of his ministers, a man named Kalinin who had a bad prostate condition, from going to relieve himself in the men's room, until he finally releases his bladder in his pants. As a consolation award to his abused minister, Stalin decrees the famous city of Königsberg, birthplace of the philosopher Immanuel Kant, to be renamed Kaliningrad. Also, Stalin's recital of Kant's most important idea to a captive audience seems hubristic theater:

> Kant's most important idea, comrades, is 'the thing in itself' — in German, 'das Ding an sich.' Kant thought that behind our representations there is something objective, a 'Ding,' that we cannot know but that is real nonetheless. But that idea is wrong. There is nothing real behind our representations, no 'thing in itself,' no 'Ding an sich.'

The sobering thought is that it may be as real a representation of Stalin's thought processes as one can assemble, considering he is generally held responsible for about 25 million deaths of his countrymen in famine, war, and repression during his dictatorship.

...*Festival* was an amusing, and sometimes thoughtful novel, and shows innovative plotting by a major author.

Banshee, by D. T. Doyle, a debut novel, is a good read. The plot has interesting twists and turns, and each new development has a startling aspect that raises levels of tension and suspense. The reader sometimes wonders, where is this story going? Each leap into darkness seems to break the mold of similar horror stories from the past, and for the most part, Doyle plunges fearlessly ahead and it works. She introduces some twists concerning the traditions of the banshee. The banshee is more typically believed to be a harbinger of an impending death in a household, flying over it in the nights before a demise and crying out in frightening wails and shrieks. Doyle makes her a vengeful ghoul, which works well, and that's most of what's important in a good story. Plot is the main engine in this story, and characters other than the banshee might have been made a bit more memorable, however, the banshee is a stunner from the beginning. The syntax had more than a couple of dangling participles and forlorn modifiers, but this didn't seem a serious drawback.

PLACE

Place in Fiction

Place can play an important role in stories, sometimes almost as large a role as the characters that populate a story. It can be a character. This might be seen in an article titled "The Mushroom Hunters," by Burkhard Bilger, in the New Yorker (8/20/07). The rain soaked forest habitat of the secretive mushrooms looms as just such a character.

Picking wild mushrooms for the market began in about the Seventies, in the National Forests of Washington and Oregon, and was mostly done by locals who kept their patches secret. However, mushroom hunting exploded beginning in the nineties. The pickers in the reference article lived in a roughshod, primitive campground, and were roughly divided into ethnic groups—Hmong, Mien, Cambodian, Laotian, Mexican, and Caucasian. Most of the pickers were Asian. Matsutake mushrooms may sell for up to one hundred and sixty dollars a pound, and though a highly experienced picker might find up to seventy-five pounds in a day, an experienced Cambodian couple together averaged less than twenty-five pounds a day. In six weeks they earned ten thousand dollars. The work can be arduous and pickers search for the mushrooms from sunup till sundown. One needs a sort of sixth sense, because the mushrooms usually lie hidden beneath a carpet of pine duff on the forest floor. Pickers are very clannish and each group is suspicious of any other group. The atmosphere in the camps can be a bit like the old Forty-Niner gold miners, with guns fired in the air during evening celebrations in camp. Pickers also fire guns in the deep forest to keep up a contact with each other and avoid getting lost.

There's a story hidden in the sort of place described, and waiting to be populated with unique characters.

David Guterson populated such a mushroom world with memorable characters in his novel, *Our Lady of the Forest,* published in 2003. A frail young woman ekes out a marginal living hunting mushrooms in a National Forest in Washington. She has visions of the Virgin Mary appear to her in the deep forest, and when word gets out, people drive from all over seeking to witness the apparitions. Crowds follow her through the forest on her daily workday. A priest is dispatched by the Catholic Church to investigate the authenticity of the apparitions.

It was an engrossing story and showed the power of place in a memorable novel.

Leaving--a Theme for Writing

One of the universal themes in fiction writing is "leaving." The main character has been left by another, or he/she has left someone else. The event, whether it be a death, divorce, abandonment, or dismissal, typically sets off a powerful series of predictable emotional grief stages, which might be exploited by the writer in plotting the story arc for a novel. The stages are variously described in the literature (esp. E. Kubler-Ross's *On Death and Dying*) as including denial, anger, bargaining, depression and acceptance. Some studies have suggested adding a couple more stages, but Kubler-Ross' basic five will do for a discussion.

Wild, by Cheryl Strayed, provides a vivid example of writing a story with a theme of leaving (*Wild* is essentially a memoir). Like her mom, somewhat independent and venturesome as a young woman, and strongly attached to her mother, Cheryl is stunned when her still early-forties mom is diagnosed with inoperable cancer. At the time, the mom, with her second husband, and Cheryl and two younger siblings are living in comfortable, but spartan, homestead-like conditions in a wooded area of Minnesota.

There is the first stage of the leaving theme, where Cheryl angrily denies the likelihood of her mother dying, and vents her anger toward the medical staff, as well as toward her siblings, for failing to meet her expectations to support the mother. Then, as things look very bleak, the inevitable bargaining with God, and more anger when it seems God will not respond. A sort of depression follows the mom's death, as Cheryl, married just a couple of years earlier at nineteen, plummets into a long period of risky and sordid behavior, involving random, extra-marital sex, drinking, and drugs. She is determined to ruin her own marriage, and does, and goes on to wallow in depression. During her spiral down, she happens to read a guide book for hiking the Pacific Crest Trail, a very long trail that traverses desert and mountains across California, Oregon, and Washington, all the way to Canada. Although never having done anything like this trek, she's had a very woodsy upbringing, and feels this could be a sort of redemptive journey.

She starts out alone and with a backpack she can barely lift, at first hiking only six or seven miles a day, and gradually increasing to more than twice that. She has some mesmerizing adventures and chilling encounters along her epic eleven-hundred miles long journey of three months, traversing a part of the PCT reaching from the Mojave Desert in California to the Bridge of the Gods at the Washington state border. Refusing to quit through all the adversities along the PCT, Cheryl succeeds in finding a way through her final stages of grief after her mother's departure, and goes on to a genuine acceptance of herself.

A very engrossing, well-written memoir, with the Pacific Crest Trail providing an epic sense of Place, nicely matched to a legendary Joseph Cambell-like (*The Hero With a Thousand Faces*) redemptive hero's quest.

Journeys

The vast reaches of the open sea, and the equally mesmerizing stretches of the western plains furnish two more place settings for gripping stories. Two are non-fiction and one is fiction, but all three suggest good models for fictional stories of place.

A 17-yr. old boy, Zac Sunderland, completed a 13-month, 28,000 mile, round-the-world voyage in a 36 ft. sailboat. Zac bought his well-used boat for $6000, and set sail in June 2008 when he was only 16, arriving back home 13 months later, at Marina Del Rey in southern California. Previously homeschooled, he studied to complete his high school education while at sea. His parents--dad is a professional sailor--stayed in touch with him during the voyage, using special software and satellite updates to help track storms in Zac's path.

Zac's daring voyage is reminiscent of another epic sea voyage commemorated on a memorial plinth at our nearby Point Arena, CA wharf. The inscription describes a landing of 15 men from the town of Yawatahama, Japan, on Aug. 13, 1913. A free-hand etching done on a metal plate set In the top of the monument depicts their 15-meter, 3-masted junk, and though the boat was a bit larger than Zac's, it may not have been any more seaworthy, and certainly did not have any satellite updates of weather to help plan the safest route along the 11,000 km voyage. It did have 15 crewmen , though, which may have been an asset, or a burden. Disappointingly, the hopeful immigrants were sent back to Japan after landing; nevertheless, a sister city relationship sprang up between Yawatahama and Point Arena in later years.

All of which leads into a discussion of *On to Oregon,* by Honore Morrow. First published in 1926, it had been mentioned by a number of YA literature folks as one of their favorite books while growing up, and was compared to a couple of American classics.

John Sager, a 14-yr. old boy, with four younger siblings, and his parents, are on a wagon train leaving Missouri in 1844, and headed for the Oregon Territory. He is a difficult, rebellious boy, and the journey up through Wyoming has already encountered desolate wasteland, hunger, sickness, and marauding Indians. When both of John's parents die of disease, it falls to this undisciplined but tenacious boy to keep his remaining family together, and try to bring their wagon through to Oregon. John has elements of Huck Finn and Tom Sawyer in his makeup, but he faces much more dangerous trials in his story.

ENDINGS

Story Endings

In three short stories, novellas really, in the "Elephanta Suite," by Paul Theroux, the crafting of convincing, satisfying endings for a story come to mind. Theroux's stories, all set in India, are engrossing and beautifully written, with the endings for the first two stories powerful, seamless, and convincing, but the ending of the final story, "The Elephant God," seemed not to fit the protagonist's character. The story is gripping until that point, but though the protagonist, an American woman, looking for a spiritual life while living in an ashram and simultaneously working as an instructor of American speech patterns for employees of a tech call-center, is a resourceful, strong-willed woman, her dramatic retaliation against one of the employees who assaulted her is not quite believable. Though she's been stalked and abused by this man, her last, cold, calculating action seemed over the top, though satisfying to some degree.

Endings also come to mind reading an essay in Writer's Chronicle, Nov. 2007, "A Tale of Two Endings: Dicken's Great Expectations," by Douglas Bauer. Dickens' original manuscript ending seemed contrived in a chance meeting between Estelle and Pip in the city, and a parting between them that seemed final. Bauer says:

> if you read Great Expectations as a novel that steadily acquires real emotional and psychological traction, then Dickens's original ending—with its almost contemporary, quietly stated irony, bracingly free of his famous sentimentality; and one that's contemporary too in its

powerful truncation (all those what-ifs" that get said in all that isn't said)—is the preferable conclusion.

However, an author friend of Dickens who was asked to review the original manuscript convinced him to write a more hopeful ending. Dickens's rewrite hedged a bit, making it seem like a continued relationship between Estelle and Pip was foreseen, though the final line was left somewhat ambiguous—"I saw the shadow of no parting from her." That version got published, and the following year (1862) in a second printing, apparently now more satisfied with the idea, Dickens made the line less ambiguous: "I saw no shadow of another parting from her."

Perhaps Theroux might also have received suggestions to have his ending less extreme, a more subtle irony, but he went with a powerful truncation concept. In the Theroux story, it seemed to work well.

Some of Bauer's other thoughts on endings were interesting:

> ....any ending that succeeds both culminates and at the same time continues the story…the mix of these two factors naturally varies according to whether the writer's principal desire is, on one hand, to bring everything together, or, on the other, to leave matters more elliptically open. But both qualities, culmination and continuation, are fundamentally always present." And, "The question, then, facing the writer is how to write an ending that benefits from all the complicated momentum that has been funneled into it; one that sounds its

confidence and retains a narrower but still resounding power, even as it sings its final notes alone.

Chekov's Subversive Endings

Chekhov is often cited as one of the greatest of short story writers. Still, he may be an acquired taste, and perhaps not one to whom a reader might go for shoring up a battered psyche, or to seek some uplifting or inspirational energy. First readings of Chekhov can be laborious. Characters sometimes seem hugely stoic, and their complications never seem to resolve; indeed, they seem to arrive at the end of the story no closer to a resolution of their conflicts than at the beginning. The story seems to have no discernible end. The vast Russian settings, enormous divergence of living conditions between nobility and peasantry, and the absolute power of one over the other, can instill some powerful tensions into the stories, but basically the stories are more about recurrent ordinary human weaknesses and failings than ennobling examples of struggle and triumph.

Whence, then, the acquired taste for Chekhov's stories? David Jauss, writing in *The Writer's Chronicle*, Mar./Apr. 2010, offers some insight. His article, "Returning Characters to Life: Chekhov's Subversive Endings," examines how Chekhov tends to end his stories by returning his characters to life and the problems created either by their change or their failure to change." In his stories, even when the character changes, "their changes either fail to last, merely complicate the existing conflict, or create a new and often greater conflict."

Today's writers who have had some exposure to degree programs, seminars, or workshops, usually work within the classic model of beginning with a character who faces some sort of major conflict, the conflict intensifies, often interrupted by other sub-conflicts, until there is some climax at which the problem(s) is resolved, or not, leaving the character changed in some conclusive manner thereafter. Not so with Chekhov: "But for all of their apparent inconclusiveness, his stories do have endings; they're just not the kinds of endings favored by...the average viewer of *The Sopranos*." Nice touch there. "They are subversive endings, endings designed to undercut our expectations and, thereby, force us to examine our conceptions about life and human nature."

Jauss cites and examines a wide array of Chekhov stories to demonstrate the various categories of subversive endings used by him to such powerful effect. Jauss says "Many of today's writers write as if unaware of some of the possibilities Chekhov opened up, and thus they end their stories in highly predictable and conventional ways." Jauss's article is suggested as a worthwhile reference for writers to broaden their horizons for structuring stories. A list of Chekhov's subversive endings as categorized by Jauss will give some idea of the range and depth of the story endings dscussed:

1) Anti-Epilogues
2) Reverse Epilogues
3) Echo Endings
4) Chiastic Endings
5) False Climaxes
6) Omitted Climaxes
7) External Climaxes
8) Temporary Climaxes
9) Complication-creating Climaxes

10) Conflict-creating Climaxes
11) Extended Anti-Climaxes
12) Shifts in Address, Tense, and/or POV

The chance to revisit and appreciate Chekhov's stories will be an added benefit.

OUTLINING

Outlining With a Story Board

Some writers have only the barest of concepts in mind as they commence a first draft of a story; others prefer to work with a written outline, listing perhaps main characters, the principal and secondary problems, interim resolutions of secondary problems along the way, and a final resolution. Another approach is to engage the left brain in the conceptual process, and develop a storyboard before proceeding into the first written draft. The graphics needn't be elaborate, perhaps using only stick figures for characters and very rough sketches for the rest, but it may stir the imagination and help visualize the sequence of key scenes that are most dramatic in telling the story. The story board might also alert the writer to how well the arc of tension rises through the story toward some inexorable release in a final resolution of the main problem.

Storyboards are most often considered for developing the very short stories of children's picture books, but they can, and have been, used for considering the skeletal structure of longer fiction, including novels. Whereas the storyboard might contain a graphic treatment for every page in a child's picture book, it might only show a panel for each major change of setting, or each complication, in the longer forms of fiction.

The partial storyboard shown above relates to a short story we will call, "The Summit." The story opens (1) with the three characters, an older scientist, his much younger girlfriend, and a local guide. They are climbing a mid-difficulty peak in northern India. Their position is precarious, having just survived an avalanche, the westerners are resorting to supplemental oxygen, and the story needs to get moving. In (2) they face the next challenge on this lesser known route--a steep escarpment requiring some technical climbing. We do not have to get bogged down in details here, but just show a scene in the harrowing climb. In (3) the climbers take refuge in a small cave on the face to escape worsening weather conditions. To pass time, the scientist draws his companions into a topic much on his mind, the existence of God. He's prone to dismiss it as myth, but seems apprehensive of newer complexities uncovered by science, quantum mechanics, that may touch on it. All this detail is just in our thought process for telling the story. The girlfriend, an engineer, offers one of the usual theological arguments for god, but has little interest in the subject. She has more immediate concerns--what to do about her recently discovered pregnancy, and the intuition that the relationship is almost over. The local guide simply tells them he is a devotee of Kali. We don't need to express all these complex issues in the storyboard, but the idea is to show a place marker for a discussion in the written story. As soon as the weather breaks a bit, the climb resumes. In (4) the route taken encounters a deep slipped-out region of rock, called 'the notch,' which they must cross on their path to the summit. The guide disappears during the crossing, and is assumed to have fallen into a crevice somewhere in the notch.

The complete story board for such a short story might only be 8 panels total, and not only might it help in conceiving and writing a draft of the story, it may be useful to aid in the revision process.

Storyboard 2

This is the final strip of storyboard graphics for "The Summit."
After taking the time to mull over the previous storyboard and
highlighting of interim complications/problems, the current
revision of the short story might seem to invite a tightening up.
We consider that the backstory of having just survived an
avalanche, should be dropped. The characters have enough
problems as is, and it might be enough to show they're hard-
pressed to achieve their goal of reaching the summit.

Similarly, the complications of insufficient supplies of
supplementary oxygen tanks, and strains of a failing
relationship, furnished enough tension without adding the
woman's secret knowledge of a pregnancy discovered just
before their expedition. We may decide to drop that
complication. The story board seems a good focusing tool for
identifying perhaps too many complications, just as it might
have been useful to alert the writer of no obvious, central or
main complication that could provide ample tension for a
reader.

Continued from the previous storyboard, in panel 5) the scene
of arriving at the stone altar to Kali on the summit now shows a
major turning point, with a debilitating decline in the physical
condition of the scientist. In 6), the descent panel, the woman,
physically spent herself, faces the daunting task of getting her
incapacitated partner down the stormy mountain. In 7) they
take shelter for the night beneath a canopy of fallen rocks in a
rock notch. Her partner is now unresponsive and she can only
guess at the severity of his condition. After a fitful night the

woman awakens to the early gray light of dawn. She checks for vital signs of her partner, but other than a still warm body temperature, she doesn't detect any. Depressed and exhausted she goes in and out of sleep and wakefulness. In one of her awakenings, Panel 8), she sees a figure at the entrance to her shelter. At first she perceives it to be their lost guide, Ranpur, but she gradually becomes aware of the typical physical features of the goddess, Kali, blue-skinned, holding a sword, and a human head. The Kali figure tells her to leave her partner and descend the mountain herself. The woman is frightened and confused--she can't just leave him without knowing if he's dead. Kali can't be consulted about it any further--she's gone.

The concept for the story arises in part from reports of the disastrous events in 1996, when 15 people died trying to reach the summit of Mt. Everest. Eight of these people, men and women, died in a confused scenario when three or four parties climbing simultaneously made a series of errors. In desperate attempts by the survivors to get off the storm swept mountain, partners unable to continue had to be left behind, whether dead or alive.

And so, the dilemma of our woman character: was it Ranpur, or the product of a stressed out imagination? Does it matter-- should she leave while she still has the strength? Would the reader?

Ekphrasis, a Literary Representation of Art

Earlier, we discussed concepts of enriching literary fiction by keeping in mind design principles used by visual artists to heighten an aesthetic appeal in their work.

For example, Alex Powers, in his book, *Painting People in Watercolor*--discusses recommended design principles to guide the visual artist. These design principles are the organizing aesthetic ideas that guide the artist's use of elements in a painting. They are listed here, with the visual art parameters alongside potentially relevant writing terms:

PRINCIPLE	PAINTING	FICTION
• dominance	• emphasis, focal pt.	• major conflict
• movement	• rhythm, gesture	• plot or story structure
• variety	• contrast, conflict, tension	• sub-plots, and their resolutions
• unity	• harmony, balance	• major resolution, denouement

Next, the important design elements discussed by Powers for a successful painting are listed, followed by a column of artist techniques, and another column shows corresponding techniques potentially relevant to fiction writers:

DESIGN shape	PAINTING	FICTION
• value	• form, mass, object, subject light/dark, tone tint	• plot, place characters, moral/ethical multi-facet
• space	• illusions of 3-D, and 2-D	• environmental
• edges	• blurred/sharp, lost/found	• certainty, ambiguity
• color temperature	• warm/cold	• emotion, environment
• texture	• surface variation	• sophistication, coarseness
• line	• drawing	• language, syntax
• color - hue	• red, yellow, etc., local/	• dialect, colloquial
• color intensity	• bright/dark	• tonal speech

The term, Ekphrasis, was discussed in a recent article in The Writer's Chronicle (May/Summer, 2014), titled "Paintings in Fiction--Ten Lessons from the Masters of Ekphrasis," by Stephanie Coyne DeGhett. First, ekphrasis is a term described by DeGhett as a "literary representation of visual art." Her article is not, for the most part, about using the principles and tools of the artist to conceive an original piece of fiction as we have been discussing. De Ghett explores the ways that accomplished writers, including Oscar Wilde, Steven Millhauser, Stanley Elkin, and A. S. Byatt, have incorporated actual works of art as focal points in some of their works of fiction. A well-known painting influences and motivates the fictional characters.   A. S. Byatt's approach to employing ekphrasis is given in *The Matisse Stories*.

The ekphrasis approach seems too derivative of the original act of creation, the painting itself. It is a little too much like the creative writing assignment of taking a newspaper story, or some topical subject, and writing a story based on the subject material. The ekphrasis idea seems not too organic to a writer's compulsion for exploring his own deeply intuitive imagination as material for a story. However, the idea of using visual arts criteria for *shaping and coloring* a literary fiction might be useful to writing a deeply personal, intuitive story.

Accordingly, our discussions have rested on an assumption that great paintings and classic works of fiction might share some of the same precepts and intuitive elements of creation, but perhaps the enterprise is doomed. From DeGhett's article we get the following:

> In an essay about literary ekphrasis, Paola Spinozzi quotes Leonardo da Vinci from his *Treatise on Painting*:
>
> Your pen will be worn out before you can fully describe what the painter can represent forthwith by the aid of his science. And your tongue will be parched with thirst and your body will be overcome by sleep and hunger before you can show with words what a painter can show you in an instant.

GRAPHIC NOVELS

Graphic Novels 1

Graphic novels have been increasing in popularity and rather than being any threat to prose novels they may reinforce reading habits for some. Graphic novels invite far more introspection than a completely passive diversion, like TV, and they invite art appreciation right along with story participation. Good graphic novels have a clean-cut similarity to attractive block prints of modern art . The coupling of art forms and expressions to the story in progress can be intriguing.

A good example is *Blankets*, by Craig Thompson. It's an engrossing memoir of a young man who has been raised in a severely strict, fundamentalist Christian family, and who meets an attractive young woman, Raina, in a Christian summer camp. Raina is a warm, beautiful, liberal-minded individual who is very popular among her similar-minded friends. She intrigues Thompson, and she invites him to spend a couple of weeks of his winter break visiting at her home in another town. Her family has some internal discord, but Thompson falls in love there with Raina, and although it becomes clear it probably can't last beyond this visit, he grows and matures in ways he couldn't have Imagined before. The artwork is great, and the graphic unfolding of the story is wonderfully done.

Another good example is *American Born Chinese*, by Gene Luan Yang. This is a handsomely done graphic novel about a young boy of Chinese immigrant parents growing up in America, mostly centered around his life and friendships in school. Episodes from the Chinese Monkey King fables are interspersed in the story, and they seem very much to belong here. Jin Wang is so intent on being "American" that for a part of the book he's drawn as a Western-looking boy named Danny, though we don't quite know what's going on yet. Danny's visiting cousin from China, a crude stereotype, mystifies us, and is an embarrassment to Danny in front of the all-American girl he idolizes. The threads come together when the Monkey King comes to visit Jin and convinces Jin he'll be a happier person if he'd just be himself. Afterward, we notice the visual appearance of Danny has changed to looking Asian, his true self. Besides the great graphics, it's a well structured story.

To extend our range of interest, it will be useful to mention just one more, *Amelia Rules-The whole world's crazy*, by Jimmy Gownley. It's a MG graphic novel, kids playing at being superheroes, and coping with life at school and at home. The story is, of course, a lot less sophisticated than the older reader books discussed, but the graphics are neat and appealing.

Graphic Novels 2

Re-Gifters is one of the new graphic novels, though one might as easily refer to it in a praiseworthy way as a mass market comic book, geared to Middle-Grade or High School readers, but also appealing to some adult readers, too. *Re-Gifters*, like some of the earlier comic books, has an authors' team, Mike Carey, writer, and Mark Hempel and Sonny Liew, illustrators. Read more about comic book author teams in *The Amazing Adventures of Kavalier and Clay*, a literary gem by Michael Chabon, .

The *Re-Gifters* story is about a Korean girl, Dixie, who would like to gain the romantic interest of her top karate competitor, an Anglo boy in her training club, or dojo. Dixie lives in a rough section of Los Angeles and in an early scene she's confronted by a group of toughs. She's on her way to being nailed, but is rescued by a cool-talking Hispanic boy with attitude, who's also a loan shark. The gang looks up to him, and Dixie now has a useful friend.

Later, she uses money her father had given her to enter a big martial arts competition, and instead, buys a statue of an ancient Korean warrior for a gift to the Anglo boy. It's a futile gesture and now she's lost her chance to compete in the tournament. In a series of misadventures, the statue comes back to her as a gift from the Hispanic boy (hence, *Re-Gifters*), and she is unexpectedly given a free 'wild card' chance to enter the big martial arts tournament. The Hispanic boy provides her with a dilapidated 'gym' at his home for training. As Dixie advances in the tournament, the Anglo boy, also moving up in the tournament, gets concerned about her potential, and tries to charm Dixie into throwing her semi-finals match. She disdains his attempt, and goes on to defeat him in the finals. In the closing, the Hispanic boy is a dinner guest in Dixie's traditional Korean household, and the future seems hopeful.

The graphics are dynamic and nicely drawn, and the story has some appealing multi-cultural aspects; however, it's a bit worrisome to contemplate Dixie's new boyfriend is, after all, a loan shark, notwithstanding his seemingly good heart. Graphic novels may never replace the deep immersion and imaginative world of prose novels, but they have an appeal all their own.

SHORT STORIES

Novellas

The generic term for a fiction story usually considered by publishers to be too long for a short story and too short for a novel is the novella. A dictionary describes the word as derived from Italian/French forms of 'new,' and means a story with a compact and pointed plot, or a short novel, or long short story. It is generally described as somewhere between 15,000 to 40 or 50,000 words.

Probably most writers think of it as being hard to place for publication: too long for the literary journals and other short story venues, and too short for hardcover book publishers. Unless, that is, you are a big-name author. An article in The Writer's Chronicle, "Revaluing the Novella," by Kyle Semmel, provides some interesting reading on the use of the form. Semmel grounds some of his views and analyses on the legendary author and writing teacher John Gardner, and his book,"The Art of Fiction." To paraphrase or quote some material Semmel chose from Gardner to describe the novella:

> The novella moves through a series of small epiphanies or secondary climaxes, usually following a single line of thought, and reaches an end where the world is radically changed.

> The novella normally treats one character and one important action in his life, a focus that leads itself to neat cut-offs or framing.

Notwithstanding the above norms, three distinctive types of novella include: (1) single stream ("a single stream of action focused on one character and moving through a series of increasingly intense climaxes"); (2) non-continuous stream, or "baby novel," ("shifting from one point of view [or focal character] to another, and using true episodes, with time breaks between"); and (3) pointillist ("moving at random from one point to another").

There are all sorts of experimentation with the structure and overlap of the types given above, and some powerful novellas have resulted. Semmel's descriptions of the basic structures, and his discussions of example novellas, will provide a good footing for the aspiring novella writer.

His discussion of the non-continuous novella, "Where the Rivers Flow North," by Howard Frank Mosher, was good. The narration moves in and out of two main characters' points-of-view, a Vermont farmer and his housekeeper, and has another third person, authorial point-of-view interspersed. That may sound hard to do successfully, but was done well.

A good example of the continuous stream novella, focused on a single character moving through a series of increasingly intense climaxes, was discussed by Gardner for the book, *The Pedersen Kid*, by William Gass.

Finally, as discussed elsewhere in this book, a classic novella recommended for its many storytelling qualities is *The Member of the Wedding*, by Carson McCullers, (about 44,000 words).

Stealth Endings in Short Stories

Occasionally as readers we encounter short stories that have 'stealth' endings. The stealth tag can relate to the USAF B-2 Stealth Bomber, designed to fly under any radar observation on the way to its destination. Sometimes the trajectory of a story is almost as elusive, and we don't quite know where or how an impact is going to be felt. We may put ourselves on guard not to be too devastated by the culmination of ominous warnings, but if the author can stay under the radar for the best possible moment to break through and deliver the unexpected, a stealth strike can be memorable.

An excellent short stories collection is *Binocular Vision*, by Edith Pearlman (2011). A couple of her initial stories had this sort of stealth effect. Another good opener for a discussion is "Million $$$ Baby," by F.X. Toole, included in his story collection *Rope Burns*. An Oscar Award winning movie was based on the short story. It was about a young woman who had grown up in a hardscrabble town in the Ozarks, and was intent on becoming a boxing champion as her way out of a bleak future. Maggie Fitzgerald wins the grudging help of a trainer/manager, Frankie Dunn. The author, Toole, had worked as a 'cut-man,' patching up fighters during actual bouts, and he is able to write vivid fight scenes of Maggie in the ring. She fights her way to the top of her division, but is seriously injured in a bout and hospitalized as a paraplegic. She has no hope, and asks Frankie to 'put her down.' Her plight is indeed hopeless, but this is way outside Frankie's religious beliefs. He would know how, though; he has frequently used legal injections to stem the flow of blood from fighters during bouts. He knows what too much can do, and it wouldn't be detected in an autopsy. Still, he refuses. Maggie seems to understand, but bites her tongue off in a later suicide attempt, which is thwarted by hospital staff. Another bedside scene, late at night, and Maggie pleads with Frankie using eye motions to do it. It becomes a devastating stealth scene. You didn't think he could, but when he did it seemed somehow right.

In one of Pearlman's stories, "Tess," a child is born to a young woman of limited mental ability. The child, Tess, has major congenital problems. Tess needs continuous life support systems and is connected by two IV tubes from the machines to her heart and intestinal system.Nonetheless she is a beautiful, though mostly listless child, who is doted on by the nursing attendants. There are beautiful written scenes of the nurses attention and the limited responses of the angelic child, but there doesn't seem to be any fulfilling outcome in store for the reader. First-person narratives by the young mother are interspersed throughout. She visits her child weekly in the beginning, while she tries to maintain her marginal waitress job, but time between visits soon lengthens. She seems to keep a loving attitude and vaguely understands her child's perpetual need for the tubes sustaining her life. In the stealth ending, she removes the slow pumping blood tube to Tess's heart and hides it beneath the sheets before she ends her final visit.

In Pearlman's story, "Fidelity," an aging travel writer with dimming sight lives with his wife near Boston. He doesn't actually travel, but writes of exotic travel adventures for a small, high-brow publication called *World Enough*. We get glimpses of his stories, which are very imaginative, and of the close relationship of the writer, Victor, his wife, Nora, and the editor in New York, Greg. The editor is always very solicitous in his calls and letters to Victor and Nora, and they were all close friends when everyone lived in New York. When an unusual antique armoire in Greg's room turns up in one of Victor's stories, Greg is aware Nora must have described it to him. In Victor's next story, which we read along with Greg, it describes a traveling couple lying in each others arms, awaiting the eruption of a volcano near their lodgings on an island, whereupon they "will sink into that blue that never changes, unlike the fitful New York sky you and she watched those afternoons, Greg, you bastard." Greg learns from their daughter that Victor dies soon afterward, then Nora ten days later, from swallowing something. A strong stealth ending, in which the infidelity unfolds at the very end.

.

Men Without Women

Our discussion is on Haruki Murakami's book of short stories, "Men Without Women," published in Japan in 2014, with an English translation published in 2017.

Some fiction by Chinese writers may require a little more effort by western readers to identify with the characters, and to adapt to choices they made in resolving tensions and problems confronting the story resolution. For certain, there are universal similarities in ways that people of the world confront some of life's hurdles, but also there may be some typical and interesting differences among us. Any particular response might be conditioned by millennia of evolutionary and cultural forces at work, and might spotlight some interesting and colorful threads in a tapestry of world literature.

In the opening story of the collection, "Drive My Car," a seasoned, middle-aged actor has his car being repaired in a garage after a minor accident. A negligible amount of alcohol may have played a role, but also a problem in his eyes, glaucoma, was detected. His studio has insisted that he hire a chauffeur until his eye problem is corrected. The garage mechanic recommends a certain woman chauffeur to the actor, Kafuku:

> "Well, how should I put this, she's not exactly the congenial type."

> "In what way?"

"She's brusque, shoots from the hip when she talks, which isn't often. And she smokes like a chimney," Oba said. "You'll see for yourself when you meet her, but she's not what you'd call cute, either. Almost never smiles, and she's a bit *homily*, to be honest."

Kafuku is not in the least a misogynist and feels women can be quite competent. He agrees to give the woman, Misaki, a trial, and is impressed by her driving skills. She quite fits Oba's description, but also proves to be an engaging person. Gradually, in hurried transits of Tokyo as they drive from one stage venue to another, Kafuku listens to his collection of Beethoven tapes or practices his lines from a stash of cassettes, and their rapport grows. Kafuku's wife, a fine actor also, has died some years before, and Kafuki is often lost in thought about her. He was never unfaithful to her, and she loved him, but she had four brief affairs during their marriage. He never understood what it was she was missing in the marriage, and it still bothered him. Misaki asks him as they're enroute to a studio if he had any friends? Kafuku tells her the last time he became friends with anyone--or someone like a friend--was about ten years ago. He hesitates a moment, before plunging on. "To tell you the truth, he was one of my wife's lovers. He didn't know that I knew, though."

It took Misaki a long time to get her head around what she had just heard. "You mean he was having sex with your wife?" she said at last. Kafuku goes on to explain how he came to know, and why he decided to make the man his friend:

"How can I put this...I wanted to understand. Why she slept with him, why he was the one she wanted. At least that was my motive in the beginning."

In such discourses, Kafuku seems to find solace with the quiet, uncritical way that Misaki engages him to give voice to things that have troubled him in his life, and for him also to speak of things that he had enjoyed, like his acting profession. This intersection in the lives of the two characters, who bring different histories but who seem to be fortuitous for each other at this point in their lives, provides a richly rewarding reading experience.

A very engaging story. Another extraordinary story in the MWW collection that demonstrates the range of Murakami's craft is "Samsa In Love." Our character awakens to discover that he has undergone a metamorphosis, and has become Gregor Samsa. Readers may recognize that we seem to have come upon a reverse version of the famous story by Franz Kafka. Fascinating, but who had he been before he became Gregor Samsa? What had he been? From lying in the bed he must learn to stand, to move. His soft, naked form raises a fear in him that he might have little chance of surviving an attack by predatory birds. There's no immediate danger, though. The room is bare but for the bed, and the one window is boarded up. He manages to figure out how to don a robe found in a closet, and he leaves the room to grope and stumble his way down some stairs. He finds four places set at a table in one of the rooms. What has happened--where have the occupants gone--or been taken?

A woman knocks at the door and he manages to open it. She is a little woman, well, not so much little, as bent. If she were straightened she'd probably be of normal size. Plain, perhaps, but becoming, setting aside any bent. She is a locksmith, here to repair a lock, and is suspicious of this man in the ill-fitting robe standing before her, struggling to answer her questions. Gregor tries to explain that his family has left the house on some errand, but the woman is still suspicious. The atmosphere is tense; it appears these are troubled times for citizens to be out and afoot in the city.

They proceed upstairs to examine whatever lock was reported broken, and Gregor impulsively leads her to the room he had occupied. He gets an erection watching her open and examine the lock, but has no idea what it means, being unfamiliar with his physiology.

> "What the hell is that?" she said stonily. "What's that bulge doing down there?"
>
> Samsa looked down at the front of his gown. His organ was really very swollen. He could surmise from her tone that his condition was somehow inappropriate.
>
> "I get it," she spat out. "You're wondering what it would be like to fuck a hunchback, aren't you?"
>
> "Fuck?" he said. One more word he couldn't place. "You imagine that, since a hunchback is bent at the waist, you can just take her from the rear with no problem, right? the woman said. "Believe me, there are

lots of perverts like you around, who seem to think that we'll let you do what you want because we're hunchbacks. Well, think again, buster. We're not that easy!"

"I'm very confused," Samsa said. "If I have displeased you in some way, I am truly sorry. I apologize. Please forgive me. I meant no harm. I've been unwell, and there are so many things I don't understand."

"All right, I get the picture." She sighed. "You're a little *slow,* right? But your wiener is in great shape. Those are the breaks, I guess."

It was impossible not to laugh at this exchange, and yet there is a certain melancholy and sympathy for the characters that grows within us. When the woman makes ready to take the lock away to her father and brother's shop for further repairs, Samsa asks if he might see her again--to talk together. The woman is incredulous, but as Samsa follows her down the stairs, appealing to her for another meeting, she begins to soften--why not? A wave of satisfaction rolls over the reader, a sense of happiness for these two, improbable characters in very bizarre circumstances, but so thoroughly likeable.

DRAFTS AND REVISIONS

Taking the Hatchet to a Draft

Writers' conferences can provide good venues for learning from featured speakers and fellow writers which techniques worked best for them in producing their published fiction. Nonetheless, what works well for one writer might not yield good results for another. Perhaps rules for a sort of terse, active, and staccato delivery suits the range of fictional dreams at work in the mind of one writer, but may be entirely out of synch for the fictional dream flows of another writer. We've probably all heard of the need to go over our first drafts, to take out all the flab, exposition, discursive wanderings, and such, to better focus our stories. A lot of this is absolutely necessary, but the subtractive process might also become destructive of an otherwise beautifully written, fictional dream. Let's look at an excerpt from a piece by James Joyce, from his short story, "The Dead":

> A few light taps upon the pane made him turn to the window. It had begun to snow again. He watched sleepily the flakes, silver and dark, falling obliquely against the lamplight. The time had come for him to set out on his journey westward. Yes, the newspapers were right: snow was general all over Ireland. It was falling on every part of the dark central plain, on the treeless hills, falling upon the Bog of Allen and, farther westward, softly falling into the dark mutinous Shannon waves. It was falling, too, upon every part of the lonely churchyard on the hill where Michael Furey lay buried. It lay thickly drafted on the crooked crosses and headstones, on the spears of the little gate, on the barren thorns. His soul

swooned slowly as he heard the snow falling faintly through the universe and faintly falling, like the descent of their last end, upon all the living and the dead.

The imagery is gorgeous, the sense of hushed sound, and a feeling of timelessness in the arc of our lives. We might wonder if the same feeling could be maintained if our more severe draft editing rules were to be considered. Here are a few typical, random notes taken from lectures given at writers' conferences by two accomplished writers:

John Lescroart (crime fiction)
Get rid of your 'to be' verbs, like 'when' and 'as.' Don't use 'thought' to convey a character's thinking.   When reviewing a draft, do a search for 'had,' which usually signals some sort of exposition. Get rid of it, or replace. Don't use any '-ly' adverbs.

John Dufresne (general fiction)
Eliminate the progressive form of syntax; i.e., 'I was brewing coffee.' Say I brewed coffee. Don't use adverbs--you just haven't got the right verb yet.

 In the following, we've applied such suggestions to Joyce's piece as much as we dare while trying to maintain his complete thoughts and sentences:

A few taps on the pane made him turn to the window. It snowed again. He watched the flakes, silver and dark, fall against the lamplight. It was time for his journey.

The newspapers had it right: snow all over Ireland. Snow fell on every part of the dark central plain, on the treeless hills, upon the Bog of Allen, and fell on the dark mutinous Shannon waves. It fell, too, on every part of the lonely churchyard on the hill where Michael Furey lay buried. It lay in drafted heaps on crooked crosses and headstones, on the spears of the little gate, on the barren thorns. His soul swooned at the sound of the snow that fell through the universe and fell, like the descent of their last end, upon all the living and the dead.

It has lost some of its beauty and whispered softness. There are probably other ways to edit the piece with the same suggested criteria that might yield better versions, but it is hard to imagine anything that could approach Joyce's offering. So, while the lecturers have given useful advice for consideration, it need not be considered rigid for every case.

Scoring Manuscripts

Many writers will be familiar with MS-WORD's spelling and grammar check capability in its Tools menu. Other word processing programs probably have a similar tool. MS-WORD's program can be used to find a total word count, Flesch Reading Ease score, and Flesch-Kincaid Grade Level score. It may be revealing to a writer to find the Reading Ease and Grade Level of his own work compared to more than a dozen best-seller authors analyzed by author James V. Smith, Jr., in *Fiction Writer's Brainstormer*. Smith's analyses show that all his best-seller authors typically log Reading Ease Scores between about 70 and 90; whereas, a U.S. Government manual describing combat actions that "any credible fiction writer could have turned into high-energy writing," scored about 37. His best-seller authors also scored Grade Levels between about 4 and 6—which was surprising, since one of the writers, Wallace Stegner, was a Pulitzer Prize winner. So, even in good adult literary fiction, the grade level required to understand the language chosen was not necessarily high. The Gov. manual scored almost Grade 13, a difficult reading. Interestingly, brief, intensive discussions like this, and story synopses, tend to score poorly because one tries to get too much info into a short piece.

PART TWO - INNOVATIVE WRITING

Literary Conventions and Language Deconstructions

A few authors of contemporary literary fiction have used unconventional styles or non-grammatical constructions in writing novels, and it raises questions for writers about the pros and cons of doing this. A classic example may be Joyce's *Ulysses*, with its stream-of-consciousness narration, which has its delights but makes for difficult reading over a lengthy work. Another classic example can be found in Cormac McCarthy's writing, including *All the Pretty Horses.* No quotation marks enclose any of McCarthy's dialogue. It did not seem at all distracting or confusing and it could be said that it produced a cleaner, less busy-looking text. However, such an approach might need a closer editing by the author to avoid any ambiguities for the reader.

A more complex questioning arises where an author chooses to use non-grammatical constructions, as in a recent novel, *A Girl is a Half-Formed Thing*, by Eimear McBride." In a review by Fintan O'Toole in the NY Review of Books (Nov. 20, 2014), he characterizes the book as a feminist novel. He draws on a statement made by McBride that since men had already written everything, there was for the female novelist, "only one small plot left to tell: the terra incognito of herself, as she knew herself to be, not as men had imagined her."

In McBride's book, the thematic structure portrays a female narrator (she remains unnamed throughout the book) who, in the words of O'Toole:

cannot build a self because the foundations of her childhood have been undermined by sexual exploitation. The central event is the rape of the narrator, a needy, rebellious thirteen-year-old, by her uncle who takes advantage of her as-yet indistinct desires. It is an event she is compelled to repeat again and again in crude encounters with strangers, and with the uncle who abused her.

It seems there is a lot of subjective psychology used in the review, and the book, to see the girl's actions as self-punishment ("horrible can be a good act of contrition"), but let's go on to the grammatical construction that is so unique to McBride. In a passage quoted in the review, the girl tests any power she may have over the uncle by forcing him to replay the original rape:

> So he hits til I fall over. Crushing under. Hits again. He hits til something's click and the blood begins to run. Jesus he says. I feel sick. But I'm rush with feeling. Wide and. He thinks he's bad when he fucks me now. And so he is. I'm better though. In fact I am almost best.

The cognitive and grammatical form certainly elicit anguish, despair, and revulsion in the reader, but aside from questions about how reliable a state of mind might exist in the narrator, can such form sustain a memorable reading experience over some 227 pages? Evidently it did for O'Toole.

McBride is not playing with form, she is playing with what has yet to be fully formed: language caught in its moment of transition between thought and articulation...The brilliance of the book is that this linguistic strategy exactly parallels the struggle of the narrator, who is also trying to come into being.

One would need to read the book to best assess their own, overall effect of McBride's writing strategy, but it will be difficult reading. Some captivating literature has included works of the protagonist as victim, though the most compelling seem to show more hope and energy of the protagonist, if not native intelligence, in trying to find personal closure or epiphany. Perhaps in the end, that makes this all the more a dramatic and soul wrenching reading experience.

Innovative Story Concepts

Some novel plots are audacious, but good writing can make the story entertaining, and perhaps even memorable. "I'd tell you I loved you, but then I'd have to kill you," by Ally Carter, has an audacious plot concept—the students at the 'Gallagher Academy for exceptional young women' are actually pursuing rigorous academic and field training to become spies. The secretive academy is off-limits to outsiders, and even the town in which it is situated has no idea of its nature. In addition to normal studies, the high school level girls learn to be fluent in up to fourteen languages, and are trained in covert operations including the use of lethal force on adversaries. This would be an ambitious set of plot elements for any writer to keep in play while selecting and pursuing a story conflict and resolution. It could be addressed seriously, or as a spoof. Carter seems to have alighted somewhere in between. The story is nicely written, often humorous. Gallagher graduates were responsible for inventing such useful spy materials as 'Velcro' and 'duck-tape,' and some national heroes—e.g. Amelia Earhart—are revealed as graduates. But the underlying storyline is also about Cammie, the girl protagonist, falling in love with a lower middle class boy from the nearby town. Accordingly, all the esoteric spy elements can be dealt with as points of intrigue, and not treated too strenuously. It's slightly quirky but the writing moves the story along.

Art as a Literary Device in Fiction 201

Some novels have been based on a "literary representation of visual art." The writer Stephanie Coyne DeGhett explored, among other things, the ways that accomplished writers, including Oscar Wilde, Steven Millhauser, Stanley Elkin, and A. S. Byatt, have incorporated actual works of art as focal points in their works of fiction; i.e., in Byatt's Matisse stories.

There are many ways that visual art might point the way to creating interest and satisfaction in literary constructs, and it has been a topic in several of our discussions. In this discussion we'll explore how some creative energies that seem evident in a particular work of visual art might prove useful in drawing out a main character's own emotional space in a natural manner.

We'll use an excerpt from one of my novels, *Leaving Major Tela*, about a young woman, Caitlin, the daughter a strict army officer mother, who gets an opportunity to find a greater independence while living temporarily with her divorced father:

> The pot fumes were most fragrant near a long, glassed-in porch at one side of the house, and they wandered through the doorway there. Stopping next to an elephant-leaf palm tree growing in a redwood tub, they lit their cigarettes and listened-in on the conversation. A dozen boys and girls were there, some sitting on wooden Adirondack lounge chairs, others straddled on straight-back chairs brought out from the dining room.

They passed around the last tokes of a dying roach, held by a metal clip at the end.

"When is he going to get here?" someone named Jay groused. "This roach is hereby pronounced dead."

"Product's been a little tight lately," his friend said. "Wouldn't surprise me if he asked for a price jump on this run."

"Yeah." Jay looked over at the newcomers. "What kind of junk are you two smoking?"

"Regular old tobacco-stuffed coffin nails, sorry," Luka said.

"Come over here and let's get a look at you," Jay said. "Do I know you?"

The two girls walked over to where he sat in a propped-up lounge chair. "We've met before," Luka said. "You came to a showing at my mother's art gallery a few months ago. We talked, remember?"

"Oh yeah, got it; you were the chick passing around the finger food and champagne. You know, that artist really sucked. Did you sell any of his stuff?"

"My mom said he had the third biggest opening night sales of any artist she'd handled over the last two years."

He scowled and turned to Caitlin. "Were you there, too? Did you see all that welded brass rod and polished aluminum tube crap? Do you like that sort of sculpture?"

"Well, I didn't see the exhibit, but no, it's not my favorite."

"Oh yeah--what is?"

Caitlin studied him. He could have been twenty or so, a tangle of dark hair, long angular face, nice mouth. He was so edgy though, and he had her on shaky ground about sculpture. "Well, I haven't seen all that much sculpture, just in Art Appreciation, but I often think of Verrocchio's 'David,' and—"

He interrupted. "Verrocchio's? You don't mean Michelangelo's?"

"No, I've seen Michelangelo's too, but it's so muscular, almost too perfect a male body. Verrocchio's was this slender, bushy-haired boy dressed in a sort of kilt, holding a sword, standing relaxed and with Goliath's severed head lying between his feet. Even just the screen image projected a whole room full of qi."

"The severed head must have done it for you. What the hell is qi?"

"Oh, well, you can think of it as his inner energy."

"Hey, Jay, he's here," his friend said. "Grab your money belt and let's go. He's dealing in the kitchen."

In this scene, Caitlin and her friend, Luka, are at a neighborhood party gathering material on student use of recreational drugs for a high school newspaper article. Caitlin's brief meeting and discussion with the new character, Jay, was an opportunity to explore a number of his personality traits, and to suggest possibilities for a future relationship with Caitlin. The statue of David, by Verrocchio, was introduced to show Jay has a sensitive nature--he sometimes attends art shows--and knows something about art. He affects a macho attitude toward Verrocchio's powerful sculpture, but was interested in Caitlin's own response to it. He'll be a sort of Verrocchio's David, himself, in the story.

Love In All Its Dimensions

Writers are usually vigilant for spotting storylines with a unique spin in depicting vulnerabilities of the universal condition. That's the case with the absurd but tenderly poignant 2007 movie, titled *Lars and the Real Girl*. The storyline depicts an emotionally challenged young man who resorts to buying a life-size inflatable doll to be his companion and ease his loneliness. When the movie was first released, the concept seemed off-the-wall, bizarre, and a bit kinky, with an unsavory connection to sex toys. Still, it seemed to garner some modestly good reviews, and so there was some interest in how the writer and director handled the material. The movie proved to be rather enjoyable, and the acting seemed especially good. Well, the humans acted well; the doll was rather weird.

Lars, a thirty-something, is living in a garage apartment behind the home of his married brother Gus. Karen, Gus's attractive wife, hurries across the snow-covered yard in her robe to knock at Lars' door; she invites him to eat breakfast with her and Gus. Lars seems too shy to even open his door. They carry on a one-sided conversation through the glass pane, until Karen thinks she has his agreement. But instead, Lars drives off to work. He dresses neatly, and works at a computer station in some sort of large technology firm. His cubicle mate calls him over to see the assortment of sexy, inflatable dolls he has on his monitor. Lars is disapproving of his associate's waste of company time. Another associate, Margo, a charming young woman, tom-boyish good looks, comes over to flirt with Lars. She's obviously very interested in him, but he keeps a cool distance. So far, nothing too weird.

Days later, a crate is delivered to Lars apartment. Gus and Karen are inquisitive, and Lars is evasive. Karen again tries to get him to come to dinner at the house, and, surprising her, Lars accepts—if he can bring his girlfriend. Karen is ecstatic; of course he can. Lars tells her the girlfriend, Bianca, is from Brazil, the daughter of a missionary, and has had an injury that requires her to use a wheelchair. No problem; Karen is so happy for him. The next scene alone is worth the price of admission. Karen and Gus are seated at one side of the table staring across at something that grips them in a sort of catatonic trance. The camera pans around to show a smiling Lars at dinner, with Bianca, the life-sized, inflated doll, seated at the table in a wheelchair beside him. From time to time, Lars speaks to the doll, shares food from her plate, and carries on a conversation with Karen and Gus as if there was nothing unusual at all.

Getting kinky yet? Not at all. Lars explains later to Karen that since he and Bianca are not married yet, it wouldn't be right if she stayed with him in his apartment, and so could she stay in the extra bedroom in the house? Of course, yes, of course, Lars; no problem, says a shell-shocked Karen. In what seems a good writing strategy, the back-story is unfolded after an intrigue has been built-up wondering what is Lars's problem. Gus gradually pieces it together for Karen. Their mother died when they were very young, and it devastated their father who remained drowned in grief and remorse afterward. As soon as he was old enough, Gus, unable to bear it, got out of the house. Lars, the younger brother, was left to live with the depressed father until years later, and it apparently has taken its toll on him.

Karen decides they have to get Lars to see a local doctor-psychologist in this small, mid-western town. The ruse is that they're going to have this woman doctor check out Bianca to be sure that everything necessary is being done for recovery from her 'injury.' Lars is persuaded, and the office visits are humorous, but more than that it's moving to see how the doctor is actually probing into Lars' own state of mind. Exceptional acting in what could have been just comedy.

Just as compelling, it seemed believable that the whole town was pulling for Lars, accepting Bianca as an everyday reality, especially by Lars' church-going community, and his office mates. Yes, the doctor, Margo, stays threaded into the storyline. It was a good, out-of-the-box concept for a story keyed to coping in modern times.

Fictional Sex Redefined by Technology

A topic discussed earlier, "Love In All Its Dimensions," explored new directions by movie scriptwriters and urban subculture artists into imaginary sexual relationships between sentient and insentient characters. This usually involved a man playing his own real-life character, and a female-themed art object, like a puppet or a 2-D art piece, playing a role as his love interest. A movie discussed in that topic was *Lars and the Real Girl*, and the subculture world has a term for the phenomenon, called Otaku. This is a Japanese slang term for "reclusive computer nerds, who often post screenshots of their (insentient lover) or go on real-life dates with them on their video-game console," as discussed in a NYTimes article, 13Dec2013.

The same Times article, "Interactive Gets a New Meaning," by Alex Hawgood, besides other intrigues, discusses the movie, "Her." It involves the Otaku-like relationship between the actor and the artificial-intelligence voice of a woman programmed on his smartphone operating system:

In "Her," written and directed by Spike Jonze, there is an awkwardly remarkable moment in which the lead character, Theodore (played by Joaquin Phoenix), has an intimate encounter with the phones digital entity, Samantha (Scarlett Johansson) after returning home inebriated from a failed blind date with another woman. Filmed with a close-up lens, it shows Theodore gently edging Samantha into arousal by telling her what he wishes to do to her. As things become increasingly explicit, the screen turns black, leaving the audience lingering in darkness as the characters reach their aural climax.

The relationship depicted in "Her," between Theodore and Samantha, seems eerily close to a rapport one can already notice between the driver of a vehicle, and the ethereal voice of the *Siri* woman emitted from the car's speaker system, as she carries out the driver's spoken commands to dial phone numbers, look up information, check the weather, etc. Siri is uncomplainingly efficient, and pleasant too, so that it has become a de rigueur option for the purchaser of a newer, upscale auto.

This concept of the interactive personal escort could be fertile ground for some stunning new fiction.

Magic Realism

The Golem and the Jinni, by Helene Wecker, is rather unique and hard to categorize. Some of the magic realism of Latin American authors comes to mind, as well as a few North American writers, but Wecker's story is a bit different. Her characters are not ordinary humans, and supernaturally appear out of a past time and place to animate a work of fiction set in today's time and place.

Wecker's golem and jinni are no ordinary humans, but they are not exactly the usual stuff of fantasy or science fiction novels, either. The golem is a human-like creature, but is fashioned from clay and imbued with immense strength, through employing Kabbalistic formulae derived from a mystical interpretation of the Bible. In Jewish folklore, golems have been created to protect the Jewish community at times of great external danger. So, by authenticating our character with a religious underpinning, where supernatural forces provide a working rationale for such a strange creature, the story has a solid, built-in basis for the "suspension of disbelief," so necessary to the reader's enjoyment of compelling fiction. That is, we have the prior legends of golems, with a semi-religious imprimatur, and so are more ready to go along with a new one.

The jinni is a little more problematic. Here we have a human-like, male figure who has been imprisoned in a metal flask for perhaps a thousand years, and is released when a metalsmith in a Syrian immigrant neighborhood in New York City repairs the flask. Of course, there is some precedent for this sort of fable too, notably in the old, *Arabian Nights* stories, with a genie imprisoned in Aladdin's lamp. However the jinni myth doesn't quite have the same level of historical credentials; we just need to believe in the magic. Wecker's jinni, unlike Aladdin's, doesn't grant wishes, but he has various powers, some of which have been diminished by a losing battle with a wizard who imprisoned him in the flask about a thousand years earlier. Though human in form, the jinni's essential nature is fire, and so even to walk in a downpour of rain can be life-threatening to him.

The golem and the jinni both arrive in NYC from foreign shores, Poland and Syria, respectively, in the year 1899. With these sorts of bizarre natures, we are intrigued as to how Wecker will navigate such characters through the teeming immigrant communities of the city. Throw in an evil, failed rabbi, who created a female golem and has followed her to the New World in search of the secret of eternal life for himself, and we, as writers, are anxious to see whether Wecker is going to be able to tie it all together into a satisfying package. From the beginning, one suspects these two unusual creatures will have to eventually meet, but many trials take place beforehand. Moreover, what is Wecker going to do for any romantic encounter between a creature essentially composed of clay and one of fire? Does she pull all the disparate elements together for a satisfying conclusion? You may or may not think so, but it's a fairly good read, and a useful experience for a writer in constructing and tracking an intricate plot with plenty of mysterious elements.

High Concept Plots

Good stories are typically character-driven, or plot-driven, though the best ones generally have both elements. A good author, John Dufresne, in "The Lie That Tells a Truth" suggests setting your character in motion and just watch what happens. Get it down. That would certainly get a story started, but not really having anything yet for a plot is daunting. Then there are the writers for whom the plot is all consuming. "What I'm Reading Now," a blog by Allisa Lauzon, is a useful collection of YA book reviews, and the most compelling feature of her stripped down reviews is usually the plot. Some seem so pumped-up and bizarre that we're coaxed to read them to see if the author really pulled it off well. We earlier discussed the high-concept plot of *I'd Tell You I Loved You, But Then I'd Have to Kill You*, by Ally Carter. Let's discuss this again in comparison with another high concept plot to see the similarities and differences.

> "From the outside the Gallagher Academy for Exceptional Young Women appears to be a boarding school for rich and snotty young women. The school, however, is actually a training school for future spies. Cammie is a Gallagher legacy and the daughter of the school's headmistress. By her sophomore year, she is already fluent in fourteen languages and knows how to kill a man seven different ways and is starting her first covert operations course..."

The concept is almost outlandish—and yet, it's totally intriguing. Is it going to be tongue-in-cheek, or serious stuff?

Ally has another spy-themed book in her credits, so she probably knows her genre. The other intriguing high-concept plot is *Blue Bloods,* by Melissa De La Cruz. Like Carter's book, an elite group of young adults from wealthy families are embarking on secretive, bizarre callings:

> "The most powerful and elite families in New York City are hiding a secret- a secret that their children are about to discover as they are inducted into The Committee. They are Blue Bloods- an ancient race of Vampires. Schuyler's life changes dramatically when her invitation arrives to join The Committee. She soon discovers that they are hiding things- especially after a young Blue Blood turns up dead- her life force goes completely drained. It's an interesting new take on a vampire novel. *Blue Bloods* moves quickly, capturing readers' interests from the beginning."

A belief in vampires today is almost a rational stretch, though the concept has a long history in storytelling, books, movies, and TV, so that the readiness of readers to suspend disbelief is already at work for the author. Melissa has a great plot, but she'll have to work hard to keep the reader caught up in the "fictional dream," as per writing guru John Gardner.

High Concept Plots 2

Earlier we discussed a theme of high concept plots, including the Gallagher Academy for Exceptional Young Women. The school is a training school for future spies. An audacious plot premise, however it's close to the concept of a movie made later, in 2011. *Hanna*, stars Saoirse Ronan, as a 16 yr. old girl being trained in a remote, isolated setting by her father, an ex-spy, to be an assassin in an international operation. The fiction writer for the 2007 novel proved to be the seer of a compelling plot.

In another high concept plot we discussed, the most powerful and elite families in New York City are hiding a secret- a secret that their children are about to discover as they are inducted into The Committee. They are Blue Bloods- an ancient race of Vampires.
Vampires are probably not that much of a high concept entity anymore, but varying the setting or place of the novel, as done here, and proceeding in compelling steps, can give it an overall high concept score.

Vampires in the Lemon Grove, by Karen Russell, 2013, is a collection of short stories which include a few that could qualify as high concept models, including her vampire title story. The vampires consist of a kindly, very old man who whiles away his days sucking lemons and playing dominos in an ancient lemon grove in Italy, and his partner, a woman vampire who nightly transforms into a bat to return to a nearby cave. The old man is an unpaid fixture at the grove, kept on to amuse the tourists.

The lazy pace and idyllic setting are dream-like, and hardly prepare the reader for the shocking ending, which helped give the story a high concept rating.

"Reeling for the Empire" was another story in the volume that was even much more a high concept. Poor, rural girls in early industrial age Japan are recruited from their needy families by a company agent for two-year contracts at a silk-making mill. The agent describes to the parents how it is their patriotic duty to help their country compete with foreign industrial textile giants, and offers an advance payment to the impoverished parents. On the journey to the mill, the agent encourages the girl to drink a ceremonial cup of tea to celebrate her good fortune. At the mill, after meeting the other workers, the new hire soon realizes her special cup of tea was drugged, and she and the other women are at various stages of transforming into silk worms. Each night their stomachs swell with embryonic silk threads, and the next day they draw silk threads from their hands to feed the giant spinning machine. Their output dwarfs what could be accomplished with traditional silkworm culture. Each day the women are fed bowls of mulberry leaves, the food of natural silkworms, and each day they grow more body fur and their physical features continue to slowly morph into silkworms. The reader may be reminded of Kafka's story about the man who became a cockroach during his sleep.

Another story in the *Lemon Grove*.., "The Barn at the End of Our Term," concerns nineteen past American presidents who have been reborn as horses at a ranch somewhere in the western states, and these ex-presidents are aware of their past identities. A writer can go anywhere with an original high concept plot like that.

Cellphone Novelists

An amazing writing phenomenon began in Japan somewhere around the early 2000s. Cellphone novelists, mostly girls and young women, were posting serial installments of their work on special (free) web-hosting sites. Imagine trying to tap out a 100,000-word novel on a cellphone, using your two thumbs, while commuting to a job on a crowded bullet train. Some of the writers have no idea of the structure of novels when they begin, but, increasingly, their on-line works were making it into manga (graphic novels), books, and movies. A published novel written by a previously unknown cellphone author sold 2 million copies. A movie version of another cellphone novel earned 35 million dollars At the end of 2007, cellphone novels held four of the top five positions on the literary bestseller list!

Some of the examples discussed in *The New Yorker* (12/22-29/08) generally portray passive, emotionally painful, often masochistic, romances, written with very simple word and sentence structure. The editor of a literary journal is quoted as saying,

> The author's (real) name is rarely revealed, the titles are very generic, the depiction of individuals, the locations— it's very comfortable, exceedingly easy to empathize with. Any high school girl can imagine that this experience is just two steps from her own. But this kind of empathy is largely different from the emotive response —the life-changing event—that reading a great novel can bring about. One tells you what you already know. Literature has the power to change the way you think.

In a panel discussion hosted by the same magazine, the question discussed was "Will the cellphone novel 'kill the author'?" A panel conclusion was that the novels weren't literature at all, "but the offspring of an oral tradition originating with the mawkish Edo-period (*1603 to 1868*) marionette shows and extending to vapid J-pop love ballads." The journal editor concluded, "It's not a question of literature being above it. It's just—it's Pynchon vs. Tarantino. Most people have a fair understanding of the difference."

Perhaps, but the connection of Japan's cellphone bare-bones novels to the Edo marionette shows seems pleasingly rhapsodic. Perhaps some American bare bones, genre novels are offspring of our ubiquitous Eighteenth and Nineteenth Century "Punch and Judy" puppet shows, staged on sidewalks in many of our urban-immigrant centers. No literary pretensions, just economical, brief respites from grim realities pressing in on all sides.

PART 3 - PROBLEMATIC FICTION

Inauthentic Writing

Imagine a storyteller, a seanchai in the Irish tradition, who unwinds his tale from the darkened corner of a smoky cottage. Though he remains partly obscured in the shadows as he tells his tale of 'long ago and far away,' the audience judges his appearance and words to decide for themselves whether he's an 'insider' or an 'outsider' to the people of the story. If he speaks intimately of the ways of the 'Tuatha de Danaan,' the faerie people, he may take care to validate how he comes by such knowledge. He might claim for himself a special relationship to the faeries, but in that case his audience might wonder why he has come to be wandering their countryside, hungry and in need of shelter for the night. Whatever his claim, the storyteller needs to stand ready to defend it. If his story suggests an intimate, personal tale of the Tinkers, a gypsy-like subset of the Irish population, the storyteller's own appearance, dress, and dialect may be the key in winning over his audience.

In modern times, the novel, with its acceptability of author pseudonyms, a wider world of social and cultural complexities, and various degrees of removal between author and audience, the audience is in a more uncertain position to decide on whether it may be 'inauthentic' writing. Some cases discussed here will clearly involve 'inauthentic' writing, as in the case of an author of a memoir which did not in any way represent his own, personal experience. A much lesser degree of inauthenticity might be ascribed to the author James Frey, who was shown to have allowed some amount of non authentic personal experience to creep into his memoir. In such cases the storytelling could have been more rigorously honest, and still compelling as first-person fiction. Indeed, most 'memoirs' probably have at least some, if minor, amounts of fiction, which would not necessarily move the memoir into being seriously inauthentic.

The subject has provided the media with a lively topic, wherein misrepresentations of a book have raised interesting issues for the reading public.   In most if not all cases, the misrepresentation is solely by the author, though occasionally the publisher also contributed by being remiss in fact-checking. In a few books the representations were a hoax, with the writers presenting themselves as Holocaust survivors, or survivors of drug addiction, or of urban violence, and their book was offered as a memoir, or a personal experience. However, in other cases the misrepresentation might consist only of a false representation by the author of his ethnic identity, presumably intended to establish credentials for writing the story and so gain access to market quotas thought to exist for a certain cultural or ethnic identity.

An interesting survey and a writer's discussion of this topic are given in "Real Fakes and Inauthentic Others," by Alyce Miller, in The Writer's Chronicle, V5 No. 41, March/April 2009. Curiously, some of the same fakes and inauthentic others were discussed in *Guilty*, a 2008 bestseller by Anne Coulter, a political conservative who suggests that some authors feel a modern need to identify with victims in their stories.

Hoaxes dealing with the Holocaust include the award-winning *Fragments*, by Binjamin Wilkomirski, published in 1995, and comprising memories of his imprisonment as a Jewish boy in a

Nazi concentration camp in Poland. He was uncovered as a hoax in 1999. He'd actually spent the war years with adoptive parents in Switzerland, and wasn't Jewish. Another two hoaxes of the genre exposed in 2008 included *Misha: A Memoire of the Holocaust Years*, by Misha Defonseca, and *Angel at the Fence*, by Herman Rosenblat.

They had all seemed to reviewers to write with authority, but their stories had come unraveled, either when backgrounds were checked, or some pertinent detail didn't stand up. Rosenblat couldn't repeatedly have met his blond angel at the camp fence as he described, because someone who knew better, an actual camp inmate, pointed out the physical inaccessibility of that fence to any prisoner. Nonetheless, these were stories that were apparently well crafted, and were praised by critics and readers—until the matter of authenticity had come up. If the story had been labeled as fiction, would it have succeeded as well? It might have lessened the presumed authority of the writer, but if the protagonist had been developed as a sympathetic character and the story had gripping obstacles and resolutions, well then, it may have been a successful story, nonetheless.

An example of the false memoir and false ethnicity issues, which were treated in both of the references given above, and which also appeared in a NY Times book review, unfolded after the publication of *Love and Consequences: A Memoir of Hope and Survival*, by Margaret B. Jones. The memoir's protagonist is a half-white, half-Native-American girl, who grows up in an African-American foster parent's household in South Central Los Angeles. She runs drugs for the 'Bloods' street gang, raises pit bulls to sell to gang members, and loses her foster-brother to gang warfare. In the Times interview, Margaret has escaped her past life, now has a small daughter and a new home in Washington, bought using proceeds from a Starbucks investment, and attends college. It seems incredulous, but why not?

The interview includes a photo of a young black man who is a guest in her home and is said to be recovering from a gun wound. In another photo Margaret is sitting on the stoop with her child, Rya, with one of those mean-looking pitbulls she used to raise in the 'hood.' Unfortunately for her, it was later discovered that Margaret B. Jones is really Peggy Seltzer, who grew up in an affluent section of southern California and attended a private school there. Nevertheless, she opined that she'd done some good with her fictional account of life in the 'hood, by giving voice to an oppressed minority who are usually ignored. If she'd only called it fiction, however, it might have been almost as successful as social activism along with imaginative storytelling. Undoubtedly, the false identity gave it at least a little extra kick.

Another interesting literary ruse occurred with the publication of *My Own Sweet Time*, by Wanda Koolmatri, supposedly an Australian Aborigine woman, but which was really written by Leon Carmine, an Anglo-Australian male cab driver in Sydney. He was disarmingly honest about it when the ruse was discovered: "I couldn't get published, but Wanda could." Before being discovered as an ethnic outsider, his book "took the publishing world by storm."

318

There were many other interesting cases discussed by Miller in her article, including *The Education of Little Tree,* by Forrest Carver, a hugely successful 'autobiography of a Cherokee Indian,' although Mr. Carver was later discovered to be white; and *I, Rigoberta,* an autobiography by Rigoberta Menchu, a renowned Guatemalan human rights activist and Nobel laureate, but relating experiences Rigoberta never had. Though not the poor, uneducated person she had claimed to be, she said she wanted to speak out for those voiceless, oppressed people of her country who had suffered such genocide. Ms. Miller makes some interesting points when she surmises that:

> "the...hoax may, in part, function as a reminder of the consequences of condescending to work from "previously silenced or suppressed voices" by presuming it looks like a particular thing," and, "The notion that an 'outsider' appropriates, while the insider never does, is false and simplistic."

To sum up, the inauthentic author might run the gamut of a repugnant hoax, to someone who only made a venial marketing decision.

Cultural Appropriation

Let's discuss the concept of 'cultural appropriation' as applied to fiction writing. There are some who frown on, or even censor the rights of any author to create characters and speak in the voice of people ethnically or culturally different from themselves. It seems such a view might may have become more strident in our current era of political correctness.

Such a climate of pc didn't give any pause to Lionel Shriver, best known for her 2003 bestseller (and movie), *We Need to Talk about Kevin*. *She* gave a keynote speech at the Brisbane Writers Festival in Australia in 2016, that treated fiction and identity politics, and criticized contemporary forms of political correctness. A cogent article discussing the lecture and its aftermath was written by Jonathan Foreman in the Journal, COMMENTARY, Nov. 16, 2016. It appears Shriver's lecture drew widespread criticism from identity politics activists, but Foreman was generally supportive of Shriver:

> She (Shriver) excoriated contemporary forms of politically correct censorship with typically astringent fearlessness and rubbished the whole notion of identity politics: "Membership of a larger group is not an identity. Being Asian is not an identity. Being gay is not an identity. Being deaf, blind, or wheelchair-bound is not an identity, nor is being economically deprived.

Points Foreman made that are germane to our discussion include the following arguments opposing the ideas of identity politics:

320

At the beginning of October, at Britain's Bristol University, a production of the musical *Aida* (an adaptation of Verdi by Elton John and Tim Rice) was cancelled because student protesters claimed that having white actors play Ethiopian and Egyptian characters would be "cultural appropriation."

By their logic, black actors should not be allowed to play Lear, Macbeth, Julius Caesar, or other "white" roles in Shakespeare, and nonwhite performers should be completely excluded from taking part in any opera or classical ballet given that both are "white" European art forms, in the same way that jazz or blues music could be said to belong exclusively to black people.

As Shriver pointed out, literature would be impossible if writers were forbidden from imagining and creating characters of different gender, race, ethnicity, age, or sexual orientation to their own.

Shriver is surely correct in this. Writers should be free to imagine whatever fictional character they wish for their story, and there ought to be no realm of ethnicity, race, religion, or whatever, reserved only to writers bearing the same genesis. Fiction writing has always been and will continue to be the richer for it.

Sensitive Language

Let's briefly discuss the writings of V. S. Naipaul: *A House for Mr. Biwas*, *The Mystic Masseuse*, et. al. Naipaul can be an enigma at times. Joseph O'Neill has an interesting article about Naipaul in a 2011 issue of *Atlantic Magazine*. The early novels by Naipaul are of life and people in his homeland of Trinidad, and the characterizations are vivid. Naipaul has had some bad press here and there from critics, chiefly it seems about his colonial and racial attitudes, and his personal, marital life. However, his writing has earned him a Nobel Prize for Literature (and a knighthood). Some well intentioned people can be quick to censor others on a number of sensitive social issues, particularly those that may deal with race, class, or religion. In the long run, our First Amendment, dealing with Freedom of Expression, seems to have it about right. We may not like what a person says or writes; still, we might gain something from it. There's at least a possibility that critics can be overly narrow, or too ideological themselves.

A party was given years ago at the home of my brother and his wife. My sister-in-law, and her brother, who was there also, are first generation Asian Indian-descent immigrants to the U.S. from a Caribbean nation that is populated by mostly Asian Indian- and African-descent people, all of them people of color. My brother and I are white. In this party atmosphere the word 'nigger' was occasionally used in a friendly, affectionate manner. My brother-in-law noticed I was uncomfortable with his use of the word with his black friend. He laughed and said the word only meant 'ignorant,' and I shouldn't be worried about using it in a friendly way. Of course, the word has become too loaded with baggage in this country for me to do that. Still, it's odd for a certain word to be accepted in good humor between some people, and be sanctioned for use by other people. Naipaul would be quick to challenge any sanction like that.

It's In the Character's DNA

Some characters claim our hearts from the very start. Wherever a story steadily loads challenges and sordid abuses on our protagonist, but we detect a tenacious quality in her personality and expect she may find a way to fight clear of victimhood, we're better able to follow her down dark alleys as the story tension progresses to its resolution.

News of the World, by Paulette Jiles, has a wonderful young girl character, Johanna, whose Texas pioneer family had been ravaged and slain by a Kiowa war party before her eyes when she was only six years-old. The Kiowa carried her off as a captive, and perhaps as a resourceful young child might do in such circumstances, she came to think of herself as a Kiowa over the next four years. She forgot her English language, as well as the German of her immigrant family. The U.S. Army eventually wrests her back from the Kiowa when she is ten, another huge disruption in her life. The army offers to pay $50 to have Johanna escorted back to her relatives in south Texas. It was a significant sum back then, and Captain Jefferson Kidd, late of the Confederate forces defeated in the Civil War and now a solitary wanderer in the southwest, decides to take the job. He has otherwise earned a living charging admission to public readings of national newspapers, which he purchases and carries to isolated towns along his travels.

During the initial journey south, Johanna rarely tries to speak and stays hidden in the wagon whenever they meet with army patrols, or stop near rough towns. She is at first unfriendly with the Captain, but he tries to help her recall English words and she gradually opens up and teaches him Kiowa words. Their friendship grows steadily. Gradually in the isolated towns, Johanna begins monitoring admission and collecting the dime fee for the Captain's readings. In one of the towns, a sleazy businessman tries to buy Johanna from the Captain, to place her in his brothel. However, they slip out of town that evening. Later, the man and his cronies follow after them and ambush them on the trail. The assailants remain out of range of the Captain's pistol and light, 20-gauge bird-hunting shotgun. However, Johanna has learned how to improvise for warfare from her Kiowa days. While the Captain keeps the assailants at bay with his pistol, she hand-loads shotgun shells with stacks of dimes from the readings, and adds double powder charges. When the Captain topples the remaining assailant with his supercharged shotgun, Johanna gives a war cry, grabs a knife, and leaps up to go scalp the enemy. The Captain has to call back his impetuous young warrior.

There is a dilemma awaiting them in south Texas, where it becomes obvious the uncle and aunt are not too keen about taking on the responsibility of an uncivilized young niece. Johanna doesn't want the Captain to leave her with them, but shall the honorable Captain Kidd now become the child's third kidnapper?

It's a great story about the resilience and courage built into the DNA of memorable characters in a bygone way of life.

News of the World is probably not going to disturb readers anywhere near as much as our next story, *My Absolute Darling*, by Gabriel Tallent. Although, there is arguably as much violence and moral turpitude implied in the former as is explicitly described in the latter. The savagery of the rape and mutilation of the pioneer family by the Kiowa was terrible in its brief detail, but the reader might be reminded, too, of the brutal destruction by the army of entire Indian villages, women and children included, contained in other historical sources. *News* did not pause to weigh-in on either of those earlier-in-time calamities. Instead, its story focused on a more recent story time, and the courage, loyalties, and honor of the two admirable main characters: the Captain and Johanna.

The situation is quite different and significantly more complex in *Darling*, however. Turtle, a nickname for Julia, is the fourteen year-old daughter of a survivalist, libertarian, hippie, physically powerful, gun culture person, somewhat learned philosopher, cynic, and social Neanderthal, named Martin. They live in a dilapidated, unfinished house in the woods, with plenty of weapons and ammunition at hand, constantly on guard against some indeterminate catastrophe that is presumably expected by Martin in an uncertain future. He has trained Turtle to carry out a 'house-clearing' tactic on arrival home from school each day when he isn't at home. This involves her grabbing a weapon and maneuvering from room to room in the house while clearing each room with bursts of actual gunfire (the ammunition expenses must have been horrendous). It seems a little over the top, but there are probably more than a few unusual such folks scattered around the forests and mountains of our rather sparsely settled northern California county. The author, Gabriel Tallent, is, presumably, from New Mexico, but he describes the northern California environment with a knowing familiarity, part of which must owe to one of the local college professors of ecology whom he credits in the book. Tallents descriptions of place are quite good.

The eight hundred pound gorilla in the redwoods, though, is the shock revelation that Martin is perpetuating a sexual relationship with Turtle. It is a consensual thing, but this is a fourteen year-old intellect navigating a vastly uneven power balance, and it transgresses one of society's darkest taboos. We're angry with Martin for exploiting her but we endure the tension, waiting for Turtle to recognize him for what he is, and to somehow bring him down. Turtle has one confidant, Martin's dad, who lives in a nearby trailer. Grandpa knows his son is bringing Turtle up all wrong with the son's survivalist paranoia, and may suspect worse, but he's an old man and just being critical doesn't do the job.

Angry with life as she sometimes gets, Turtle goes on a long, overnight hike in the woods. She encounters two lost youths her age, and helps them find their way out. Though she does attend school, this begins Turtle's first normal association with anyone her age and she begins to care about one of the boys, Jacob. Martin eventually finds out about her new interest. He knows the families of the boys and moves to thwart any further contact, throwing away letters, monitoring telephone calls, and carrying out other contemptuous actions. About this time Martin also comes home with a new, ten year-old girl, Cayenne, to live with them. This arouses a jealousy in Turtle, despite her growing confusion about her own relationship with Martin. Things become increasingly paranoid with Martin, and Turtle fears for Cayenne going through the same history she has had with Martin. She later flees the house with Cayenne in tow, and instinctively knows Martin will come looking for her at the boyfriend, Jacob's, house. She plans her defensive strategy, and the epic of all shootouts takes place at Jacob's house and along the rocky beach, between the two firearms experts engaged in search and destroy tactics.

This was a stunning read. It had only been out about a month and there were already many at the Goodreads website who had read the book and written reviews. Considering the controversial material, it was interesting to note that the great majority of ratings were quite good.

Martin is surely a case of a character whose DNA has run amok.

PART FOUR - PUBLISHING

Writing Like It's the Day Job

Writing, for most writers, is an existential pleasure that needs to be supported by a day job and maybe that's not such a bad thing. Most of us would like our books to be published and read, but except for a select few, any public rewards are apt to be modest for the long hours and energies invested in the writing.

The writer, Don Lee, describes a common chain of thought and events accompanying publication, as told in an interview by Jeanie Chung (Oct./Nov. 2011,*Writers Chronicle*):

> Maybe this will be big. And most of the time, it's not big. Most of the time, it goes all right. You get some nice reviews, maybe some not so nice reviews, and you sell a few copies, or not, and you move on. It's just a little blip. The purpose for your writing cannot be for that moment of publication. It has to be about writing the book itself.

It's a good, sobering reflection. It has to be about wanting to spend time alone with a particular exploration of thoughts and feelings, all channeled through a handful of characters and places dragged up from the subconscious mind. Sometimes it may be to explore past experience from other viewpoints, or to visualize outcomes if different directions had been taken, perhaps along totally new paths to see what might happen next. Most of the time, if we see our way through to finishing a manuscript, we can benefit by an enrichment of our conscious and subconscious being. Publication might only be a potential, added bonus.

Chung comments about a Lee character's commitment to making a huge sculpture that can never be exhibited, and might not necessarily even be 'art.' For him, Chung surmises, it was all about the process:

> In some ways, (the character, Lyndon) may be advocating more of a workmanlike approach. Like it's your day job; whatever you do for a living, most people aren't working toward one big moment. It's just what you do every day.

Lee agrees, as might many other writers. A project one works on as an engineer is not usually viewed as heading toward any one big moment; it's the day job, and we do the best we can at that stage in our career. In a related way, the fiction we write outside the normal day job doesn't have to be aimed at any one big moment, e.g., publication, and blockbuster sales; we do what satisfies the creative drive best. Like Lyndon, maybe it's sufficiently rewarding to just engage in the process.

Publishing

In the past it was a growing problem for a writer to keep up with the publishing houses and agents to know who was accepting queries, and whether the first few chapters had to be included, or who required the complete unsolicited manuscript (Ms.), or whether they would return a Ms. in a self addressed stamped envelope (SASE,) or even whether they would send a form rejection in a SASE if included with the Ms. Some publishers or agents required the writer to submit a complete Ms., and if they were interested, they'll let the writer know. Or if you did not hear from them in x days, you should assume they were not interested.

Some of the older ways of querying and submitting sample chapters, or the whole Ms., have changed for the better in the present digital age. One can research publishing houses and independent agents using an internet search. Once the writer has an internet address (URL) and visits the publisher or agent's website, there will generally be a webpage that gives specific requirements for submittals, either by email message and attachments, or at some sites they provide an opportunity to make a query directly online, where the writer can upload sample chapters of a Ms. or the complete Ms., as specified.

It has also become very easy for a writer to publish independently of a publisher or agent. Some of the big name tech firms, like Amazon, Google, and others have online capabilities for writers to upload their manuscripts, prepared to certain required formats, and after technical review the firm will make the book available for purchase online as an ebook, and/

or as a paperback (print-on-demand). The process usually does not require any cost from the writer, and the writer will receive a royalty for each book sold online by the firm. The most important thing the writer will be missing is the physical distribution of the book by a traditional publishing house to a national network of bookstores, and some expertise in securing publicity. The independent publisher must carry out his or her own publicity campaign, perhaps using social media, like querying and sending files of the Ms. to readers' blogs, or perhaps using the online advertising offered by the tech firms, at a price.

Publishing ebooks

Elsewhere we've discussed the new development of authors in Japan using cellphones to write and publish serial novels, some while commuting to work on the bullet train, and with occasional word counts up to and above 100,000 words.

 A similar development had gotten underway in Canada in 2006 when two tech entrepreneurs started Wattpad, a new website service envisioning a mobile reading app, initially hosting about 17000 public domain books. However, until the introduction of the iPhone and the Kindle, the Wattpad venture struggled to gain any momentum.   Thereafter, writers were able to post original works with the app and it took off.

An article by David Streitfeld, NY Times, 3/24/2014 in the NYTimes muses: "This is writing re-imagined for a mobile world, where attention is fragmentary," and wherein Allen Lau, Wattpad's chief executive stated, "Almost all our writers serialize their content. Two thousand words is roughly 10 minutes of reading. That makes the story more digestible, something you can do when standing in line."

The Wattpad app allows for reader comments, and for some authors this may involve huge numbers, generally positive, since the author can moderate any comments before they are published and can use the delete button to eliminate any brutish trolls. For a conscientious author trying to keep up with responding to comments by fans, the task can be staggering. One author reports 14000 unread messages pending in her Wattpad inbox.

One of the most popular Wattpad authors is Ali Novak, a 22-year old Wisconsin writer who has serialized four mobile novels. Ms. Novak was forced to limit her own involvement with her fans, some of whom apparently would like her to read samples of their work:

> I am no longer taking reading/interview/trailer/cover requests, so all related messages will be ignored. Sorry, but I just don't have the time.

A pullback that is quite understandable. Ms. Novak's biggest hit, *My Life With the Walter Boys*--about a girl who moves in with a family of 12 sons--was later published by *Sourcebooks* in revised and edited form as a paperback. Ms. Novack reflects:

> Since I was little, I've been obsessed with reading and collecting books. I always dreamed of seeing my book in Barnes and Noble and picking it off the shelf and holding it in my hands. That's one thing I could never do with Wattpad.

There is something magical about hefting that physical, material thing that you've imbued with something of your own imagination, and to know it will continue to sit safely on your bookshelf even if your computer becomes obsolete, or the internet implodes into a black hole. However, since the earlier days of Wattpad, the internet tech firms like Amazon and Google do offer the author's print-on-demand paperbacks right alongside the ebooks. Nonetheless, some accomplished authors have begun to publish exclusive ebook offerings. These authors have already made their mark in the traditional hard-copy publishing world, and include writers like Stephen King, Neil Gaiman, and many others. Anyone who has gone down the road of submitting countless query letters with catchy hooks, brilliantly honed synopses or summaries, and sample pages, to literary agents or traditional publishing houses, whom these days may or may not choose to acknowledge your submittal, might perhaps view the ebook publishing opportunities as a liberating development. The traditional gatekeepers may have been breached.

Of course, relative to the more intensive pre-publishing reviews of literary agents and traditional publishing houses, perhaps only a smaller percentage of what is independently published may have superior literary quality, but writers might hope that independently published books might just as readily rise to the top if they are well written--and noticed.

Independent Publishing Platforms

Several earlier posts discussed independent self-publishing platforms (ISP) for both ebooks and printed books. After creating and making the book available through an ISP platform, the role of marketing the book seems to be left more or less to the author. A wide gamut of ISP platforms, like Amazon Books, Google Books, Barnes and Noble, and others, can be chosen by the author to list the book and collect the agreed royalty amount for the author on any sales; however, there may be very little effort by those vendors to find and direct readers to the book. This had been one of the valuable services provided by traditional publishing companies.

Besides being gatekeepers of which books can be published, the traditional companies would generally send out copies of the finished book to their lists of nationwide book reviewers and media columnists to help generate an awareness and demand for the book. They might also arrange book tours (one has to smile to think of them trying to get J. D. Salinger to do a book tour). To some extent, the ISP author can do some of this work by searching for independent or organizational reviewers on the Internet, and providing them with the necessary digital or print copies of the book to review. Some reviews might be provided by small, independent reviewers free, and others by larger internet organizations can start at a couple of hundred dollars. The author has better prospects to enlist an independent reviewer if the book is newly published or has been published within the last two or three months. Consequently, one can see from all this that it might be most effective if the author had some sort of marketing plan, and/or arrangements made, before he ever clicks on the 'publish' button with an ISP.

Some of the pros and cons of the ISP option for an author are illustrated in an interview with author John Edgar Wideman, reported by Sejal Shah in *The Writer's Chronicle* of May/ Summer 2014. Wideman has a son, Danny, who worked for an ISP, named Lulu, and decided to publish a book titled *Briefs* with them.

> *Briefs* was an experiment. It got all the reviews you could want, under the circumstances. And also because Danny worked there I got a lot of services that if you self-published in Lulu, you'd have to pay for. For example, the expensive business of sending books to reviewers. My self-published electronic book was treated a bit like the old way that my hard copy books had been. A publicity service sent books to the media and tried to get me interviews. A publicity person promoted and followed the book's progress. Books were made available in conventional hard copy format, so that was cheating in a way. The results don't tell a lot about self-publishing or electronic publishing per se. My conclusion after the whole thing was that even with the extras I got, a self-publishing venture was premature. It still is premature, for a person of my status, used to having a certain kind of attention. You're taking a real leap of faith and financially, you're giving up, in my case, what might be a substantial advance.

Not being on bookstore shelves killed *Briefs*. Someone browsing in that nice bookstore ...is not going to see *Briefs*. A bookstore has to pay for copies of *Briefs*, and then they own the copies, can't return them. The other thing is the Times refused to review *Briefs*, because it was self-published ...They did run a story about the manner in which *Briefs* was published, but it was not a review. Almost all the articles about the book were not reviews; they were general interest pieces about the publishing industry. That meant no reviews of the book, and at the same time no one was going to trip over the book in a bookstore. So why would anyone buy it? Where would they find it? As far as merchandising strategy, *Briefs* fell into very predictable cracks. I was disappointed, but I'd do it again. I liked the adventure; I liked working with Danny; and I learned a hell of a lot.

As might be concluded from the foregoing discussions and interview excerpt, ISP is a works in progress. There are pluses and minuses in it for most authors, but the business model of the traditional publisher has contemporary issues that need to be addressed, also. One thinks of the music recording industry, which had a business model that served them handsomely for many years and did well for a relatively small number of artists, too. However, the internet opened up possibilities for many more artists that had been shut out by the traditional gatekeepers' system, and brought with it upheavals to the business model that are still ongoing. Now, the traditional book publishing model's turn may have come.

Hooks in Queries

At the point where we finish our novels, if we're going to submit our manuscript to an agent or publishing house, we're faced with the need for the dreaded query letter, with its required 'hook' content. The hook must lure the publisher or agent to think for a moment about whether to consider this wonderful opportunity a little further. How are we going to do that? How can one possibly condense the excitement and thrills of this literary gem that we've labored on for the past year, or years, into a make or break attention grabbing, terse invitation to read our entire story. Or at least to ask for a synopsis and partial. Criminal, we think, shouldn't have to be done. But it does, and even if the novel is a fairly good read in its entirety, we may as well accept that the preliminary hurdle must be overcome, with class, with élan, before anyone might invite us to the next hurdle, the equally dreaded synopsis.

Some recommendations tell us to consider the hook as a movie trailer for our story. That seems an apt approach. Get a clear sense of the problem, and of the people we'll want to care about up and running, and show some emotional conflicts they'll face in gaining a resolution to the problem. But don't shoot ourselves in the foot by using unfortunate language while doing it. Easy? Well, no, but It's a necessary skill set to acquire. A few days of browsing some of the online readers' websites, like *Goodreads*, *Readers Favorites*, Agents websites, and other websites that might be currently available from a search of keywords, would be useful to check on a current emphases and interests in contents of queries.

You may discover some contests in writing queries, such as had been posted by Fangs, Fur, and Fey, an authors' blogging site, which proposed to accept up to 180 hooks, in specified genres, 300 word maximum length, and would post on-line comments made by published authors who reviewed the hook submittals. Could be another learning experience, and thankfully, submitters would not be identified.

Email Queries

Many of the literary agents invite email queries from authors. Some accept only email queries, while others accept only postal mail. Email offers a convenient, economical means of reaching an agent and getting a faster reply, but it has some pitfalls which writers should be aware of. If a writer drafts his query letter in a word processor program, like MS-WORD, and then copies and pastes it into an email, problems can and do occur. This may happen because email does not recognize your word processor's formatting codes. In reviewing many agent blogs and writers' comments, the most common problem is the use of 'smart quotes' by WORD. These are the curly-shape quote marks that have different shapes at the beginning and end of a quote. Many writers recommend turning this feature off in WORD and use standard quote marks. The email recipient will see smart quotes reproduced as a clump of strange symbols on his end of the transmission. Other WORD formatting that will be lost and replaced by other strange symbols are italics, bolds, and em symbols (conversion of double dashes into a single long dash). To avoid these problems, the writer can save his WORD document as a Text file, then copy and paste from the text file into the email. This should resolve those particular problems. Some writers advised an intermediate step of first copying the WORD file into a Notepad, or other Text-editing file, and then copying from there into the email. However, that shouldn't be necessary; copying from a WORD file saved in Text format should be sufficient.

The next problem occurs if the agent requests sample pages be included after the query, and within the body of the email. Indents and double spacing within the paragraph will be lost when copying and pasting from the WORD manuscript into the email. It appears that the best the writer can do to improve the appearance for the benefit of the agent-reader is to manually insert a blank space between paragraphs. The email format does not allow providing double spacing within paragraphs, as is customary when submitting hard-copy manuscripts.

The situation is a little daunting, and has led some agents not to accept email queries, but hopefully things will improve in the future.

Probabilities and Agents

Writers may want to search out and enlist the aid of an agent to try and improve the chances of marketing a Ms. However, many agents prefer a novelist with published credits, so an unpublished writer may prefer to submit their unsolicited Ms. to a traditional publishing house where it is possible. If you're not going to do simultaneous submissions, which many houses say they do not accept, it's a pretty time consuming process. Whether submitting to an agent or a publishing house, the writer might hear back within a few months, but it can also take up to a year for a reply.

There was an interesting article written by an associate editor at a literary journal on the success rates for short story Ms. He figured there was an average one-percent chance of being accepted, and he gave himself at least a five-percent chance of having his own stories accepted at any given journal. He had a math instructor do the statistics and he figured he needed, on average, to submit his Ms. up to 56 times, if not using simultaneous submittals, to have his story accepted.

One might have thought with a probability of five-percent it would have been twenty submittals, but in any case the odds are daunting. If the percentages are the same for books, and it took on average about six months to hear back from a book publisher, you might not learn whether you had a viable novel for up to ten years, if not doing simultaneous submittals.

Increasingly, publishing houses prefer submittals only from agents, A writer can often meet and interview with agents at the many writing conferences held each year in all parts of the country. If a writer can interest an agent at such a conference, he stands a better chance at having a manuscript given serious consideration when it is invited by the agent for review.

Book Ratings

On many book readers' websites, a general practice is to arrive at a 'star' rating for each book under discussion. This may be because most Indie reviewers feel a star rating is expected--the convention. No doubt it's a lot better than simply giving a thumbs-up, or thumbs-down, opinion of a book an author has put a lot of passion into writing, but is it a 'best' practice? Notice for example that the weekly *NYTimes* book reviews do not use a star rating; however, they select from a market-tested, best-sellers list reported by the booksellers and publishers. Presumably public opinion has already narrowed the universe of recently published books to ones that typically would receive at least a four-star rating. Consequently, public opinion having already spoken, the professional reviewer's job is eased into discussing what in the book works for them, and what does not. This critique usually avoids murdering any personally disliked book--more or less.

If a book gets, say, a three-star rating by volunteer literary critics on internet sites, even though the reviewer may have discussed a few things that were done well, the book probably will have a much diminished chance of being picked up by a reader. Perhaps it's all for the best, so many books, so little time. Readers may miss more than a few jewels if they only read four and five-star books, but it's a reasonable starting point, along with the brief description material on the cover. Once we find an author we like, odds are that we will generally like his future work. Cover all your bases, though, and don't forget the artful cover graphics and title.